perfectly charming

ALSO BY LIZ TALLEY

Morning Glory

Charmingly Yours

Home in Magnolia Bend

The Sweetest September

Sweet Talking Man

Sweet Southern Nights

New Orleans' Ladies

The Spirit of Christmas

His Uptown Girl

His Brown-Eyed Girl

His Forever Girl

Bayou Bridge

Waters Run Deep

Under the Autumn Sky

The Road to Bayou Bridge

Oak Stand

Novellas and Anthologies

perfectly charming

a morning glory
novel

LIZ TALLEY

Montlake
Romance

Published by Montlake Romance, Seattle
www.apub.com

Amazon, the Amazon logo, and Montlake Romance are trademarks of Amazon.com, Inc., or its affiliates.

ISBN-13: 9781503936201
ISBN-10: 1503936201

Cover design by Laura Klynstra

Printed in the United States of America

To my husband, who has loved me since I was thirteen years old. Thank you for not looking for any other experiences and choosing to love me every day. Sometimes you meet your soul mate in eighth-grade English class and get a happily ever after.

Chapter One

Jess Culpepper, formerly Jess Mason, stared at the envelope sitting in the center of her table and then slid the final documents inside, sealing them with the double prong. In her craptastic handwriting, she scrawled *Divorce Papers* across the front. There. They were now ready to be added to the filing cabinet beside her cramped desk, filed somewhere between business receipts and federal income tax returns. Just another chapter in her life relegated to a file.

"That's it. Finished," she said to the apartment she'd occupied for the past six months. Her austere apartment didn't answer back. She'd never added any homey touches to the place, preferring the white walls and utilitarian carpet over anything that might look like she gave a damn. She hadn't wanted to live here anyway. Sky Oaks Condominiums. A romantic name for a bunch of boxy, plain apartments.

She picked up one of the salt and pepper shakers Lacy had brought back from New Orleans when they were fourteen. A comical gift typical of her late friend. The pepper shaker was a frog groom; the salt was the bride. When lined up properly, the pair kissed.

Silly like Lacy.

Her friend had laughed and said they reminded her of Jess and her boyfriend, Benton. Lacy had wiggled her eyebrows. *Maybe he'll kiss you finally.*

No one had thought it strange that Jess had used the cheap ceramic shaker set atop her wedding cake. She even had a cute picture of her and Benton kissing behind the cake, mimicking the frogs. People had loved the personal touch, the fact that two childhood sweethearts had married each other. Till death do them part.

Or rather, until someone changed his mind and screwed their florist.

The doorbell rang, the door opening immediately after. "Yoo-hoo?"

Eden.

"Hey," Jess said, rising from the table, catching the swish of Eden's black pageboy from the corner of her eye. "What are you doing here at this hour?"

Eden scooted inside the apartment and shut the door. "You shouldn't leave your door unlocked, Jess."

"We live in Morning Glory. The biggest crime wave we've ever had was when those high school kids came over from Jackson, knocked down mailboxes, and left a dead cow carcass on the high school football field." Jess went to the fridge and grabbed a bottle of white zinfandel and waggled it. "Vino?"

"God bless you," Eden said, tossing her flip phone on the coffee table and dropping onto the plush couch, toeing her sneakers off and wiggling her toes. "I'm not sure how much longer I can work at Penny Pinchers."

Jess smiled. Eden said that every day. Seriously. Every day. The woman had been working at the local discount store since the age of sixteen. She was now the manager at twenty-eight. "Youngest manager in Mississippi," her regional manager liked to crow as he ogled Eden's boobs.

"So quit."

"You know I can't," Eden said, accepting the glass of sweet, cold wine and curling her feet beneath her. "Mama's with Aunt Ruby Jean. We had the annual Voorhees reunion at the church today. Honestly, we're lucky lightning didn't strike when we stepped in the place. It was a potluck, and Aunt Ruby took Mama home and gave me the evening to pretend I'm a normal person."

Eden Voorhees had been Jess's first friend, smiling at the new girl who was tall, skinny, and slightly bucktoothed as she balanced her lunch tray and looked desperately around for someone to sit with that first day back in fourth grade. Eden had patted the round stool attached to the lunch table and told Jess to sit down. Jess had adored the shy Eden ever since.

Her friend wore her crappy life like a backpack, strapped on and never complaining. Well, at least not much. Bless her pea-pickin' heart. Since her mother was a former stripper/crack addict and her stepfather was in prison for armed robbery, it was a bloomin' miracle the girl had blossomed into the kind, hardworking, beautiful woman she'd become. Eden liked to credit her surviving hell with the friendships she'd made with Jess, Rosemary, and Lacy. But Jess knew goodness such as Eden possessed didn't fade away under the duress of hardship. Goodness like Eden's was a flower in a bed of weeds, stretching up toward the sun, refusing to be choked out.

Presently, Eden worked at the local discount store and took care of her handicapped mother. She'd missed out on frat parties, keggers, and beach trips to stay home and mark down cheap crap from China and change her mother's diapers. Eden deserved a medal. Or at least more than what she'd been handed.

"So it's final. Are you okay?" Eden asked, eyeing Jess with concern.

"I'm not suicidal, if that's what you're asking," Jess said.

"Why would anyone be suicidal over that jerk face?" Eden picked up the remote control. "You talk to Rosemary yet?"

"Yeah, but she's busy having fun in NYC. I don't want to piss in her punch," Jess said, frowning when Eden settled on a rerun of *Bones*. She was so not in the mood for gore. But then, the idea of a rom-com made her want to hurl.

"She's never too busy for you. You know that. But I'm so glad she's met someone fun. She got a tattoo," Eden remarked, hooking an eyebrow inquiring about the programming.

Jess shook her head. She didn't want to watch TV or talk about the fun Rosemary was having with a certain Italian guy in SoHo . . . even though she was truly happy for her friend. And she damn sure didn't want to look at that envelope sitting on the table like a knot on a log. And she didn't want to drink last night's wine.

No, Jess wanted to forget about the reality that was her life.

"Let's ditch the flesh being dumped in a tub of worms"—she gave a shudder—"and go to the Iron Bull."

Eden blinked. "I'm not exactly dressed for a bar. I'm wearing tennis shoes."

"So? You look cute. And I need to do something that says I'm not pathetic."

"You're not pathetic. Besides, I do not look cute. I look like I work at Penny Pinchers."

"I'll loan you a shirt. And some hoop earrings. Hoop earrings always make a gal look stylish." Jess rose and walked toward her lonely bedroom, which looked like the rest of the place—uniformly uninteresting, the antithesis of the three-bedroom cottage she'd shared with Benton for the past six years. Their house had been adorable. Everyone said so. Three months after Benton left, she'd sold it to a man who worked for the paper mill. The new buyer was divorced and had let the flower beds go to weeds. She could barely bring herself to drive by the place.

"I don't have big enough boobs for your shirts," Eden called out.

"I have some clingy things that will work," Jess said, opening the closet, feeling determined to do something about her pseudodepression. So Benton didn't want her anymore? So he'd divorced her? Said he needed to experience life . . . whatever. So did she. The divorce was done. Over. So why the hell not?

"Hey," Eden said, appearing in the doorway. Jess looked at her petite, lithe friend. She did, indeed, look like she worked at Penny Pinchers. She wore simple, cheap khaki pants and a T-shirt that read, "We Save You Money." At least the red Converse sneakers were somewhat cute.

"I know what you're going to say," Jess said, pulling out a sleeveless white top with pearl buttons and eyeing it. "I'm fine."

Eden watched her for a few seconds before saying, "Things have been hard these past few months. Lacy and—"

"I don't want to talk about Lacy," Jess said, pushing away the grief. At one time there had been four best friends, pretty, simple, happy girls who believed life was good and walked in sunshine. Until cancer came knocking. Until a husband came home and said he didn't want a baby—he wanted a divorce. Jess didn't want to talk about losing her friend or her husband. She talked about loss every Thursday at four with her therapist. Enough talking, damn it.

"Fine. We'll go out and celebrate Jess Culpepper," Eden said, padding into the room and taking the shirt from Jess's hands. She held it up against her torso. "Does this look too long?"

"Yes, but you need something to cover the travesty of those pants," Jess said, wiggling out of her scrub bottoms and kicking them into the empty corner. She jerked a pair of tight jeans she'd been unable to wear for years off the shelf and slid into them. Buttoned easily. Huh, an upside to grief.

Eden rolled her eyes and jerked off her Penny Pinchers shirt and tugged on the white shirt. "Ugh, my bra." She tugged on the straps that showed.

"Take it off. You've got little boobs."

"Thanks." Eden made a face and unhooked her bra, pulling it through the arms holes. "Can you see my nipples?"

"Only the outline. I think guys consider that a turn-on. Just don't stand beneath the AC vent." Jess yanked her scrub top off and pulled on a tight T-shirt with a sequined pocket. She never wore sequins, something her flamboyant former mother-in-law could never understand. But when a girl went out for liquor, dancing, and flirting with big country boys, she could damn well wear sequins. *Thanks, Lydia, for buying me something I'd never wear as your son's wife, but will wear as a newly single woman. You rock. Sorta.*

Eden bent and rolled the khakis at the ankle, turning her discount pants into something somewhat fun. Then she knotted the two sides of the shirt, lifting the collar '80s style. "Where are those hoop earrings?"

"How do you do that?"

"Do what?"

"Look so damn cute all the time," Jess called as Eden walked to the small bathroom with its shower/tub combo and lone spot of color—the shower curtain Eden had bought at Penny Pinchers.

"It's because I'm barely over five feet. I'm practically a toddler." Eden might be small, but the woman had more talent in her pinkie than most people had in their entire bodies. When Eden slid into a costume and painted her lips red and the spotlight hit her, she became larger than life, a devilishly sexy siren who could croon, dance, and seduce. Her performance in Jackson's community theater production of *Gypsy* had had critics lauding her performance. Eden could be a spitfire when needed.

Jess pulled out a pair of pumps and put them on. God, they pinched. She was so accustomed to wearing running shoes or clogs. One of the best things about being a nurse was wearing scrubs and comfy shoes to work . . . and saving lives, of course. She walked back and forth in front of her closet, catching herself in the mirror. The pumps made her look tall, lean, and sexy, but if she had to hobble around, it defeated the purpose. She tossed the eff-me heels back into the closet and dragged out a pair of sandals she'd bought when she and Benton went to Cabo. They had a heel but weren't potential ankle twisters.

Eden emerged from the bathroom wearing red lipstick and an extra layer of mascara on her lashes. She looked like Annette Funicello in one of those '60s beach movies. "I like those shoes. You know, I can't remember the last time you wore pretty shoes."

"Says the woman who wears this." Jess picked up the discount store T-shirt.

"Point taken," Eden said, giving her a toothy grin. "I have only a couple more hours before I have to be back home. If we're going . . ."

Jess hustled past Eden and grabbed a pretty plum lipstick and swiped it on. Then she gave an extra swipe of deodorant and a fluff of her curly hair and winked at herself in the mirror. She really didn't want to go out. But she had to. She needed to do something that said she was okay. So everyone would stop looking at her like she was pathetic. So everyone, including her best friends, would stop asking her if she was okay.

She wasn't.

But she would be. Eventually.

"Ready," Jess trilled, her kitten heels clacking on the cheap bathroom tile. "Wouldn't Lacy be proud of us? Two gals about town."

Eden's head jerked up from her phone. She still had to punch numbers to text and refused to waste money on an updated smartphone. "I thought you didn't want to talk about Lacy."

Jess shrugged. "I'm just saying."

Eden smiled and nodded. "She'd be proud. And if she was still here, she'd be firing up Earline so she could be the designated driver." Jess laughed. Lacy had loved her old truck, which she called Earline, even though she'd cried when her parents had given it to her for her birthday during their junior year at Morning Glory High School. The bouncy class president had longed for a cute convertible Volkswagen Beetle and was certain the stepfather who worshiped her would buy that for her. Instead, he'd found an old Ford a coworker had for sale. Lacy had been horrified for all of a week before she embraced the truck, swore she loved it, and started saving to get a bright-orange paint job. Everyone in town smiled when they saw her coming. Something about Lacy and her orange Ford made people want to be a part of Lacy's world.

Their friend had succumbed to cervical cancer months ago, but in typical Lacy fashion, she'd left her three best friends letters and money to fulfill something they'd always longed to do. Rosemary was on the first leg of that mission, using the money Lacy had left her to go to New York City for three weeks. Didn't seem like such a big deal to most people, but Rosemary had been coddled, swaddled, and locked down her whole life by her crazy-assed parents. Going to the Big Apple alone was a big deal for the old-fashioned Rosemary. And her embarking upon an affair with an Italian pizza maker was a mind boggle for Jess and Eden. But they were relieved for their friend. If anyone needed to get laid and—well, hell, they all needed to get laid and feel good about themselves—it was Rosemary.

Leave it to Lacy to understand just what to do to shake up her three besties.

"She would so do that. Probably wear that blue wig, too," Jess said, remembering how they'd laughed when Lacy had bought a blue wig to cover her bald head. It was common knowledge Lacy had been born with a pointy head after her mother had labored for eighteen hours and twenty-three minutes—something her mother was known to tell perfect strangers—so when Lacy started to lose her hair, she wasn't about to take any chances. And somehow, Lacy had looked right in the blue bouffant wig. Lacy's mother, however, had been horrified. She'd bought Lacy a nice blonde wig to wear to church, in which Lacy had tied a big bow just to tick her mother off.

Eden giggled, meeting Jess's gaze. Something passed between them. A sort of sadness. A sort of happiness. They'd loved and lost, but they were alive and doing what their friend would want them to do. Move on. Wear red lipstick. Talk about the fun times. Choose to be bold. Lacy had admired boldness in a person.

"Let's go," Jess said, walking back into the kitchen to get her purse and cell phone. She glanced at the screen and saw that her mother had called twice. Her brother once. They were all worried about her, knowing she'd gone to court that day. Wondering what Benton said or didn't say. Wondering why Jess hadn't wanted them to go with her. Why she'd refused to eat dinner at her parents' that night. Why she'd wanted to be alone.

She scrolled down and saw she'd missed a call from an unknown number.

"Jess," Eden called from the living room. "Let's go if we're going."

"Just a sec," Jess said, seeing that whoever had called had left a voice mail. She pressed the button and listened.

"Mrs. Culpepper, this is Jill Grover with Staff Pro. Sorry for the late call, but a position has come available I think you will be interested in. It requires availability for at least three months and is located in Pensacola, Florida, where you are licensed. If you'll call me in the morning, I'll relay the details—they need someone who can start in a few weeks' time. I think this is exactly what you've been looking for. And as a bonus, the hospital is five minutes from the beach."

Jess couldn't stop the smile that curved her lips.

The beach?

Oh hell yes. She'd always longed to fade off to sleep to the sound of waves crashing on the beach. To be tanned and sandy. Make a seashell collection. Be a beach bum.

Just a week ago she'd signed up with a company providing contract medical staff to hospitals. She needed to get out of Morning Glory for a while, away from her past so she could decide her future. With her mother suggesting nice men she could date, including poor gay Chris Haven, who'd just moved back to Morning Glory to take a job at the bank, and her brother inviting her over to watch his kids scream and run around the backyard while he talked about various hardy grass varieties, she was at her wits' end with all the good intentions whirling around her. She needed a break, but she also needed a break where she could make money. No longer could she depend on Benton's income, and the job she'd taken at the local pediatric office last year in preparation for becoming a stay-at-home mommy didn't pay enough to allow her any savings. And a newly single gal needed savings, plenty of wine, and, according to Carla Minnis at the dry cleaner, a good vibrator.

She'd never had a vibrator before and didn't know how to go about getting one. Maybe the Internet. Or one of those sleazy stores that dotted the interstate.

But regardless of battery-powered loving, she had an opportunity tossed into her lap. If she could get away from seeing Benton at the grocery store, get away from the idle gossip of him dating Deirdre Perot, get away from all the damn pity in the eyes of every bank teller, she might be able to heal. And with the money Lacy had left her, she could afford to rent something right on the beach.

"Jess!" Eden cried impatiently. "Come on. I turn into a pumpkin at eleven o'clock."

"Not midnight?" Jess teased, sliding her phone into her back pocket.

Eden's red lips turned down. "Come on, if this were a fairy tale I would not be wearing my cousin's hand-me-down khakis or a borrowed shirt."

Jess gave her friend a smile. "If this were a fairy tale, I wouldn't be a nearly thirtysomething divorcée wearing sequins."

Chapter Two

Ryan Reyes stared out across Pensacola Bay and flipped a beer top across his deck. Part of him hated himself for doing something so cavalier. What if someone kicked it off the deck and it ended up in the sand, a potential hazard for a bare foot? The other part celebrated that it was his own damn deck and he didn't have to pick up after himself if he didn't want to.

He took a long draw on the beer as he propped his feet on the top of the wooden fence surrounding the deck that sat off his bedroom. The sun waved good-bye to his right, streaking the deepening darkness with a last hurrah of pink and orange ribbon curls flung out above the white-capped waves below. It was gorgeous, like so many sunsets he'd watched over the past year. Sometimes he felt moments like these—when he sat on the deck and watched the sun set—were like a nod of approval for the choices he'd made. Other times it provoked regret.

He always dashed the regret away, because he'd decided over a year and a half ago, shortly after he'd received that call from Tarrant

Biometrics, that he would be exactly who he was today—just a regular guy who didn't wear white lab coats, who drank domestic beer, and who didn't care about having a long list of scientific accomplishments.

The sea breeze coming off the Gulf made his hair wave against his forehead, and he liked that feeling. Windblown, loose, and chilled. Yes, that was who he was now.

"Yoo-hoo," a feminine voice called from below.

Ryan leaned over to find Morgan Mayeaux standing below him wearing a sarong and holding a pitcher of margaritas. "Hey, whatcha got there?"

She held up the chilled pitcher. "Dinner."

"In that case, come on up," he said with a smile. He'd met Morgan at Peg Leg Pete's last fall. She'd been wearing a tube top that barely held up her admirable rack and a pair of cutoff shorts that left little to the imagination. She had bouncing dark hair, a round face, and friendly brown eyes. They'd hit it off right away, discussing Tom Petty and the Heartbreakers and their favorite kinds of Life Savers candy. She'd given him a slightly sloppy drunken kiss and then invited him back to her place, which belonged to her parents and was ironically only five condo units down from his. He'd turned her down, an oddity for him, because he liked her and didn't want a one-night stand with someone he'd see on the beach or around the neighborhood. And because she'd told him she wanted a boyfriend, someone to share her world with. She was tired of dating and hooking up.

And that was *not* what he was looking for.

Morgan pulled the gate open and sashayed up the wooden stairs he'd added over the winter. He hated sand getting into his house, and the deck was a natural catchall when he or friends walked up from the beach. "My famous recipe, perfected when I was a bartender at the Sand Trap in Destin."

"I'll grab some cups."

"Got 'em," Morgan trilled, pulling two plastic cups wrapped in motel cling wrap from her beach bag.

Ryan poured himself some of the frosty concoction, nodding as he took a sip. "Perfect."

"I know, right?" she said, unwrapping her own cup, filling it to the top, and sinking onto a deck chair. "Now, let's plan your birthday party."

"You really don't have to do this."

"Are you joking? I love a reason to throw a party. I bought some cool lanterns and Andrew said he'd spring for the keg. Sara is borrowing a beer pong table from her brother. He goes to Georgia. It has a Kappa Alpha crest on it, but you don't care, do you?"

"Nope. Beer pong is beer pong." Or at least he thought it was. Was there something sacred about a fraternity crest? He didn't know. He'd entered Stanford when he was fourteen, so being in a fraternity hadn't been an option. Med school didn't have social fraternities, and he'd still been so young he was rarely asked to any event. And if he'd gone, he wouldn't have been able to drink anyway.

"Right. And I've invited about twenty people. Of course, it could turn into more if some of them bring dates or friends or something. But anyway, I sent out invites via e-mail and told everyone to BYOB if they didn't want beer and bring a snack or something. It will be epic."

Epic. His favorite new word. Or at least one of his favorite new words. "It's nice of you to do this."

"Sure. That's what friends are for," she said with a shrug, but he could hear something in her voice. He knew she wanted to be more, but Ryan didn't do girlfriends. Not because he had anything against the concept, but because he was still on year one of his new life. Technically year one. In a few weeks he'd turn over to year two, which held the possibility of a relationship but nothing too serious. He didn't want true commitment until he was at least thirty, preferably thirty-three or thirty-four. Maybe even forty. Or never. He liked his life as it was. Why rush into anything complicated?

"So what's been going on?" he asked, changing the subject from his twenty-sixth birthday party taking place in two days' time.

"Not much. Let's see, I worked today, went to visit Zsa Zsa, and made margaritas. I'm calling it a win."

Ryan held up the cup with the words *Holiday Inn* inscribed on the side. "Hear, hear. How's your sexy grandmother, by the way?"

"Still chasing the men who can actually walk around the complex." She touched her plastic cup to his and took a drink, propping her bare feet next to his on a weathered board. "I have a new neighbor."

"Yeah? They finally rented the Dirty Heron?"

"Unfortunate name, huh? Yeah, it's a nurse. I saw her unloading her car today. She looks really sensible, but I invited her to your party anyway."

"Why?"

"I don't know. 'Cause she's new to the area? From some small Mississippi town or something. She's working at Bay View General doing . . . contract work? I don't know what that is."

"That means she's working for an agency that fills positions temporarily for understaffed hospitals and clinics." Small Mississippi town, huh? Just like him. Of course, most people he hung out with at the marina or down at Sid's Beach Hut thought he was from California. He let them think that, though he knew sometimes his Mississippi dialect slipped through. Not to mention some of the idioms he'd picked up being raised in his small town. Didn't seem pertinent to mention he'd been born to two ambitious educators who'd raised their intellectually gifted only child to do something more than cut up bait and take spoiled businessmen out to catch fish they'd likely not even bother to take home to eat. Of course, his clients took pictures with the fish. Facebook and all that.

"Oh, well, she seemed nice enough. Of course, she was kinda pretty, so I hesitated to ask her to come to the party. I don't want any competition." Morgan slid a sly glance toward him.

"Oh, come on, who's prettier than you?"

She sniffed and pushed her thick, brown hair off her shoulders. "No one."

"So did she say yes?"

"She said she'd try. But I won't be surprised if she doesn't." Morgan drank a few more sips. "You want to go swimming?"

"No. Fat Sam saw some sharks feeding last evening."

"You scared?" Morgan asked.

"Hell, no, but I ain't dumb. Why chance it?"

"So you can get naked with me," she said with a flirty smile.

"Morgan, I'm not opposed to getting naked with you, darlin', but I *am* opposed to ruining a perfectly good friendship."

"It's not like we can't screw and still be friends." She tried to sound nonchalant, but he could hear the yearning. Thing was, she had a smoking body and was fun to be around, but he'd already tried that with a waitress at Curly's. Anna had gotten possessive and then gone a little crazy, spray painting the word *bastard* on his fence when she caught him with another woman. Thing was, Anna had sworn she hadn't wanted a relationship when they'd first hooked up, too. Obviously she had. And he'd had to paint his pretty, naturally stained fence white to cover up the offensive word. Sometimes he imagined he could still see the scrawled red through the fresh white paint. And he could no longer hang at Curly's, which was a shame because they had awesome wings and a nice selection of imported beer.

He patted Morgan's arm but didn't answer. He liked having friends, too. There were plenty of fish in the sea. Maybe he'd invite a few barracudas from the marina that might suit Morgan . . . and keep her from scratching his vintage Mustang or smashing his windows. Women were incredible, but some had a temper that scared him more than the occa-sional tropical storm or hurricane ripping through the Panhandle. *No strings* seemed to mean different things to different people.

"The tide's going out," he commented as the glowing orb of orange sank into the dark blue. The waves pulled at the beach, churning the sand. Tomorrow morning would bring plenty of crushed shell, but he wouldn't have time to go down and wade through to look for any beau-ties. He had a deep-sea charter booked for 6:00 a.m. and he would need to cut bait and check the reels before they went out. Usually his deckhand took care of that, but Vic had to go to court tomorrow, so he was borrowing a deckhand for the day. Thankfully, he'd already fueled up *Beagle*, his forty-six-foot charter fishing boat. Might be rough in the morning with heavier winds, so he'd need to bring a few more buckets for the pukers.

"Since you're not interested in my rocking your world, I'll head back home. I have a slight headache," Morgan said, sounding disappointed.

The woman needed to get laid. She rose and stretched, her chest thrusting out, making hot lust shoot straight to his groin. His good intentions wavered. What would it hurt? But then he caught sight of the fence and thought about never seeing Morgan again because she was pissed at him. He liked her too much for that. He'd find someone else to scratch that itch and pray one of his guys found the brunette to their liking. "You don't have to."

"I know, but I can see you're in a weird mood, too."

"What do you mean?"

"You're such a cool guy, but sometimes you get this look. Like you're somebody else."

"Because I don't talk?"

She shrugged. "It's hard to explain. Most the time you're you, but sometimes you're so different. Like you're above all this."

Uh-huh. He knew what she meant. Sometimes his good-time-Charlie demeanor slipped and he drew into himself. Being social wore him out. A natural introvert, he often craved downtime, especially after he spent several days in a row hanging at beachside bars, shooting pool and carousing. Oh, he liked the carousing, all right. After spending his entire childhood and teen years studying and participating only in activities designed to pad his résumé, he wanted to be exactly who he now was. But sometimes it wore on him. "I'm me, Morgan. And I'm looking forward to the party tomorrow night. I do have an early morning, so I guess I'm winding down. Thanks for the margaritas."

"Sure," she said, glancing down at him with that damn yearning again. Her eyes took in his open linen shirt, sun-faded cutoff khakis, and his bare feet. He knew he looked the part. Beach bum. No worries. Totally cool.

He was no longer Dr. Ryan Reyes, MD, PhD, major nerd.

"See ya tomorrow, darlin'," he drawled, flashing a dazzling smile thanks to his home bleaching kit. He liked the way his white teeth looked against his tanned skin. Being on the water every day had its advantages.

"'Night, Ryan. Don't worry about bringing booze tomorrow. I got your favorite tequila."

He saluted her and watched as she carefully made her way down the steps. She'd put on those weird shoes women wore . . . uh, wedges. They did wonders for her nice, tanned legs. But they'd not accomplished Morgan's goal of seduction. Ryan congratulated himself on his self-control. Normally, he'd take what a girl like Morgan was selling. And no one could look sideways at him for making up for lost time. After all, he'd gotten two doctorates before he'd ever even gotten laid. He was due some fun.

Maybe tomorrow night he'd meet a girl who didn't want anything but a good time.

A woman who knew the score.

Jess pulled the heavy glass door closed and made her way across the rental to the front door. It had taken her all day to unpack her few suitcases and stock the empty fridge with healthy foods. She'd studied all the good stuff—Oreos, Cheetos, and Fruity Oh's—at the grocery store, but knew if she indulged in them she wouldn't fit into the new clothes she'd bought in preparation for beach living, including the cute red bikini with the anchors on it. Yeah, she hadn't worn a bikini since spring break in college, but she'd bought the skimpiest damn one she could find at the semiannual clearance sale at the Dillard's in Jackson. And why the hell not? She'd lost enough weight grieving her marriage. Might as well surf the silver lining.

She winced as she bumped into the ceramic sculpture of a heron. The top of the bird's head was missing. Maybe so she could store her umbrella? She wasn't sure.

Okay, so the condo wasn't something out of *Southern Living*, but the location more than made up for the kitschy decor and bright-yellow paint. Yes, view trumped tacky every time. And she had two of them. A string of ten condo units sat facing the bay on the narrow strip of land called Gulf Breeze, which split Pensacola Bay from the Gulf of Mexico. Thankfully, her particular condo sat across from the Gulf, giving her a view of the crashing waves from the back of the house and the gentle lapping bay from the front. She had only to cross the two-lane highway and follow the gangway before she emerged onto the wide beach.

Once Labor Day rolled around, she'd have to give the rental up to "the nice couple from Jersey" who spent every winter in the Dirty Heron. That was the name of the condo. Dirty Heron. She had no clue why anyone would name a condo something so absurd, but it had a certain ring to it, she guessed. After the holiday weekend, the rental company would find something else for her. Her only requirement was that it was either beachside or beach view. She wanted the crash of the waves on the beach to lull her to sleep every night and the silky sands only feet away when she needed the particular therapy of sun and salty waters. Which after a long day was exactly what she needed—a hello to the beach.

Crossing the highway and traversing the weathered walkway between the dunes, she emerged onto the wide stretch of sand. Jess stared out at the dark waters lapping at the white powder sand. The moon was full tonight, making the beach glow. Small crabs sidled sideways across the sands, and sea oats danced in the night winds.

Paradise.

And exactly what she needed to soothe away the hurt.

Something about the sea made a person feel small, her problems insignificant. So her husband had walked out on her? Big deal. So she had to start over careerwise and relationshipwise? Wasn't like she was totally dead in the water. Much. She was still young—not even thirty yet. And she had a good job. Contract work paid well. And her boobs didn't sag. Much. And she didn't have stretch marks from being pregnant. Or a C-section scar. Or crow's-feet. She was good. She could start over. No big deal.

Jess walked down to the water's edge, marveling at the gulls dipping and diving like acrobats, chasing their evening meal before roosting somewhere. Where did the gulls go? They must go somewhere when they weren't greeting beachgoers each morning and wishing them farewell each night. The water was cool, but not cold. It was August, which meant warm gulf waters. The waves rolled in, covering her feet.

Though her stomach felt jumpy about being on her own, she knew she could do this.

She'd gone to the hospital that day to fill out paperwork. After which a very pregnant nursing supervisor had given her a brief tour of the surgical suites, supply closets, and ever-necessary break room. Bay View was an older hospital with an intentional retro vibe. The tour and quick staff meet and greet had whetted Jess's appetite to get back to what she loved. She'd spent the past year and a half working for a pediatrician. She'd thought it perfect for a woman looking to grow her family—no commute, easy access to day care (a.k.a. her mother), and less stress. But that was before Benton had come home with flowers. The man had brought her flowers. A mixed bouquet with too many carnations.

She'd taken one look at the bouquet in his hands and felt thrilled. She was ovulating, and he'd tried to make it an occasion. She'd taken them to the sink and pulled a bottle of his favorite wine out of the fridge. But when she turned back to kiss him, he's had this look on his face. Like a dog that had pissed on the floor.

She'd jabbed the flowers in water, a sour feeling in her stomach, and then asked him what he'd done.

Turned out he'd done Brandy Robbins, the florist she'd always used.

The fucking florist who'd wrapped up the flowers he'd brought to apologize to Jess. The flowers that he'd handed her like an apology. Like an arrangement for a funeral.

Then he'd told her he wanted out.

O-U-T. Out.

As in he didn't want her, a baby, or an SUV that could fit a growing family. As in he had regrets about not dating any other people in high school and college. As in he'd made a mistake when he married her, and he was really sorry but he couldn't help the way he felt. Which was trapped.

Jess had stood there staring at his handsome face, at this man she'd gone to prom with, given her virginity to, given up a dream job in Birmingham for, and wanted to laugh. Because it sounded like a joke. A big fat gotcha.

But it wasn't.

Benton had fallen for Brandy . . . or so he'd said. He didn't want to be married any longer. He'd missed out on too much by dating only one girl his whole life. *Experiences.* That's what he said he wanted. Like they hadn't had experiences together. Like they hadn't shared each other's notes in English III or seen the sun sink into the Pacific Ocean while sipping champagne to celebrate their nuptials. Like she hadn't squealed with glee when he scooped her up and carried her over the threshold of the cottage they'd restored or painted the nursery a pretty, soft green in preparation for their someday baby. Like everything they'd dreamed, whispering to each other in that poignant moment after soul-stirring lovemaking, hadn't been an experience. No, an experience obviously was fucking Brandy on the counter in the back of Flowers for You.

'Cause that's what Benton had wanted.

Jess kicked the wave, causing droplets to explode into the air, peppering her bare legs with the spray.

She didn't want to think about the hurt anymore.

It was a new day. A new Jess. She'd had a year to cry, hurt, rail, throw things. Her therapist said she'd gone through all the steps of grieving the loss of love. But what the therapist hadn't told her was how to fill the enormous void inside her. Or maybe Dr. Richardson had. She'd encouraged Jess to try new activities, relish her friendships, cherish her parents. Essentially, she'd told Jess to appreciate the life she had, not grieve the one she'd built up in her mind—the picket fence, the dimpled baby, and the carpool lines. *Stay in the moment. Live each day without planning the next. Be spontaneous. Be open to love.*

Horseshit.

Jess shook herself, trying to beat off the cynicism, trying to embrace her new adventure.

So maybe she should go to that party tomorrow night. Her new next-door neighbor, a sunny brunette with skimpy clothes, had asked her to come over and celebrate her friend's twenty-sixth birthday. They were making Jell-O shots and playing beer pong. That should be fun, right?

Jess sighed and glanced back as the water rolled over her toes. Dark, foamy water, nothing clear. Just like her future. But beneath murky waters lay pretty things—smooth shells, delicate sand dollars, and iridescent fish. Or things with teeth. Things that tore and stung. Only time would tell what lay beneath for her.

Turning away from the introspection, Jess headed back.

She looked up and down the beach, wind tousling her hair, and caught sight of a figure standing much as she had about a hundred yards down the beach. A man quietly assessing his own life. A moment of kinship struck her. *Such is the human condition.*

Finding her flip-flops, she brushed the sand from her feet, sinking briefly on the weathered wood of the walkway to dust her legs off. Her gaze snagged once again on the man framed against the inky sky, like a portrait painted as a study in loneliness, which seemed suitable for her reflective mood.

She rose and walked back toward the Dirty Heron, determined to embrace her own new experiences.

Chapter Three

The next evening Jess punched the unfamiliar pillow and muttered a really dirty word—one that would have made even her father blanch. And her father had been a sailor . . . even if it was as a dental officer in the navy. The music from the condo next door was ridiculously loud. And Jess was tolerant, damn it. She'd never been one to get pissy over a little noise. But tomorrow was her first day at Bay View, and being comatose for her shift would probably be frowned upon.

A roar of laughter temporarily blocked AC/DC screaming about shaking them all night long. Final straw. Jess sat up and blinked at the red numbers glowing on the alarm clock—2:04 a.m.

Freaking 2:04 a.m.

Whipping the covers back, Jess pulled on a pair of athletic shorts she'd tossed on the bamboo chair and struggled into a T-shirt. No bra, but for God's sake, it was the wee hours, and she didn't really care if she looked like a wild demon rousted from slumber. 'Cause she was a wild, mad demon . . . who had to work the next day. Time to be *that* neighbor. The grumpy stick-in-the-mud who complained about noise.

Grabbing the key so she didn't lock herself out, she pushed out the front door and emerged onto the graveled concrete that dug into her feet. She tenderfooted it over to the next set of steps and climbed up to the condo that had a cute little sign that read, "Beach Blanket Bingo." Much cuter name than the Dirty Heron.

Jess knocked on the door, but the music and laughter overshadowed a simple knock.

So she banged her fist against the yellow door.

Nothing.

A cacophony of Bruno Mars and shrieking conspired to stifle her knocking. She had to admit Bruno Mars was more tolerable than '80s headbangers, but he'd still keep her awake, uptown funky or not. Trying the doorknob to no avail, Jess leaned her forehead against the locked door in momentary defeat.

Who locked a door when there was a party?

Sighing, Jess spun around, pushing her frizzy brown hair from the corners of her mouth. A dull headache pressed against the back of her eyes. She'd look like hell tomorrow, no doubt. Determined and growing more and more pissed by the rude, inconsiderate, too-young-to-realize-people-needed-sleep-to-function-the-next-day partiers, Jess went back down the steps, cutting beneath the raised pier-and-beam condominiums, heading toward the deck that faced the Gulf. She could see the soft shadows of people clustered in groups above her, hear the Richter-scale laughter and conversation. Because she was looking up, trying to find Morgan, her new neighbor, she didn't see the large body lying a few feet from the bottom of the steps.

She snagged her foot on a leg and went sprawling. Her windmilling arms did nothing to stop her from landing with the grace of a hippo facedown in the sand.

"Jesus," Jess whispered, lying still a moment, flexing her muscles and checking for any injury. Nope. The soft sand had cushioned her.

"No, not Jesus. I told you. Ryan. My nameth Ryan," someone slurred.

Spitting sand from her mouth, Jess pushed herself up, wiping her face. When she finally cleared her wild curls from her eyes, she found herself sitting a foot from a naked man. In fact, her right foot had landed across his bare thighs. Squeaking, she jerked her foot back, shuffling back in order to put an extra foot or two between her and the nude dude.

"Krista?" the man asked, his words noticeably slurred. "Krista!"

Jess poked him in the ribs with her foot. "Stop yelling. I'm not Krista."

The man cracked an eye at her. She couldn't tell the color, but she got the general idea he was young. He lay on his back, gloriously splayed as if the gods had given birth to him. Like in that *Clash of the Titans* movie where Perseus washes up. Or was that *Blue Lagoon*? Or some other '70s flick she'd watched on the AMC channel? Whichever. Same result. Young, hot, and naked on a beach.

"Where's she?" he asked, his one open eye on her.

"Who?"

"Krrrrrista."

"I don't know."

"Okay," he said and closed his eyes, resting his hands on his chest like a corpse.

Jess was a nurse and had seen plenty of naked bodies. Some were finely honed, beautiful to gaze upon (not that she ever forgot to be professional), and some were not so finely honed—in fact, far from it. This guy was in the former category. Hey, she was professional. Not blind. "What are you doing out here? The party is upstairs." And too loud.

He grunted before saying, "Watching stars."

"Your eyes are closed."

He opened them as if alarmed. "Well, I was watching, but then I had to rest my eyes."

"At least someone's sleeping through the party." Jess spit some more sand out of her mouth. "Why don't I help you up? You're, ah, missing some clothing. We can get you some water and perhaps an aspirin or two."

"I don't wan water. I wan rum. It's my birday."

His massacre of the English language told her all she needed to know. The guy was way over the limit. "But it will make you feel much better tomorrow, birthday boy."

So here lay the birthday boy who had caused her to miss her beauty sleep and face-plant into a dune. Hadn't anyone upstairs realized the guest of honor was drunk, naked, and stargazing?

"Okay," he said, pushing himself up. His smile was wide and goofy, reminding her of a puppy . . . if puppies had scruffy chiseled jaws and dark slashing brows. Grains of sand clung to his tanned shoulders, and his eyes looked light—maybe green or maybe blue—but not the boring brown she dealt with in the mirror each morning. White teeth flashed, and brown hair highlighted by either the sun or a good stylist tousled in the sea breeze.

"Where's my clothes?" he asked. His gaze was sincere, as if he had absolute faith she knew the answer to his question.

Jess struggled to rise in the shifting sand. Dusting her hands, she glanced around but could see nothing but a pair of flip-flops that had been orphaned close to the surf. "I see your shoes."

"Good, good," he said, nodding, his head falling forward like a sleepy child's.

Jess strolled over to the two flip-flops and scooped them up, but she didn't see his actual clothes. Padding back, she nudged him with her big toe. "Hey, I don't see your shorts. Did you go in the water?" She peered at his hair to see if it looked damp, wondering why she even bothered.

She should leave him naked under the stairs, march upstairs, and make the complaint to Morgan. Then she could get two or three more hours in before she had to go to work. She looked down at the man, whose head bobbed against his chest. Someone stupid enough to get that wasted didn't deserve help, but still she felt obligated to assist him. Probably because she'd been raised by a Sunday school teacher . . . and had taken an oath to devote herself to those placed in her care. She'd tripped over him, and now he was hers to aid.

"We went skinny-dipping, 'cept I forgot about the shark Fat Sam saw. Then I yelled, 'Shark.' She didn't think it was so funny . . . and she didn't come back to watch stars with me . . . and she didn't give me any on my birday."

"Good Lord," Jess muttered as the man fell over and curled up like a child. Of course his hard ass wasn't chubby and cute like her nephew's. Not even close. "I'm going to get a towel off my deck. Don't go anywhere."

"Okay," he managed before releasing a huge sigh.

Jess stomped over to her set of steps, thankful she'd left a towel out on the glass-topped table earlier that day. She'd spent the day running errands and familiarizing herself with the area, finding a local branch of her bank, popping in to a beach store for a couple of towels, sunscreen, and a six-pack of beer. She'd splashed around a bit in her new bikini, feeling conspicuous in something so . . . not there. Then she'd made a big salad, watched some Netflix, and hit the bed early, electing not to show up at the party next door. She knew she should have forced herself to mingle if only for half an hour, but she wasn't ready to go to parties and make small talk with people. She wasn't ready to be "out there." But that would have been better than playing mommy to an overgrown kid who couldn't handle his liquor.

She stopped just as she reached for the towel draped over the side of the table.

Kid?

She was probably only three or four years older than the drunk. And probably only six or seven years older than Morgan. So why did she feel so ancient? Hazard of her job? Or maybe it was her nature. She tended to be pragmatic . . . reasonable . . . too comfortable. That was why Benton had left, right? Because she was boring. Booooooring.

"Shit," she said, angry at herself for not going to the party. For labeling the people at the party as kids. Jerking the towel free, she marched back over to Morgan's. The naked guy now snored softly against the sand.

"Hey," she said, again using her foot to nudge him.

He didn't move.

"Sleeping Beauty?" she said, leaning down and setting a hand on his shoulder. Gently she moved him side to side.

He rolled over, opening his eyes. "Hey, you."

"Hey," she said trying not to smile at his expression, which was boyishly sleepy. "I brought you a towel."

"You're so sweet," he said, giving her a drunken smile that somehow looked adorable. "And this should totally cover my 'nads."

Jess nearly laughed. "You're welcome . . . what's your name?"

"Ryan."

"You're welcome, Ryan." She held the towel out, and he looked at it for a few seconds. "Here. Cover yourself."

He grabbed the towel, pulled it over his shoulders, and lay back down, snuggling into the sand.

"No," she said reaching for him again. Clasping his now towel-covered shoulder, she shook him again. "Get up. You can't sleep here."

"Yeah, I can," he sighed, closing his eyes.

"Ryan." Jess tried again, shaking him. "Come on. Let's go inside. Morgan will be worried about you. Maybe we can find, uh, Krista. You can get you some."

"I know you," he said, still not opening his eyes.

"Sure you do. I'm the nice girl who is helping you, and you're the guy getting up. Come on," she said, slipping an arm beneath him the way she did when she had to lift patients to slide them onto a gurney. She didn't have sheets to use, so she tried to position the towel. Ryan shifted and wrapped her in his arms.

"Hey," she said, pushing against him as his hands moved toward her butt.

"You smell good. I knew you'd smell so good," he said, nuzzling his nose into the valley between her breasts. For a slight moment a jolt of pleasure hit her, which was so freaking weird, because the whole thing was so inappropriate. She didn't know this dude. He was a total stranger—a drunk, naked stranger—and he was sticking his nose where it absolutely didn't belong.

"Stop it," she said pushing against him.

"What's a matter, babe?" Ryan muttered, reaching halfheartedly for her again. "Come on. It's just Ryan. You know me."

Jess shot backward and landed on her butt. Then she got pissed again. Scrabbling up, she gave him a hard kick with her foot. "Okay, listen, Ryan. You either get your ass up or I'm leaving you to the crabs and whatever else moseys along. You've got until the count of three to get up. One . . . two . . ."

"Okay, okay," he said, struggling up, the cute lime-and-pink towel draped over his shoulders. Jess kept her eyes on his shoulders, because she sensed the flopping of certain parts of him. Parts that she shouldn't look at. For any reason.

He rolled over onto all fours, and she jerked her eyes to the huge wooden beam nearest her. "Put the towel around your waist, and I'll help you up the stairs."

She heard a lot of grunting and watched him stumble against the piling nearest him before he said, "Okay. I got a towel on."

Chancing a glance, she sighed in relief. He'd managed to rope the towel around his lean hips and had even managed a tuck that looked secure. Standing up, he looked even more gorgeous. And more drunk. He listed to the side and said, "Why're you movin'?"

"I'm not. You are," Jess said cautiously, stepping to his side so she could loop an arm about his waist. She felt a bit uncomfortable, considering he'd tried to snuggle with her mere seconds ago, but if she were going to get him up the stairs, it was a necessary evil.

She didn't want to notice how firm and warm he was, nor how he smelled like both the sea and a nice cologne that hadn't come from a discount store. 'Cause, again, weird.

"I may have had too much to drink," he said, throwing a heavy arm about her shoulders.

"You think?" she said, allowing some lightness into her voice.

"Yeah. I think," he said, looking sheepish.

Jess was used to people's embarrassment. After all, when you've inserted a catheter or aided someone in using the toilet, you develop a certain sensibility about delicate situations, not to mention compassion and humor.

"Morgan went to all that trouble making Jell-O shots shaped like li'l boats. Then someone wanted me to funnel beer. Seemed like I should be a good sport and all, 'specially when they just wanted to make me happy on my birday." He managed to make it to the stairs. Once there he clung to the handrail, trying to alleviate some pressure from her shoulders. "I think I should go home."

Jess shook her head. "You're in no condition to drive . . . you're barely in enough condition to walk. I'm worried about the stairs."

"Hey, Morgan, there he is," someone shouted from above.

Glancing up she saw a guy hanging his head over the railing. Seconds later, Morgan's long brown hair swung over. "Ryan, where in the hell have you been?"

"The beach," Ryan said, his concentration on lifting his legs.

"Why?" she asked, scooting around to the opening of the stairs and trotting down. "Someone come help Ry."

A handsome guy jumped to attention and leaped down the steps, moving Jess out of the way so he could support Ryan.

"Oh, hey," Morgan said, pausing a few steps from the top, her gaze landing on Jess. "You made it to the party. Come on up and grab a beer or whatever."

Jess pressed her hands to Ryan's broad back as he stumbled back. "Uh, not really. Look, I knocked on the front door."

"Yeah, I locked that. My mom's all paranoid about the painted wood floor in the foyer. She had it done to look like a bingo card and it's, like, not something she wants all scuffed up. Everyone came through the back. What do you want to drink?"

The woman was so friendly, Jess almost acquiesced. But it was now way after 2:00 a.m. The first slivers of dawn would sneak up on her like a ninja. "Nothing. I actually came over to ask you to turn down the music. I start a new job in the morning, and it's hard to sleep with the music blaring."

A flash of irritation swept Morgan's face, but she quickly covered it with a smile. "Sorry. I didn't think you'd mind. You didn't seem . . ." She hesitated for a moment, letting the implication that Jess was a whiny bitch sit there. Then she turned and screeched, "Tanner, turn down the music."

The guy who'd jumped to help Ryan had managed to get him to the top of the stairs. Morgan looped her arm around Ryan's shoulders and gave a shake of her head. "You're such a lightweight."

The music shut off, and several people made their way out onto the deck.

"It's okay," Morgan said to the people peering out at Jess standing in her Morning Glory Fun Run T-shirt and bleach-stained shorts. "Ryan got lost."

"I'm gonna head out," one girl said, looking at her watch. "Didn't realize how late it was."

"No, don't go yet. We still have to have the championship round of the beer pong tourney," Morgan said as Ryan stumbled against her.

It was time to go. Jess started creeping down the last five steps. Party looked to be winding down, so maybe she could finally get some sleep.

"Me, too. I got class tomorrow morning," someone else said. Several others affirmed they had to leave, calling out happy birthday to Ryan, who looked to be falling asleep where he stood.

"Come on, y'all," Morgan called, trying to steady Ryan. "Ryan wants to play spin the bottle. Seven minutes in heaven. Or naked twister."

Ryan straightened up and opened his eyes, glancing down to where Jess stood poised to make her escape. "Thanks for getting me this . . . whoops," he said, grabbing the towel at his waist. "Almost lost it."

Morgan jerked her gaze to Ryan's waist. "If everyone's leaving, you can let it fall, darlin'." She sounded like she was joking . . . a little.

Ryan frowned, his glazed eyes never leaving Jess. "Thank you."

Jess waved. "Sure. Good night."

"'Night, Jess," Ryan said, stumbling away. Morgan watched him with a look of longing, and Jess could definitely see the lay of the land. Morgan was into Ryan, but he wasn't into her. Or perhaps he was merely too drunk to appreciate the suggestion.

Jess lifted her hand lamely and then headed back to her house. Out front she could hear car doors opening and closing and people calling out good nights. Of course, they should have called out, "Good morning." She walked back to her rental and knew she wouldn't sleep. She was too awake, and after the exertion of helping the birthday boy up half the steps, her heart was pumping. Slipping back into her now blessedly quiet condo, she put on a kettle and found the tea bags she'd purchased earlier. Minutes later she folded her long legs into one of the chairs on the deck and stared out at the bay gently lapping at the sand surrounding it. Almost three miles away, the bay bridge stretched out, lights lining the way to the mainland full of grocery stores and modern conveniences. On the side where her rental sat there were beach shops, small boutiques, and restaurants specializing in shrimp and crab. The bay had its own particular charm.

Lacy would have loved it.

Lacy.

Jess rubbed her face, thinking about her late friend. The woman had been so full of life. She would have gone to that party and made tons of friends within the first hour. With her chubby dimpled cheeks and wholesome charm, she'd automatically seemed like a person's best friend. Everyone loved Lacy.

Jess missed her friend.

Since junior high Jess, Lacy, Rosemary, and Eden had been the best of friends. They'd gone through the whole bra-fitting thing, getting periods, and crushing on Benton . . . yes, they'd all liked Benton in the eighth grade. They'd struggled through geometry and physics together, traded prom magazines and cheered for the Morning Glory Mavericks, except for Rosemary, who was the editor of *The Bloom*, MGHS's yearbook. They'd been sisters, linked arm in arm, bound by innocence, wrapped in self-involvement, fresh-scrubbed faces ready to conquer the world. And then life happened. Eden couldn't go to college, Rosemary opened a store, Jess got married, and Lacy got cancer.

At first they'd thought it would be okay. Lacy was eternally optimistic. They made T-shirts and held races and fund-raisers. There were late-night hospital pajama parties and wig-shopping trips. Lacy smiled through it all, so sure it would be a story she could tell her grandchildren one day, about that time their grammy had cervical cancer and wore blue wigs to embarrass her parents. But it hadn't happened that way. Lacy's cancer spread. All over. And nothing worked. Not chemo, not radiation, not the experimental drugs. Finally, Lacy accepted hospice care and waited to die. It broke Jess's heart, especially since she stood next to a surgeon day in and day out helping to save people.

But this time, Jess could do nothing but watch Lacy waste away.

"Don't look at me that way, Jess," Lacy would say. "Like I'm dying."

"I'm not," Jess would say, though both she and Lacy knew she lied. Because Lacy was dying. But they wouldn't talk about it. So as she sat with Lacy, they'd talk about the tramp Benton was dating or about spring fashions or the frickin' weather. But never about how hollow Lacy's eyes looked or how gaunt she grew. Somehow it was easier for Jess to be a friend and not a nurse in those moments.

On the day of Lacy's funeral, she, Rosemary, and Eden had slipped away from the somber reception held at Fulbright's Funeral Parlor, grief weary and empty of tears, and gathered at their table at the Lazy Frog coffee shop, the place where they'd met almost every day for over ten years. There behind the counter, Lacy had left them a gift—a cheerfully wrapped box containing Lacy's treasured travel charm bracelet along with letters and money for each friend. In each letter she encouraged her friends to do what she could no longer do—live out a dream, have an adventure, be bold—and then buy a charm to represent what they'd done. Once the bracelet was complete, they were to gift it to someone who needed hope. Something about the hokey gesture struck Jess.

One of Lacy's favorite movies had been *The Sisterhood of the Traveling Pants*, so it didn't surprise Jess that her late friend would do something similar, directing it from, as she called it, "the great beyond." She knew they wouldn't refuse her request. In fact, Rosemary had already attached her charm. The Empire State Building charm was a fresh reminder that good things could happen. Rosemary was now engaged to Sal, who was set to open Sal's New York Pizza in Morning Glory the last week in September. Lacy's first mission had been accomplished.

The charm bracelet sat in its paisley ditty bag in Jess's makeup case, waiting for Jess's turn. Jess hoped renting a house on the beach counted. It had been something she'd always dreamed about but never had a hope of accomplishing. Benton had been set on staying in Morning Glory and professed to hate the beach. But Jess loved the waves washing over her feet and the splendid sunsets sinking into the waters.

Somehow she didn't think using the money to rent a beach house would be enough. Lacy would want her to find more, discover a strength she'd never known, heal . . . move on. In the letter she'd written, Lacy had reminded her friend that she was her own person, strong and courageous. Her failed marriage didn't define her, and Benton being an asshole (yes, Lacy had actually said a bad word) hadn't anything to do with any shortcomings of Jess. Her friend's last words had brought fresh tears and somehow a conviction that Jess wouldn't be content to be a victim. She'd find a bigger purpose, starting with living where the ocean could splash on her legs.

Staring out at the dark water and sipping the warm tea, Jess wondered what that purpose could possibly be. If Rosemary had found love, would Jess find herself again? Because love seemed unlikely at this point. She wasn't ready to risk her heart. But she did want more than existing in Morning Glory.

Question was, did life care what she was ready for?

Chapter Four

Ryan woke with a foul taste in his mouth and a strange towel wrapped about his waist. Beneath the pink flamingos and bright-green palm trees, he was naked. Blinking, he looked around. He was on Morgan's couch, and if the streaming sunlight was any indication, it was mid-morning. Maybe close to noon.

"Morning, sleepyhead," Morgan said from the galley kitchen. "Thought you'd never wake up. Coffee?"

He clutched the towel and sat up, wiping the sleep from his eyes. His stomach rolled from the colossal amount of booze he'd consumed, and an army of hammers tapped away inside his skull. "Ugh."

"Tell me about it," Morgan said, wearing a T-shirt that barely covered her silk-clad rump. The bright-blue panties left little to the imagination, and he figured she'd designed it that way. She looked like the girl next door with naughtiness on her agenda, which was usually irresistible to him, but he'd drawn that line two months ago. A pair of blue undies wouldn't make him change his mind. When he settled on friendship, he settled on friendship. Done deal.

Ryan grunted and made sure his junk wasn't hanging out.

"I made some cheesy eggs because it was the only thing that sounded good to me. You're welcome to some." She lifted onto her toes and snagged a ceramic mug, setting it on the counter.

Ryan scratched his head, feeling the grit of sand against his scalp, and the antics from last night came roaring back. He'd thrown his clothes in the surf and howled at the moon. And a girl had been there. Black hair and big tits. She'd called him crazy and kissed him in the spray of the surf. There had been dancing and more tequila shots and talk of constellations. And then . . . Jess?

Jess Culpepper.

He'd not thought about her in forever, but somehow she'd been in his dreams last night. Or maybe she'd been real. But that couldn't be right. Jess was in Morning Glory, married to Super Jock. The last time he'd talked to his mother, she'd said Jess was painting a nursery, but, of course, that had been a while ago. Still, she had to be a figment of his imagination. Except she'd been so real. And she'd kicked him in the ribs. Had he tried to kiss her? He couldn't remember. It was like watermarks smudging his memory, running everything together.

He probably shouldn't have funneled the beer.

"I'm going to take a rain check, Morgan. I feel like something vomited me up. I need a shower and my own bed," he said, rising from the couch, his neck stiff from an unnatural position.

"You sure?" she said, turning toward him. She held her shoulders back so the snug T-shirt stretched across her breasts. Dark hair spilled around her pretty face, and damned if her lips didn't look freshly glossed. "I make good eggs."

"Uh, yeah, I need a shower." He stood, clutching the towel, wondering how he'd get home without his clothes. He could wear the towel home, he supposed.

"We do have a shower here," she teased, her gaze running down to where he likely still sported a slight morning erection.

He'd wear the towel. "No worries. But thanks for the party. It, obviously, was too much fun."

Morgan shrugged. "There's no such thing, Ry. I'll see you later?"

"Sure. Salty Gull?"

"Maybe. Though I do owe Luke Simmons a game."

Ryan knew what she was trying to do—use Luke to make him jealous. Luke was a bud of Ryan's, and the golf pro had been after Morgan ever since Ryan had introduced him to her at Peg Leg Pete's. Luke was a good guy, not necessarily ready to settle down with anyone, but definitely looking for a relationship. Or at least that's what he'd told Ryan one night when they'd sipped too much scotch. Luke had said he was lonely.

Ryan had scoffed at the thought, mostly because he liked being by himself. Having been raised by two parents who abhorred pedantic small talk or excessive noise, he relished the solitude of his own place, being alone in his boat on the water and—note to Morgan—showering by himself. Case in point, he moved toward the door that would take him back to his own condo. "I'll look for you."

Morgan stared at him, twisting her lips. "Where'd you get that towel? It's cute but not mine."

He looked down at it. "I don't know."

"Oh, it's probably my new neighbor's. She helped you up the steps . . . before she totally shut the party down." She shook her head and rolled her eyes.

"I'll take it back to her later. Thanks." He slipped out the double doors into the hot Florida sunshine. It was midmorning, according to the sun's position, and the world bustled around him. Plenty of vacationers frolicking on the bay side, screeching kids and a yellow lab galloping over the sand, tennis ball in mouth. The units in Del Luna were at the end of the busy beach highway near the national seashore, so it was a relatively peaceful area, but in the summer it was still moving. When Ryan had first bought the condo, he thought he'd hate summer here, with its minivan loads of tourists. But something about the brightly colored beach balls rolling past with sun-kissed kids chasing them, parents strolling with frosty drinks in hand was . . . homey? Or something like that.

He made it to his deck and stomped up the steps, shaking the sand from his feet. No one had looked askance at him, strolling with a towel about his waist, even if it was a girly beach towel. Morgan had said her neighbor had helped him up the steps. He squinted his eyes and tried to remember. Curly dark hair? Wide mouth like Julia Roberts? Maybe that's why he'd thought of Jess, his former Morning Glory High chemistry lab partner.

He ran a hand along his ribs. The woman had kicked him. But not hard. No bruise. What had he done to deserve it?

Ryan knew he hadn't tried to take advantage. His parents might have been weird, but they were moral and had instilled manners in him. Her scent came back to him. She'd smelled soft, like baby powder, and her skin had been silky. Oh God, had he sniffed her or something?

He couldn't remember, but he probably owed her an apology and a thank-you for loaning him a towel.

Pulling the key from its hiding spot within the old iron sea bell, he unlocked his French doors and stepped inside the dim coolness of his place. He'd gone with gray and black, which seemed contrary to the beach outside his window but suited his personal aesthetics of cool, modern, and acceptable to women who might come home with him. His decorator had tried like hell to bring pops of color—whatever that meant—to his world, but he'd waved the red pillows and blue rug away. Yeah, he'd never thought he'd do something as asinine as hiring a decorator, but before he'd moved to Florida, he'd papered his California apartment with posters of *Star Trek* and whiteboards full of notes on cellular membrane attachment. His unmatching furniture and action figure collection weren't exactly screaming *hot, young, available dude*, so he'd written the check to Helen Fabrizzo, interior decorator, to make the new place in Del Luna more socially acceptable.

Sometimes he missed his nerdy world.

But not enough to give up the boat, the gym, the casual sex, and the new man he was. Maybe it was shallow, but he didn't care. He'd missed his entire self-involved adolescence. No groping in dark movie theaters with a bubble-gummed fourteen-year-old girl trying to score a first kiss. No homecoming . . . or prom . . . or graduation party. No hanging with his buds. Or drinking and puking up his first six-pack. No warm, fuzzy memories of high school.

Or college.

Or anything other than lab coats, graphing calculators, and copious note taking through mind-numbing lectures. His world had been white, austere, unpainted for years upon years. And then, one day, he said enough.

And he quit his world and traded it for the life he had now.

Shutting the door, he dropped the towel. Then turned and looked at it. Because he wanted to pick it up and not leave it lying on the floor. He made himself walk away, padding naked into the kitchen. Then he forced himself to unscrew the lid of the 2 percent milk and drink from the carton. He even scratched his balls while doing so. Because he was a man. A regular dude. Not a genius. Just a dude.

Shutting the fridge, he looked over at the pink-and-green towel. It looked like a tourist casualty against the black-and-charcoal rug. Too out of place. He picked it up and took it to the laundry room. Choosing unscented detergent, he tossed it in with the soft gray towels he'd placed in the laundry basket yesterday. He didn't like doing laundry naked, but he did it. Because a regular guy didn't care. They liked being unclothed and wearing things like flannel shirts untucked. They farted, belched, and did disgusting things like trim their toenails on the bathroom rug, not bothering to pick up the trimmings. He knew this only because his freshman year at Stanford, he'd ended up misplaced in the athletic dorm for a week and had lived with Sherman Hilliard, an all-American running back who could have used some instruction on personal hygiene. Ryan had existed in a corner of the room, breathing through his mouth most the time, until the dean of engineering (personal friend of his parents) could get things straight with housing. Ryan had been suitably traumatized by Big Sherm and his profusely sweaty bros. But the upside was he'd learned how guys rolled. A bit disgusting but now useful for his new role as a dude.

He was a dude. Not a nerd. Or a dweeb. Or a geek.

Dude.

Gym time assured his body was similar to those guys modeling underwear and cologne in magazines. Owning a big boat and hooking big fish gave him street cred. Or was that marina cred? Drinking beer and shooting pool ensured he seemed normal . . . even if he kept a mental tab of pocket accuracy, which, by the way, was up to 83 percent thanks to watching YouTube videos posted by pool sharks. His collection of *Mystery Science Theater 3000* and *Dr. Who* videos were well hidden beneath titles like *Bull Durham* and *Rocky*. Although to be honest, he'd never made it all the way through *Bull Durham*, probably because of the trauma he'd suffered at the hands of Morning Glory High School's all-district catcher Bruce "The Goose" Mahoney and his all-state pitcher bud Benton Mason. Everyone loved Goose and Benton because they could crush beer cans with their heads, charm teachers with Jim Carrey impressions, and lock dorks in the storage closet. 'Cause that was cute. Except when Goose and Benton forgot to let the dweeb out of the gym storage closet. Ryan had spent five hours inside hyperventilating because he was seriously claustrophobic before he pissed on himself and passed out. Yeah. Good reason not to like baseball movies. But *Rocky* was okay.

Some would call him a poser, but he wasn't. Not really. He liked his boat and fishing. Loved beer. And the women? Well, he really liked them. When he'd left his old life in the lab at Caltech, he'd slept with only one woman. The results had been disastrous, because for male virgins the amount of time actually spent in the vagina is usually infinitesimal. And Sarah, who had proposed having sex as a way to alleviate the stress of waiting for the results of the variable test group, hadn't seemed too impressed. He'd half expected her to fetch a notebook from the pocket of her lab coat and plug in the minute amount of time it had taken Ryan to achieve orgasm. So once he'd decided to leave nerddom behind, he'd purchased every book on tantric sex he could find, along with the *Kama Sutra*, not to mention books that relayed what women really wanted in a man outside the bedroom—confidence, charm, and decisiveness. He had to be the whole package.

And it had worked.

Ryan pressed the button on the washer and walked toward his bathroom and the massaging shower he needed after a night on Morgan's couch. He had no charters today and would need to run some errands. And he needed to return the freshly laundered towel and give an apology to the woman who'd rented the Dirty Heron. Since she had the Julia Roberts thing going, maybe he'd take some apology flowers. Or maybe that would be too trite. Wine? No, too forward. Maybe something clever like a bottle of sunscreen or some funny sunglasses to welcome her to the beach community. Or not. Maybe just a clean towel and a sincere apology.

Turning on the shower, Ryan stepped inside. After hydrating himself and popping some aspirin, he'd be good to go. Another day in paradise being a regular guy.

∽

Jess was exhausted.

She struggled up the steps of the beach rental carrying her gym bag, a sack of essentials she'd need for her locker at the hospital, and a paper sack of wine she'd scored on the way home from the hospital. She'd circulated on four surgeries that morning—two gallbladders, a knee replacement, and a bowel resection. Wine, sesame chicken, and season three of *House of Cards* would be her reward . . . as long as she could find a decent Chinese takeout place. Not that Morning Glory had one. Such were the perks of living in a city for the next three months.

Shifting the bags, she dug into her purse, searching for the house key. Just as her fingers closed around the pelican key chain, she heard a snore.

Whipping around, she found a slumbering man in the hammock swing. How she'd missed him, she didn't know. Her heart galloped in her chest as adrenaline shot through her body. But then she noticed her new beach towel folded on his chest and a pitiful planter of scraggly begonias sitting beside the hammock. Her gaze darted back to the man sound asleep on the shady porch, and she clued in fast.

Sleeping Beauty, mouth open and chuffing a snore, was her drunken stargazer. This time he wore clothes, thank Jesus, and shoes. The cutoff khakis had a frat boy/Jimmy Buffett thing going, as did the linen-blend shirt with the light-blue stripes. Those weird hiking sandal things all the high school kids wore were on his feet. He looked masculine and sexy but somehow approachable. Well, at least he did when he was asleep . . . which was the only way Jess had approached him to date.

Jess cleared her throat, but he didn't stir.

"Hello," she called in a soft voice.

Nothing.

Oh for goodness' sake. She shifted the bag in her hand and walked over to where he lay. Lifting her foot, she nudged him in the ribs. "Ryan, wake up."

"Mmm?" he murmured, not bothering to open his eyes. He smiled sleepily. "What?"

"Wake. Up," Jess said.

His eyes flew open, and finally she could tell they were a beautiful golden green. Like the color of grasses along a lake or the first colors of fall. Shifting, he tried to sit up too fast, and the hammock rocked, making him lose balance. His arms shot up to steady himself, and his large body rocked back and forth. Since her hands were full, she could do nothing to help him. She watched, prepared for the worst—Ryan crumpling into a heap at her feet.

But he didn't. Somehow he managed to steady himself and get his feet planted. Looking up at her, he grinned. "Hazards of the hammock." But then something in his eyes flashed, making them more golden. His smile widened. "Well, I wasn't dreaming."

Jess didn't know what he meant by that. Probably couldn't remember much from last night. "What are you doing here?"

He pulled himself from the hammock, scooped up the towel and plant, and said, "I'm returning your towel." He waved the folded towel. "And I'm bringing you a welcome-to-Del-Luna gift–slash–apology for whatever I did last night, which I don't exactly remember but think I got a kick in the ribs for."

"You're a stubborn drunk who was intent on sleeping on the beach."

He lifted a shoulder. "I don't regularly drink that much, but it—"

"—was your birthday," she finished, moving toward her front door. The key still dangled in her hand.

"Yeah, let me help you with that," he said, taking from her the pharmacy bag filled with tampons, leave-in conditioner, and a box of condoms. The condoms were only precautionary and probably not necessary. She didn't think she was ready for that kind of intimacy yet, but having them on hand reminded her she wasn't dead. She could meet someone at the hospital . . . or anywhere, for that matter. Hell, she had a guy with flowers standing on her porch waiting for her. Of course, his flowers were welcome/apology flowers, but still.

She unlocked the door, hoping she wasn't being too trusting by letting a stranger into her rental. She'd read books about this very thing—a guy pretending to be nice and carry packages inside before locking a gal in the basement and skinning her with a knife. Her stomach clenched, but she forced herself to relax. He was Morgan's friend. And she was too damn paranoid. "Thank you."

He slid past her and set the bag on the counter. When he did, the damn box of condoms tumbled out. Picking them up, he turned to her. "Extra large? High expectations, huh?"

Jess blushed, something she rarely did. "Uh, those are for, uh . . . why don't you just put"—she dropped the gym bag and set the bag of wine on the counter. Grabbing the box from his hand, she jabbed them back inside the plastic bag and moved it onto the counter away from him—"them back."

"Hey, I'm kidding," he said, taking the sad begonias to the kitchen sink and running some water in the container covered with gold foil. "These poor flowers were the last they had at the store. I started to get fresh flowers, but that seemed like something you wouldn't appreciate. Bet you're the kind of girl who likes something that lasts longer."

Yeah, she was. But so much for that. "They're . . . lovely."

Ryan set the leggy plant with the coral flowers on the granite bar and shook his head. "Not yet, but I bet they will be with a little care."

Jess wondered if this was some kind of weird analogy for where she was in life. Like the universe was sending her a message. But that was silly. Ryan couldn't know that like the sad begonia she needed water, sun, and time to renew herself so she could bloom again. He was just a guy who'd gotten drunk, tried to kiss her, and thankfully hadn't puked on her. By the looks of him, his sensitivity meter was likely on the low end.

"Well, thank you for returning my towel and bringing me the welcome begonias. Very kind of you." *Now go away.*

She'd had a long day, and though he was cute with his apology and all sexy with his smiles and teasing, she wanted to get out of her clothes . . . uh, alone. Her stomach growled, reminding her she'd been too busy for lunch.

"Sure," he said, looking around the place. "So this is the Dirty Heron, huh? Always wondered what it looked like on the inside. Is there green shag carpet in the bedroom?" He peered around the hanging cabinets and into the dim hallway.

"No. It's Berber. And the color of sand."

His gaze returned to hers. "Want to go out to the beach? It's not too hot, and this time of day is the best time to go."

Jess shook her head. "Uh, actually, it's been a long day, and I . . . uh, need to eat."

"There's a good seafood place about a mile or so toward town. Peg Leg Pete's. Kinda touristy, but their food is good, and they make a great cocktail. I could take you there. As a sort of extended apology and welcome."

"That's not necessary," Jess said, wondering why in the world the guy would ask her out. She was older than him and very obviously not like him. No, wait. Wrong attitude. This was what she was trying to change—her pragmatic nature. Her propensity to be boooooring.

"It's because I tried to kiss you, isn't it? I mean, I think I did. I distinctly remember the way you smelled. Which was good, by the way." Ryan shrugged, looking sincere and friendly. Not like a guy who was asking her *out* out. But a friend saying, "Hey, let's go get a drink. No big deal."

She was deluding herself if she thought it was anything more. Better to stick to her original plan. "Look, you were drunk and—"

"It's just I always wanted to kiss you, you know? Call it a crazy leftover adolescent fantasy or something." He picked up the map of Pensacola she'd studied in preparation for embracing her new city for the next few months.

"I beg your pardon?" Adolescent fantasy? Wait. How old was he? Her mind flashed to that Jennifer Lopez movie in which the character slept with a high school kid before she realized she was his teacher. Was Ryan younger than she thought? Could he actually be in high school? Dear Lord. And besides, how in the world had he always wanted to kiss her? She'd moved in a mere three days ago.

Ryan froze, his pretty eyes narrowing. "Wait. You don't remember me, do you?"

Jess shifted her gaze away, her mind reeling over how she was supposed to know him. Had she passed him when she grocery shopped? Perhaps glanced over at him when she got gas at the 7-Eleven? Perhaps he worked at the hospital? She had no clue.

Ryan started laughing.

"Why are you laughing?" she asked, crossing her arms and giving him her no-nonsense nurse stare.

"Because you really don't know me. I mean, I know I've changed, but I thought you would clue in. It's not like we didn't sit across from each other for a whole year in lab."

Jess looked hard at him. He hadn't been in nursing school with her. Nor had he gone to Mississippi State. She didn't think. Of course, her freshman year at Mississippi State was a bit of a blur. Benton had joined a frat, and they'd spent a lot of nights going to beer busts and shooting tequila. She and Ryan might have had a class together, but how would she have forgotten a guy like him?

Not only did he have a chiseled jaw and gorgeous eyes, but she'd seen his body. He was out of her league, with a broad chest sporting a sprinkling of sun-bronzed hair, abs that belonged in a workout magazine, and, uh, really toned thighs, among other well-proportioned things. Okay, so she'd sneaked a peek, and he was fairly well endowed. She wasn't a saint. To say Ryan was the cat's meow was like saying chocolate was delicious. True and true. "I don't think I've ever had a class with you. I'd remember."

He arched his eyebrows. "Oh, we had class together. You're not that old, Jessica."

"I know I'm not that old. I'm not even thirty." Even if Benton had accused her of acting like his parents. So she liked knitting. And gardening. That didn't make her old. It made her hippie chic.

"I know how old you are. I also know your birthday is July third, your favorite color is blue, and you have a scar on your knee from a freak diving board accident in fifth grade."

Jess felt alarm uncoil in her stomach. She stepped back, wondering which drawer harbored the knives. Obviously this guy was a stalker or something. Was he some vague Facebook friend she'd forgotten about who studied her postings in order to track her down? Or maybe he'd seen her on Snapchat? But she would know, wouldn't she? Oh God, she was about to be that woman. The one who let the killer inside just because he showed up with a smile and a stupid nearly dead pot of begonias. Her father was going to kill her . . . even if she ended up dead. "Uh, I think you should—"

"Oh no." Ryan waved his hands, his laughter so benign for a serial killer. "I'm Ryan Reyes. We had chemistry together at Morning Glory High. Go Mavs?"

Jess froze.

Ryan Reyes?

"The Brain?"

Ryan laughed and held out his hands. "I finally went through puberty."

Chapter Five

Ryan watched as realization unfolded in Jess's eyes like a long-forgotten note folded up to pass in that chemistry class they'd taken together in high school. He hadn't been dreaming last night when he saw Jess. She was here . . . in Pensacola . . . and had obviously seen him naked.

Not exactly how he'd envisioned being seen again by one of his old classmates.

Jess Culpepper had been a pretty cheerleader with tons of friends and a popular boyfriend. Ryan, on the other hand, had been a skinny nerd with exactly two friends—one of whom he'd met in an online calculus forum—and a binder full of Pokémon cards. Because he'd skipped several grades in high school, graduating when he was fourteen, and hadn't hit puberty until he was a junior at Stanford, no doubt the memory Jess had of the Brain was vastly different than the man who stood before her today. Even so, the knowledge he'd been so secondary in her world that she didn't recognize him in the slightest caused a tiny ping of hurt inside him.

Jess stood in her kitchen, hand hovering over the nearest drawer pull, staring at him like he was a specimen in a petri dish. Her soft mouth hung slightly open, and her amber eyes blinked as she processed that he had, in fact, been her high school chemistry lab partner. The seconds ticked by, uncomfortable as wing tips a size too small.

"Uh, could you say something?" Ryan asked.

"I'm sorry. I just—" Jess snapped her mouth closed and moved toward him. Then she actually circled him, like an appraisal. "It's amazing. You don't look anything like the kid who—"

"Sneezed into your chicken noodle soup?" he finished.

Jess gave up a laugh. "Lord, I had forgotten about that."

"And you'd forgotten me," he added.

"No, I hadn't forgotten you. But I never expected you'd end up looking like this." She stopped, peering up into his face, her gaze catching his. Amazement on her face. "I mean, you're gorgeous."

Ryan felt heat flare in his cheeks at her comment. He'd never been a blusher, but maybe something about his once-upon-a-time fantasy girl circling him the way she was and telling him he was gorgeous made him itchy, embarrassed . . . blushing. "I wouldn't go that far."

"I would. Don't forget I've seen you naked. As a nurse who sees a lot of naked bodies, I'm an expert on what goes for gorgeous, and I gotta tell you, it's freaking me out a little. The Brain grew into a hottie." Jess laughed, her eyes sparkling. "I'll be damned."

"Yeah, well, people grow up," he said, wanting to shift the conversation to something other than his hotness. Sure, he worked hard to be what he was on the outside—tan, fit, and somewhat slouchy. Wearing his shirt untucked nagged at him all day long.

She sobered at that thought. "I guess they do."

"So, do you want to grab dinner? Even though seconds ago you thought I was a creeper who'd been stalking you," he said, searching for the tried-and-true charm he'd learned to use around women. No longer was he the geek who'd crushed on Jess, stammering around her and turning the color of lithium chloride when set to flame. "I could sort of see the panic in your eyes when you were looking for a weapon."

She tilted her head, and her curls fell forward to frame her face. Still so pretty. "I prayed there was a butcher knife in the closest drawer."

"I could have taken it away from you," he said. Because he could have. Thanks to gym time and training in judo, tae kwon do, and mixed martial arts, he was proficient, quick, and strong.

Jess made a face.

"I have a black belt." He'd achieved that several years ago, when he still wore a lab coat.

"Of course you do," she said with laughter in her voice. Then she swiped a hand over her face. "This is surreal."

"So, dinner?"

"Honestly I really don't want to go anywhere noisy. It's been a long first day for me," she said, gesturing to the brown bag of wine. "And I have a date with a wine bottle."

"Not a great conversationalist," he said, pulling the wine from the bag and reading the label. Sauvignon blanc. Decent vintage. Nothing soul stirring. "We can order takeout and spend some time catching up. Or I can leave. I'm not trying to force my company on you. I guess it's nice to see you again. I don't run into too many fellow Morning Glorinians."

"Is that what we are? Glorinians?"

"Best I can guess," he said.

Jess took the bottle from his hand. "I'd love for you to stay. We can catch up, and you can tell me how you ended up here. I figured you'd be curing cancer or something by now."

"Nah, I'm just a regular guy. I have a boat—a charter fishing business," he said, taking the bottle and the bottle opener she'd pulled from a drawer from her hand. He had a need to be useful. She looked like she might argue with him about taking over the chore of opening the wine, but she gave up in favor of finding glasses.

"So you're a fisherman?"

"No. More like a guide. I find fish for people who want a memorable vacation. Late spring all the way into fall is my busy season, but I took the day off on account of the birthday blowout. Morgan goes all out for every event. You should have been here for the Fourth. There was a slip and slide."

"I can only imagine. So are you and Morgan . . ." She trailed off with a question in her voice.

"Friends. Just friends." He wanted to make that emphatically clear. Not sure why, because he hadn't carried a torch for Jess Culpepper in years. When he was a kid sitting across from her in that too-tight cheerleading uniform, he'd practically drooled on the desk they shared. She'd never acted annoyed with him like other girls had—in fact, she'd always been kind. Tolerant of his mooning over her. Made him wince to think back on how lame he must have been. He'd brought her silly pencil erasers and her favorite candy bar. She'd always acted so pleased with his thoughtfulness, and now he knew she must have thought his adolescent crush so annoying. He'd made a fool out of himself for her. But that had been long ago. Now he was a different person.

Jess snagged a pair of wineglasses with flip-flops painted on them. "This is all I can find."

"That'll do," he said as the cork made a satisfying pop, coming loose.

"Since I'm new, what are the good takeout places?" she asked.

"Partytime Pizza and Little China are two safe bets. What are you in the mood for?"

Jess took the wine from him and poured a hefty portion into a goblet. "Definitely Chinese."

Ryan pulled his cell phone from his pocket and hit his favorites list. Little China delivered to him at least once a week. A cook he wasn't. "Hey, Lin."

His friend Henry Lin responded with, "You want usual?"

"Yeah, and add . . ." He arched a brow at Jess.

"Sesame chicken, one spring roll," Jess said, handing him the glass with the lukewarm wine. He took it and relayed her order to Lin, giving the man the unit number for delivery.

"Ah, you with girl tonight, player?" Lin asked a bit too loudly.

"You know it, bro," Ryan said into the receiver, winking at Jess.

"You so lucky, Ry. I work all the time. No time for honeys." Lin sounded disgusted.

"Lin, I'm having dinner with an old friend. No being a player tonight. Can you deliver for seven?" he asked. After confirming the order and telling his friend he'd see him at the tennis courts soon, Ryan hung up.

"Player?" Jess drawled, opening the freezer to fetch an ice cube, which she promptly plopped into her wine. "Want one?"

He nodded, and she slipped an ice cube into his wine. "I've cultivated a certain reputation among delivery guys." He lifted his glass, clinking it against hers. "To old friends and new beginnings."

She lifted her glass. "I'd rather drop the old, thank you very much."

They each took a sip. Ryan allowed his gaze to wander over his "old" friend. Jess had thick, curly hair that often stuck out in riotous curls around her face. Her skin was golden, her eyes a sleek feline brown, her chin pointed elfishly. She was taller than most women, about five foot ten, and her breasts were a nice size, slightly out of proportion with her long, slim-hipped angularity. Back in high school, Jess had had an untouchable vibe, a sort of innate coolness and confidence. Her smiles weren't easily given, but when she did smile, it was as if the heavens opened. Her words were measured, her intentions always clear, her tongue razor sharp. He'd thought she was all that and a bag of chips.

"So what brings you to Pensacola?" he asked, sliding onto a bar stool.

Jess leaned her elbows on the granite countertop and glanced past his shoulder out at the gulf water rolling onto the beach. Several seconds ticked by in which she seemed to weigh what she wanted to tell him. "Well, let's see, my husband left me, Lacy died, I got divorced a month ago, and the medical company I work for sent me to fill in for a surgical nurse on maternity leave at Bay View."

Whoa. "Uh, Lacy Guthrie died?" The image of a round friendly face, blonde hair, and a funny orange truck named something absurd appeared in his memory. Lacy had been a nice girl. "How?"

Jess swallowed and didn't bring her gaze back to his. Instead she stared hard out the window. "Cancer."

"God, that's terrible."

"Yeah, it was. It is," she said softly.

"And you're no longer with Benton?" Something inside him gave a standing ovation to that notion. He'd never liked the cocksure Benton Mason, with his rolled-up Oxford button-ups and flask of bourbon in his back pocket. As the son of the mayor, Benton had strolled through Morning Glory secure in his position, unafraid of the Barney Fife cops in the small town. Fourteen years ago there had been no social media justice, antibullying campaigns, or people willing to stand up to fat cat Mayor Mason. Benton was an apple who'd not fallen far from the tree. Ryan knew all too well what it meant to be on the receiving end of Benton's attention.

"Weird, huh? We were always 'Benton and Jess.' Still feels strange to me."

"You were together a long time." He wanted to ask what had happened but didn't think it polite to push. Sometimes his southern upbringing emerged to strangle his curiosity.

"Yeah," she said, taking a big gulp of the wine. She looked sad, and he didn't want her to be sad so he was relieved when she asked, "So do you like living in Pensacola?"

"Love it. The weather's nice, even in the winter. Early spring can be rough with the constant cold fronts, but even at that, Mother Nature gifts us with warm days to remind us of what's coming. I've only been here for a year and a half, though."

"Oh," she said, her gaze finally locking on his. He could see so much in those eyes—regret, longing, grief, and a sort of gameness, as if she refused to sink too far into the mire within her soul. That was something he'd always liked about Jess—she was a fighter. "So before here you were in California? Think that's what my mother told me."

"Yeah, California. Similar gorgeous weather, except for the humidity."

"But the downside is earthquakes, forest fires, and health food."

Ryan laughed. "True. Never been much of a tofu or kale guy."

"You told your friend to deliver the food at seven. You want to take a quick walk on the beach?" she asked, her face now impassive. "I need some beach therapy."

"If that's what you want," he said, meaning every word of it. Something told him Jess needed time and space. Any possible thought he had of taking things to another level with his fantasy girl fizzled like cheap champagne in Christmas punch. Jess needed a friend . . . even if it was an old one she hadn't recognized.

"You know how rare it is to hear a man say that?" she joked.

Ryan smiled. "Well, I was always your puppy."

Jess paused, her face dimming. "You knew we called you that?"

"I'm not stupid," he said—truer words never spoken. He wasn't stupid. Far from it. Hadn't that always been what separated him from everyone else? The fact that he was a genius?

Jess touched his shoulder, light as a moth wing. "No, you're definitely not stupid."

Jess watched a group of teen girls stroll ahead of her and Ryan. She'd left her shoes at the end of the walkway and rolled up the jeans she'd slid on after dumping her scrubs into the laundry at the hospital. Her white cotton shirt caught the wind and ballooned, so she tied the shirttails together at her waist. Ryan looked suitably like a beach bum.

Ryan Reyes.

She still reeled at the thought that the skinny kid with the runny nose and strange comic book obsession had evolved into the hunk ambling beside her. Now that she knew, she could see traces of the boy he'd been. Same brown hair, even when burnished caramel by the sun. His eyes were the same golden green that had stared unblinkingly at her from behind the microscope. He'd been such an odd duck, smarter than his teachers, always sharing strange facts. And he'd watched her. Like, all the time. And he'd followed her around school, peeking out behind lockers. She'd known he had a crush on her and tried to be nice about it. Benton? Not so much.

Her ex-husband hadn't been the most tolerant of Ryan's public adoration of his girlfriend. Cocky, smart-aleck, and a bit wild, Benton took exception to the kid her friends had dubbed her puppy. Jess hated when Benton got jealous and resorted to bad behavior. They'd broken up several times over his possessiveness, but then Benton would do something endearing and beg her forgiveness, and she couldn't resist. Perhaps her desire to fix people had led her into nursing. She'd always thought she could patch the holes Benton had inside him and use the balm of love to help him be the man she knew he could be. And she'd loved him. He'd crack a smile at her, nose her shoulder with a little whimper. Then his warm brown eyes would fill with an apology, and she'd take him back. She'd never been able to resist Benton's charm, his dashing good looks, and the way he could play her. And when it came to playing her, Benton had been the genius.

Love was a funny thing. But after the pain, the heartache, the refusal to believe she and Benton were over, her love had finally withered. Love didn't last if it wasn't watered, given sun, or tended. Love didn't last when one of the people stopped giving a damn and walked away. Now her love for Benton was a brittle tree waiting for a strong wind to blow it over.

"So why fishing?" she asked, kicking at a wave and drawing her thoughts from Benton and the tearing in her heart every time she thought about what they used to be.

Ryan shrugged his broad shoulders. "I never went fishing as a kid. Always wanted to."

She didn't know what to make of that answer. This guy, a veritable genius who'd scored perfectly on the ACT, blown the SATs out of the water, and skipped three grade levels, ran a fishing-charter service. Of course, there was nothing wrong with that, but everyone had always thought the Brain would do great things in the scientific community. His parents had always pushed him to excel. Her mother took yoga with Ryan's mother at the Calvary Church of Christ community center, and she'd occasionally mention Ryan's accomplishments at Stanford and Caltech. Every now and then, when Jess caught an episode of *The Big Bang Theory*, she'd think about skinny Ryan in a lab coat writing formulas on a whiteboard, hanging out with other geeky friends. That vision made her happy, like Ryan was doing what he was meant to do. Not shivering in some locker somewhere, deemed a loser because he didn't play football or crush beer cans with his forehead.

But this Ryan—the one who lived in Florida, did Jell-O shots, and passed out naked (splendidly so) on the beach—was something she never expected. Things didn't compute.

"But what about your other work," she persisted.

"What other work?" he asked, turning to her, his eyes crinkling as he faced the sun. Sliding on the sunglasses hanging around his neck, he hid his gaze from her.

"Don't you have a doctorate, and you discovered something to do with stem cell research or something like that?"

"Yeah, I have an MD and a PhD. The scaffolding for stem cells was a side project I got lucky on. I sold the procedure to a biomedical company and retired from science." He stopped and turned to stare into the horizon. The sun hovered over his right shoulder, and his hair feathered in the sea breeze. He looked strikingly gorgeous, the antithesis of what he should have been—pale, erudite, with feverish eyes. He looked like a guy who should be standing on a boat, wearing tropical fashions and drinking imported beer from a bottle. "I like fishing."

So much weight sitting in those three words. They said, "Back off," "I don't want to talk about it," and "Don't define me." Jess decided to let the conversation go.

"So what else do you like to do besides find fish and play tennis?" she asked, moving to the other side of him and stopping to pick up a tiny shell that resembled a unicorn horn.

"I shoot pool. And I teach a beginner karate class for kids on Thursday afternoons." He paused for a moment before saying, "and I kill it on ESO."

"Eso?"

"Elders Scroll Online. It's a MMORPG—massively multiplayer online role-playing game. I'm a sorcerer, but I don't usually tell girls that, you know." He smiled at the water, looking a bit sheepish. "But since you already know I'm a dork, I can be honest."

"You're not a dork," she said, laughing at the very idea of anyone thinking this guy with his tan legs and hard body, not to mention her next-door neighbor fawning over him, was anything but—what had the Chinese-takeout guy called him?—oh yeah, a player. He certainly looked the part. He had a veneer—bright and shiny like his smile.

"Not any longer. Or at least not much," he said, those teeth so white against his tanned face. "Look."

Her gaze followed his pointed finger out beyond the sand bar to where two dolphins rolled over the incoming waves.

"Dolphins," Jess said, awe welling inside her. She'd always loved the graceful mammals with their sweet faces and playful curiosity. And who didn't like a dolphin? Really. This was why she'd told Jill Grover from Staff Pro she'd take the job. Didn't even have to think about it.

"See them a lot here," Ryan said.

"Then I know I'll like living in Pensacola. Especially since I have an old friend with me," Jess said, not taking her eyes off the two frolicking dolphins.

"You won't tell everyone about me, will you?"

Jess jerked her gaze to him. "About you?"

"Like how I once was," he said, his gaze seemingly on the two dolphins.

Those infernal glasses hid his eyes, so she couldn't tell if he was serious or not. His tone sounded light, but it made her wonder if the idea of outing him as a geek made him uncomfortable. But she couldn't figure out why. Did anyone really care that he played video games online or had an IQ in the 150s? She didn't, but she didn't know Ryan well enough to make a judgment. Perhaps being whom he'd once been had scarred him in some way. Maybe all that time locked in the storage closet or gym locker had caused an aversion to anything geeky. Or maybe Ryan was in hiding. Like he'd invented some terrible neurological weapon and was forced to hide from the Russians or the Chinese. He was hiding in plain sight. Jess nearly snorted as her imagination ran away with her. So silly. But maybe silly was good. She needed a bit of lightness in her outlook.

"If you don't want me to say anything, I won't. I'm not sure why it's a big deal, though." She tacked on the last part so he would know she accepted him for who he'd been and who he now was.

"Thanks." Ryan turned back toward the path they'd taken. "It's almost seven. Lin is always on time."

"Then we should head back." She turned to start walking but stopped and faced him. "Hey, Ryan."

He stopped. "What?"

"You know there's nothing wrong with who you were, right? I know people teased you about being smart, but most were jealous as hell they didn't have half the brain you did. You are incredibly gifted, and I hope you're not ashamed of that." God, she sounded like her mother. She wanted to snatch the words back even though she'd given them out of kindness . . . or perhaps as an apology for not standing up for him more when he was a kid. Not that she'd tolerated anyone being mean to him, but that she'd never tried to fix it in the first place.

She couldn't read his face. He stopped walking, growing still. The corners of his mouth tilted down as he nonchalantly lifted a shoulder. "You're the first person from my old life who's shown up here in Pensacola. Guess I can be honest with you—you know too much about my past for me to be anything but."

Jess didn't say anything. She waited. Her therapist had told her she lacked listening skills, said she was too busy dashing into the fray, ready to fix things.

Be still and listen.

Ryan shoved his hands into his pockets. "I never disliked who I was. Sure, I had some scars, stayed away from guys who looked like they might torment me, but I was as well adjusted as could be expected."

"Nothing wrong with being smart," she said. "So why leave something you were meant to be?"

His brow lowered before he shrugged. "Because it was an empty life. Look, one night I worked late in the lab at Caltech. When I went out to my car, I found the battery dead. No reason. I never leave anything on, my OCD doesn't allow for it, but the battery had given up the ghost. I tried calling a few colleagues, to no avail, and the security guard couldn't help me. My apartment wasn't far, so I decided to walk home and take care of the battery situation the next day. You know, I'd never done that, just walked home. As I crossed streets and passed houses, life opened up around me. It was as if I pushed open a door and a scene would unfold. One couple was fighting, hurling nasty accusations at each other while standing beside their van. One house had a bunch of guys sitting around on the porch, drinking beer, playing guitar. A little farther down, a couple with their baby arrived home. They were laughing and singing a funny song about eating beans and farting. And then right before I reached my apartment building, I found a drunk guy sitting on a trash can talking to a skinny mutt."

Ryan stopped talking.

"So?" Jess prodded, not understanding why a walk home would necessitate such a huge change.

"The bum looked at me like he could see who I was. Then he shook his head, like he felt sorry for me. *Him* feeling sorry for *me*. I had just sold my discovery to a huge pharmaceutical company for a few million dollars, and he felt sorry for me?" Ryan paused, giving a little laugh. "At first I was offended. But then he pointed his long finger at me—and it was like something from a Charles Dickens novel, I swear—and said, 'You need a dog. Go with him, Ace.'"

"I told him I didn't want his dog. I was allergic, and besides they were messy and needed constant attention. But the bum looked at me and said, 'Well, that's what you're missing, huh? Some dirt.'" Ryan held out his hands in a *you see what I mean* gesture.

"And because a drunk bum said you needed some dirt, you walked away from—"

"No, it was more like the final nail in the coffin, so to speak. I mean, the guy was pretty wasted, and I didn't really trust his brand of therapy, but it was a lightbulb moment. I could see I wasn't truly living." Ryan drew a circle in the sand with his big toe. "As I climbed the stairs to my apartment, I realized I'd never had a fight with a woman.

Hell, I'd never had a relationship with a woman. I didn't have buds to drink with . . . I had never even been drunk. No pets. No prospect of children. No silly songs to sing. Nothing. My life was . . . a vacuum. I'd missed out on so much by living this plan my parents had conceived for me—or maybe it was one I never questioned. Either way, it pissed me off."

"So you quit your life?"

Ryan smiled. "No, I didn't quit. I started living, truly living. I became a man who didn't live for work. I needed more than scientific discoveries to keep me warm at night. I needed to plunge myself into a life worth living."

Jess shook her head. "That's . . . mind-boggling."

"Not really. It's the smartest thing I've ever done. I'm having experiences, getting dirty, making mistakes, doing all the things I never got to do because I was too busy being a prodigy . . . which, by the way, is a synonym for *nerd*."

Experiences. That's what Benton had said he wanted. Benton had gone through high school and college dating only Jess. The day they'd graduated from high school, she'd tossed her cap into the air with the rest of her class, and Benton had kissed her and told her they were in it together. And she'd believed him. They'd married six months out of college, obtained jobs close to Morning Glory and bought a fixer-upper. They'd carefully set their feet in the lines they'd sketched out.

But Benton, too, hadn't thought out what it would be like to marry the girl he'd started dating when he was a freshman. He hadn't been thinking about experiences. He'd given up being a single guy with his own place, he'd forgone dating women who didn't have curly hair and a past with him. Personally, Jess had always thought those sorts of experiences overrated. Why would Benton want anything but a woman who loved him? But Benton had wanted more, the way Ryan had.

Jess didn't tick that way. She'd always known what she wanted—a flexible career, a white picket fence, and a family smiling back on yearly Christmas cards. She'd seen her American dream laid out in a ten-step plan. *Do this. Then that. Go here. Wait. Move ahead.*

For a while, it had worked.

Until that word cropped up—*experiences.*

"So what did your parents say?" she asked, still trying to wrap her mind around the fact he'd chucked everything he'd worked for. And why? Because he thought he'd missed out on things that weren't all that great. Waking up in vomit after a huge party . . . not fun. Fighting over who didn't pay the water bill . . . still not fun. Bad guitar music, stinky dogs, and songs about farts . . . perhaps somewhat fun, but not worth tossing out winning a Nobel Prize.

"Who cares what my parents thought? I had scholarships, and though they helped me with living expenses, it didn't give them the right to control my life. They'd planned my life for me—rushing me through high school, making me go to physics and computer camps all summer long. They lobbied the counselor to allow me extra course loads every semester. My father chose the medical school I attended, and he was crushed I didn't take the surgical residency offered to me by Johns Hopkins. So, no, they aren't happy I 'threw away my career to catch fish.' In their minds I'm wasting myself. That's the phrase used every time I call. So I don't call much. They don't seem to mind."

Jess thought that sounded terrible. She loved her parents. Her father was a dentist, her mother a dental hygienist. She had an older brother who lived three blocks from her parents' house and was father to two towheaded boys who played T-ball and finger painted their aunt indecipherable pictures. Her younger brother lived with his longtime girlfriend in Oklahoma City. She talked to her family weekly. They were so tight sometimes she had to step outside to get a breath.

"I'm sorry, Ryan," she said.

"Me, too." Ryan started walking back toward Del Luna. "Let's forget about the past and focus on the lo mein."

Jess could see he was done with talking about who he'd once been. Maybe she should be doing the same thing. And she didn't need an old drunk to point out what she needed in her life.

Like Ryan and Benton, she had experiences in her future. And the first one would be eating Chinese takeout on the beach with a nerd who'd grown into a hottie.

Not a bad start.

Chapter Six

Jess set her cell phone on the bench in the locker room. Three texts—one from her mother, one from Rosemary, and one from Ryan. She didn't bother reading her mother's text because she saw the name *Aunt Sally* embedded within. Her dotty aunt's eightieth birthday celebration was that weekend, and Jess would miss it. Her mother wasn't accepting of the idea, but Jess couldn't ask to switch shifts when she'd just started the job. Rosemary was checking on her—

How are things going?

Ryan wanted to Hang out?

The last one gave her a little thrill even if it sounded more friendly than interested.

She texted Rosemary first.

Going good. Job is challenging. Beach is awesome.

Little dots appeared telling her Rosemary was responding.

So glad. Meet any guys?

Seriously?

Why not? You're single now.

Cause I'm trying to get over the last asshole.

No need to mention Ryan at the moment. They'd enjoyed the impromptu Chinese dinner and catch-up session just over a week ago, and since that time, she'd received only one text from him—a sort of *great seeing you* text. She wondered if that would be last she'd hear from him since he'd said it was his busy season. After all, she didn't need babysitting. Still, a teeny part of her ego was bruised. She'd thought they'd hit it off. Or maybe she wanted to cling to a little piece of home, and Ryan was all that was available.

True. But still, don't be afraid to jump in with both feet.

Rosemary loved giving relationship advice now that she was engaged.

You're talking about the ocean, right? Cause that's all I'm jumping into. Later, gator.

See you soon, you big baboon.

Jess smiled at her friend's parting comment. She missed her two buds, but over the past week, she'd settled into her new job, worked on her tan, and made friends with several of the other nurses. She'd gone to a late lunch with Becky Brewster and another nurse named Tanae Jackson on Tuesday. They'd invited her for happy hour at a local bar and grill when they cleared the operatory earlier. Felt nice to be treated like one of the girls.

"So are you going to Landsharks later?" Becky asked as she pushed into the locker room.

Speak of the devil.

Jess lowered her phone, her finger hovering over Ryan's text. She wanted to hang out with him. And that was scary, because she wasn't going to get involved with the Brain. That would be insanity. "Maybe."

"Come with us. They have excellent mojitos, which hit the spot in this heat. Tanae's boyfriend might stop by, and after a week of mourning my breakup with the biggest narcissist in Florida, I'm ready to stop being a hermit."

Though she liked being asked, Jess didn't actually feel like enduring loud noises, clinking glasses, and forced conversation. Besides, she was halfway through the first season of *Orange Is the New Black* on Netflix. And going with Becky and Tanae would mean missing her evening walk on the beach. The pair of dolphins that had been showing up all week might miss her. And then there was Ryan.

But if she chose hanging with Ryan over trying to develop a social life, what did that say? After all, she didn't know if Ryan considered her a friend, a potential romantic interest, or an obligation. Several times during the course of dinner, she'd seen him glance at her in an appraising way. His gaze caused delight to skip up her spine, giving her a tingle of anticipation, but the thought of going there with Ryan felt strange. It was hard to pull him out of the slot where she'd placed him long ago—sort of like wearing those weird aqua socks when you swam. Not uncomfortable just . . . not right. Besides, Ryan was three years younger than her, and even though she knew it was silly to let age stand in her way, she couldn't deny there was a difference between being twenty-six and nearly thirty. Ryan still partied. And Jess didn't.

Of course, something more with Ryan might not even be an option. The man had made no move toward anything more than friendship even if he'd checked her out over excellent Chinese takeout. He was a man, right? Men couldn't help checking women out. DNA and all that.

Besides, going out with her coworkers would be good for her. Sorta like eating veggies. Not appetizing, but yielding good results. Tanae and Becky were friendly, funny, and actually seemed to like Jess. She needed to expand her social circle, and drinks with new friends would be a good opportunity to put herself out there. "A drink sounds good, but I need to shower first. Dr. Singh killed me today. I've never pulled so many instruments. I actually broke a sweat in the OR."

Becky snorted. "He's a prima donna. But if I needed to have a mass or something removed, he'd be the top of the surgeon list. He's good."

"Yeah," Jess said, pulling off her top and gathering her pants. She dropped them in the laundry bin. "He is good. I guess I'll meet y'all at Landsharks. Wait, where's it located?"

"You know the shopping center with the Publix? Right past it. Can't miss it. There's a big shark head over the sign. I'll be there around four thirty. Grab a table if you get there earlier." Becky disappeared into a curtained stall, leaving Jess to do the same.

Jess grabbed her cell and typed, Going to Landsharks after work for drinks. Later? and pressed SEND. Maybe after she got home, she and Ryan could watch a movie. Or sit out on the deck and finish the bottle of pinot grigio she'd started last night. Or maybe he'd blow her off and do his own thing. She sensed he wasn't sitting around twiddling his thumbs with nothing to do.

After showering and applying what little makeup she had, she left the hospital with time to kill. Since she hadn't anticipated going any-where after work, she wore a slightly pilled cotton top and her least favorite jeans. With that thought in mind, she drove around Bayfront Parkway and spied a cute boutique. There she scored a few flattering shirts and one dress that hit mid-thigh. Her mother would have frowned at that one, but Jess had the salesgirl ring it up anyway. After all, her legs were her best feature, and her mother wasn't here.

An hour later, Jess stood outside the bar with the big shark mouth and garish beach signs. Becky had been right. Easy to find. She tossed her mostly dry curls over her shoulder and tugged at the hem of the short dress. Her tummy fluttered slightly, and she hated herself for feeling any doubt. That's what this damn divorce had done to her—shaken the foundation of who she'd always been. Before Benton broke her, she'd been so confident, so bold, so sure of herself. She'd known exactly who she was. But now? Now she was a woman who'd been spat onto the beach, blinking water from her eyes and pulling her swimsuit from her crack. She'd fallen overboard while Benton powered off into the sunset with a florist . . . and then a veterinarian's assistant . . . and currently a bartender at a restaurant in Jackson.

The upside was she was on a beach and about to have drinks with new friends.

And she wore a new dress.

And she was tired of thinking about her past. Time to eat her vegetables.

Jess pulled open the door and nearly ran smack into Ryan.

"Hey, there you are," he said, grabbing her by the elbows and grinning down at her.

"What are you doing here?" Jess asked, noting Ryan looked amazing in a black T-shirt that hung up on his biceps and jeans that looked intentionally worn. Mirrored Ray-Bans sat atop hair that was much shorter than it had been last week. "What happened to your hair?"

"Eh, a new girl at the salon cut it. Pensacola is a military town, and sometimes they get carried away. Not exactly high and tight. I'm working the officer look. If only I had the white uniform to go with it. I could be Maverick."

"And sing 'You've Lost That Loving Feeling'?" Jess joked.

"Nah. I don't sing, and I haven't lost any loving feeling. Yet," he said with a smile, his words sounding awfully flirty as if they dared her to mess with his heart. He set his hand on the small of her back and steered her into the coolness of the bar. Tanae and Becky sat at a high top and waved as she came through the second door.

Jess approached the table with Ryan right behind her.

"We didn't know you knew Ryan," Becky said, grinning like a jack-o'-lantern and pulling Jess down on the stool beside her. Becky had long, straight blonde hair and eyes that twinkled. She wore too much eye makeup and red lipstick that Jess's mother would call whore red, but not in a judgy way, because Donna Culpepper was known for her red lipstick.

"He lives in my complex," Jess said, glancing over at Ryan, who was in the process of snagging a stool from another table. "I met him at a party."

"She tripped over me. I got drunk and nearly passed out under Morgan's deck. You girls know Morgan Mayeaux?"

Tanae shook her head. She had short ebony hair and beautiful caramel skin. "But I heard there was a party for your birthday. I was going to come by, but I forgot which condos you lived in. Del Luna, right?"

"That's right. And Ryan was naked," Jess said.

"You decided to go there, huh?" Ryan asked, lifting his eyebrows. He didn't look mad, though. Smiling, he turned to Tanae. "Should have been there."

"I sure the hell should have," Tanae drawled. "So you took the birthday suit thing to heart, did you?"

Ryan laughed. "Well, I am young and stupid. Why not? And since Jess has already ratted me out, I can't deny it."

The butterflies in Jess's stomach subsided. Ryan had come to Landsharks because she'd said she'd be here. He made her feel comfortable. Included. Normal. And maybe he was a little interested in her? Something inside her hoped that to be true even as she hoped it was not true. She tottered on a fence when it came to Ryan Reyes. "Just revealing the most interesting part of the party."

Ryan leaned on the table, folding his hands and setting his chin in them. "So you thought it was interesting, huh?"

"Oh, I see what's going on. You two," Tanae said, wagging a manicured finger between the two of them, "are talkin'."

"No, we're just ol—" Jess caught herself as she was about to blurt out *old friends*. "We're neighbors. Ryan brought me a nice welcome-to-the-Del-Luna pot of begonias and filled me in on all the good takeout places. Nothing going on." *Yet.*

She winced for even thinking that last word. Doing Ryan wasn't an option. She could still remember him as a kid in his cartoon T-shirts and too-big high-tops.

Ryan nodded. "She saved my life. I had to get her a pot of begonias."

"Saved your life?" Becky asked, lifting a finger as the waitress hurried by. The harried woman didn't see her.

"Yeah, crabs could have eaten me alive. Have you ever seen a body after crabs have done their handiwork? Vicious crustaceans," Ryan joked, smiling over Jess's shoulder at someone sitting at the table behind her. He gave whoever it was a good two- or three-second appraisal. The feeling of anticipation dampened.

"Way to be obvious," Tanae said, giving Ryan a look. "You're sitting here with three of the hottest women in this town and looking at another woman. What's wrong with you?"

"She smiled at me," Ryan said, his gaze moving over the three of them. "I'm being polite by returning the favor."

"Every woman smiles at you, Ryan. You're serious eye candy, sugar," Becky said, allowing her gaze to wander over Ryan's broad chest and the defined biceps peeking out from his sleeves. Twelve years ago, Jess would have put down a hundred bucks against the likelihood of Ryan Reyes ever being called eye candy. And she would have lost. 'Cause he was so sweet to look at.

"The waitress looks busy. Why don't I go to the bar and get you something, Jess? What do you want?" Ryan said, ignoring Becky's obvious invitation for some flirty banter.

"You don't have to do that," Jess said, sliding one butt cheek off the stool. "I can get it myself."

Ryan brushed her attempt to get up away. "I got it. What do you want?"

"Try the mojito," Tanae said, stirring her own mojito with a straw.

"Okay, I'll try it," Jess said, sliding back onto the stool. "Want some money?"

"Nah, I got it this time," he said, moving off toward the bar.

"Holy shit, I've been hungry for a piece of Ryan Reyes ever since I met him at a cookout. He was all sweaty after playing volleyball. Yeah, I sure would like a piece of that," Becky said, her eyes zeroing in on Ryan's ass as he wound around the tables. He stopped to high-five some guy, give knucks to another, and hug a woman whose boobs looked overinflated. Jess felt a stir of discomfort, a sort of odd possessiveness. All this fawning over Ryan . . . and he seemed to eat it up with a spoon.

"Mmm-hmm," Tanae responded.

"Well, you almost hooked up with him a few months back. When you and Cedric were split," Becky said, her blue eyes still on Ryan as he chatted with the bartender.

"No, I didn't. You know Ryan likes the young girls. I'm too damn old for him. Over thirty," Tanae said, spinning toward Jess and jabbing her finger, "but don't tell anyone."

"Of course not." Jess made a cross-your-heart gesture. "Everyone seems to know him, huh?" Jess asked.

Becky nodded. "Oh sure. He's just one of those guys. He plays pool over at Cuesticks, buys the ladies a drink, and he's a pretty good dancer. Remember New Year's Eve when we ended up at the country club party?"

Tanae nodded. "He looked fine ass in that tux. That bitch who brought him looked like she hit the lottery and wouldn't let him dance with anyone else but her. Pissed me off."

After that revelation Jess didn't want to talk about Ryan anymore . . . or his many conquests. Jeez, he was a gigolo, which seemed so at odds with the charming, vulnerable man she'd walked with on the beach. It was as if when he'd given up a life of scientific pursuit, he'd meant business. "So, Tanae, is your boyfriend coming? I'd love to meet him."

"No, he's got a class he can't miss tonight. He's a TA at Pensacola State."

"That's too bad. How long have y'all been together?" Jess asked. Tanae launched into an explanation of her rather contentious relationship with Cedric. As she talked, Jess looked around at the bar, noting the crowd thickening. Over in the corner, a band set up. Ryan wound his way back to their corner table, holding a tall glass of mojito. At that moment, she wanted nothing more than to get up and go back to her rental. She wasn't ready for bars, clubbing, and mixing it up with singles. And even though Ryan was a small comfort in being from her old life, she didn't want to stay and watch him flirt with every woman in the bar. This was not supposed to be her life.

But it is your life.

"Here you go, Jess," Ryan said, setting the drink down in front of her. He settled back onto his stool, swigging a beer and winking at Becky.

Yes, this was her new life . . . she didn't have a garden where she clipped zinnias and placed them in the crystal vase she and Benton had received for a wedding gift. No snuggling in the recliner and watching the Braves play. No decorating the Christmas tree with Benton's famous hot chocolate at her elbow. That life had been snipped in half, leaving her with half the furniture, the good china, and memories. So unfair, but it was where she was . . . starting over.

She pasted a smile on as Ryan chatted with the other girls about his day. He'd taken a blustery businessman and two clients out fishing. The businessman had gotten seasick and had to stay in the cabin, but every so often he'd poke his head out, try to give a sales pitch, smell the baitfish, and then promptly run to the side of the boat.

"I have to give him credit for his tenacity. Never seen a fellow puke and give a sales pitch at the same time," Ryan said, pointing his finger in a what's-up gesture to the guy setting the microphone into the stand. "Hey, Jess, you don't mind giving me a lift home, do you? My truck's in the shop. Transmission's acting up."

"Sure," Jess said, nursing her drink. The mojito was good, but she wasn't in the mood for it, either. Maybe it was too much newness, too fast. She'd never been one for going out for drinks or cruising the singles scene. Maybe because there was only one decent bar outside Morning Glory and two package liquor stores. It was easy to be a wine-on-the-porch girl in Mississippi, especially when her porch had a husband waiting on it. "Any certain time you need to leave?"

"You ready to go now? I'm hungry. We could pick up something."

"Sure," Jess said, shooting Becky and Tanae an apologetic look.

"Don't go yet," Becky said, picking up the laminated bar menu. "We can get cheese fries or wings. The band hasn't even started."

Ryan laughed. "Have you heard Harvey's band? I'd advise you to pay your tab now."

"He's not that bad," Tanae said with a wince. "And he tries really hard. That should be a point in his favor."

Jess slid from the stool. "Thanks for inviting me, but I have to be honest, I'm not in the mood today. I'll take Ryan home and go to bed early tonight."

Becky's gaze moved down Ryan's body and back up again. "I can see what you're in the mood for. Can't hold going to bed early against you."

Jess felt her cheeks bloom pink before she could think about it. And she couldn't think of how to respond to the implication she was taking Ryan home and going to bed early . . . for more than sleep. She wanted to press her hands against her cheeks, but instead she pushed the stool back in place, ducking her head. Which was so not like her. She didn't duck her head. She didn't effing blush. Who the hell was she at this moment?

"Hey, Jess's not that kind of girl," Ryan said, blinking when he realized he'd shown his hand.

"How would you know?" Becky said, challenge in her voice.

"Guess I wouldn't. Are you that kind of girl?" Ryan asked, his gaze tugging Jess's from the pattern of whorls burnished into the metal stool. His question seemed more than what it was. Was Ryan testing the waters? Or merely covering up for nearly telling her friends he knew her? Thing was, she didn't know exactly what temperature her waters were. It had been so long since anyone had wanted to . . . uh, bathe in her bathtub that she didn't know. Maybe her tub was empty. Or held lukewarm water. Or had barely enough to cover the bottom. Maybe she needed to find out. After all, Benton had pulled the plug almost a year ago.

Or maybe the real question was whether Ryan Reyes was the right guy to splash around with.

"Exactly what kind of girl are you talking about?" she asked, abandoning the tub-water analogy in her head. Jeez. Maybe she was thinking too much. After all, she was supposed to be having her own experiences.

"The kind who sells her friends out for a piece of action," Tanae teased.

"Uh, if the action is taking a man home . . . I mean, giving a guy a lift home, then, yes, I am that kind of girl," Jess said, taking one more swig of the cocktail.

Becky laughed. "Go. We'll see you tomorrow."

Jess hurried after Ryan. The sun was still hot, but then again, August was hot everywhere. At least in Pensacola a sea breeze made it less intense.

"My car's over there," she said, pointing to her blue Mustang convertible. Her new GT was her one vanity. Under the hood of the shiny car sat a 300-horsepower engine—it ate up asphalt. The blue paint sparkled in the sunlight, and she loved the way she felt with the top down and the wind whipping her hair. Everything about Jess was methodical, practical, all sharp points and rules, but her sexy car busted all that apart. When Jess let go behind the wheel, she let go.

"Nice," Ryan said, running his hand over the freshly waxed hood. "And hot." He shook his hand and grimaced.

Jess unlocked her baby and climbed inside, cranking the engine and pushing the button that would lower the top. "Thanks."

Ryan climbed into the passenger's seat. "So I sensed you were ready to get out of there?"

"In theory, no. In reality, yes." She inhaled deeply and released the tension with her breath. "Going out for drinks is not my thing. I don't care for a bunch of noise or silly small talk. The whole time I was sitting there, I kept thinking about how comfy the Dirty Heron's couch is and how good the wine I opened last night was."

Ryan hesitated for moment. Then he clicked the seat belt and said, "I get it, but how about before we settle down on your couch, I take you somewhere."

"Where?"

"Somewhere you'll like. Head downtown."

"My, you're bossy." Jess pulled out of Landsharks and followed Ryan's directions. Not ten minutes later, she pulled into parking lot where a shiny diner sat. Scenic 90 Café looked straight out of the 1950s and could have been a twin sister to Dean's Diner in Morning Glory. "It looks like—"

"Dean's," Ryan finished, giving her a wink. "I come here sometimes when I need a little small-town goodness . . . and a good piece of pie."

Jess felt warmth flood her. Ryan had brought her to a place that reminded her of home. Somehow he'd sensed what she couldn't admit—that underneath her declarations of what was good for her was a longing to connect to who she truly was—a small-town girl missing her life. How Ryan knew this, she couldn't begin to guess. Maybe he didn't. But it felt nice to be parked in front of a place that was so . . . her.

Ever since she'd signed the divorce papers, she'd been pulling on a dress that didn't fit her. Mostly because she felt she had to. People back home, her mother included, had been giving helpful advice like, "You should be over him by now," or "Get back in the dating pool," or people would say, "I always knew this would happen—people shouldn't marry their high school sweethearts." Jess had started believing them and had forced herself to be someone she wasn't. She'd gone to the Iron Bull several times, not counting that night with Eden. And she'd hated it. Even today she'd forced herself to meet Becky and Tanae. As if having a drink in a bar could help her get over everything that had happened to her in the last year.

When Ryan pushed the door to the diner open, the smell of french fries and bread welcomed her. The floors were tiled black and white, and the ceiling was lined with electric-blue neon. A metal roof and booths covered in teal pleather lent a kitschy feel, as did the waitress with the mile-high hair.

Her name tag read CINDY and she popped her gum as she chewed. As soon as she saw Ryan, she placed a perfect lipstick tattoo on his cheek. "There's my favorite boy. Ooh, who's your friend?"

"This is Jess. We graduated high school together," Ryan said, waving at another waitress across the room.

"Well, butter my butt and call me a biscuit. I'm a Mississippi girl myself, darlin'. I'm from Meridian," Cindy drawled, setting wrapped utensils on the table and jabbing a finger at the plastic menus on the table. "Menus are right there. You want a Coke, Ryan?"

"Yes, ma'am," Ryan said, arching an eyebrow at her.

"Oh, I'll take a tea."

"One Coca-Cola and a sweet tea coming right up," Cindy said, walking away before Jess could say she'd prefer unsweet.

"Guess I'm having sweet tea," Jess said, unwrapping her fork and knife and placing her napkin in her lap. Like her mama taught her.

"You could stand a few extra calories, and besides, Miss Cindy automatically assumes you're having it sweet 'cause you're from Mississippi. She's the only person who knows I'm from there. Couldn't bullshit her." Ryan picked up a menu and handed it to her. "Everything's pretty good here, but I always have a cheeseburger."

Jess took the menu and glanced around. "I love this place."

"I knew you would. It's like home, though I haven't been to Morning Glory in so long, I wouldn't know it." His green eyes scanned the menu, and she wondered why he was looking at the offerings when he said he always got a cheeseburger.

"You don't go see your mama and daddy?"

"Not since I moved here. When I lived in California, they'd come out on occasion. They knew my work didn't afford much time to travel to Mississippi. Besides, why would I want to return to a place where I lived an inferior version of myself?" he said, sliding the menu back beside the napkin dispenser. "I'm sticking with the burger."

"You hated Morning Glory?"

"I didn't say that."

"So why do you come here?" she asked, pointing down at the table. Her finger landed on the menu, specifically the all-America cheeseburger. She should go with that. But her little red bikini reminded her she probably needed the chef's salad. Eh, she'd had a protein bar for lunch—she could splurge for dinner. Maybe.

"I like it here. They make good sundaes."

"And that's it? I assumed you liked it because it reminded you of home."

Ryan lifted a shoulder. She looked at the soft fabric covering that shoulder and wondered what it would be like to lay her head there. He'd feel different than Benton. Smell different. Because he *was* different. "I have some good memories of my hometown. And I have bad ones. It's the bad ones that keep me here on the beach for Christmas."

Jess thought about Christmas in Pensacola. What did Ryan do to celebrate? Did he get a Christmas tree? Drink eggnog? Sit alone in front of the TV and watch *A Christmas Story* for twenty-four hours? Or maybe he got together with friends? She couldn't imagine not making Christmas cookies with her mom and nephews or playing Dirty Santa with the whole Culpepper family. She'd never miss the Morning Glory Christmas spectacular at the civic center and the Christmas cantata at the Baptist church. No stockings, no breakfast casserole in the kitchen, no watching *White Christmas* with her daddy. Sounded horrible.

Cindy came bopping back with their drinks. Taking a pen from behind her ear, she fished her order pad from her apron pocket. "Okay, so Ryan's having the cheeseburger, medium, with a side of fries. What about you, honey?"

"Um, I'm not sure."

"I'll give you a few minutes more," Cindy said, disappearing.

Jess had been about to blurt out she'd have the burger, but the waitress was like Speedy Gonzales. Vamoose.

Ryan smiled. He did that a lot for a guy who'd spent most of his high school days looking hunted. He should be damaged, skulking around wearing black. But instead he grinned, charmed, made her feel better than she had in almost a year. And it didn't hurt that he looked like he'd stepped from the pages of *Yachting World*.

"So, Jessica Anne, what's the plan?" Ryan asked.

"What do you mean?"

"Do I have a shot?"

Oh crap. She wasn't ready for this conversation. Ryan wanted to know the score, the parameters, the chance he had at getting into her pants. Glancing down, she amended—under her skirt. Or maybe he didn't. She hadn't actually gone on a real date before. Unless frat parties in college counted. Maybe he meant something else.

"At what?"

His lips tipped up even more, and his eyes crinkled. Crikey, he had great eyes. They were perfectly green. Burst of gold in the center spreading out into irises the color of the emerald sea. Gray ringed the outer edge, making them look like an agate stone she'd seen in a jewelry store once. "Okay. I see that you're not ready to have this conversation. That's cool."

"What?"

"You're going to hide from this," he said, his eyes assessing her.

"From what?"

"Me and you."

Jess sucked in a breath and thought about what to say. Part of her wanted to touch him and find out if there were sparks between them. Part of her wanted to shoot him down and eliminate any chance for anything more than friendship. Just be honest. "I don't know if I'm ready for anything more than what we're doing now."

His smile weakened, and something in his eyes softened. "You're still not over him?"

Jess pursed her lips. "Look, saying that isn't a cop-out or an admission of still being in love with Benton. I'm trying to get my land legs, I guess. The thing I struggle with the most is wondering why things turned out the way they did. I had a plan."

"So did I," Ryan said, tracing a rivulet of condensation on his glass. No more lightness. His words echoed her thoughts.

"I guess neither one of us got what we thought we would," she said.

"But what if that's for the best?" Ryan said, lifting his gaze to hers. "What if you can have something better than you thought you'd get?

You don't know. Life may have thrown you a curveball, but that doesn't mean you step out of the batter's box."

"Baseball analogies from the science student of the year?"

"I have a rudimentary knowledge of the sport. It helps me assimilate to my environment."

Jess couldn't help it. She laughed. "You're amazing."

Ryan showed her his teeth again. "Why, thank you."

Cindy bumped into their table as she docked. "Okay, Ryan's getting a cheeseburger, no onion, and a side of fries. What can I get you, darlin'?"

"I'll take the chef's salad—go light on the bacon," Jess said.

"Safe choice," Ryan said.

She suspected his words weren't just for her meal.

Was she too chicken to open herself up to a potential relationship? Or was she being who she'd always been? Jess didn't toss reason out the door when it came to decisions. She was always careful. Always safe. And that had gotten her heartache.

"For now," she said.

Chapter Seven

Ryan cut the limes in half and sprinkled the juice on the tuna steak, one of his favorite fish to grill for tacos. He'd bought the corn tortillas from a lady who supplied a high-end Mexican restaurant and the cilantro and peppers from the farmers' market. The tuna had been caught yesterday on an all-day jaunt out near the oil platforms. Nothing fresher than tuna that had been swimming the day before.

He whistled an old Broadway song from *Guys and Dolls*, congratulating himself on a perfect idea for late Saturday afternoon. A small cool front had pushed down, bringing slightly cooler temps and making it a perfect day for tossing an anchor into the water and having a boat party. He'd invited Jess, of course, and—

"Ryan?" she called from the dock.

He left the fish marinating in the galley and stuck his head out. Jess stood with Morgan and her friend Becky on the dock, holding a beach bag and a plastic sack with what looked to be tortilla chips.

"Hey, ladies, welcome aboard the *Beagle*. Drop your bags and grab a beer," Ryan said, gesturing to the freshly washed deck.

Jess eyed him. "*Beagle*, huh? Wasn't that the name of Charles Darwin's boat?"

Ryan lifted a shoulder. So he'd named his boat after Darwin's research vessel. Hey, you could take the geek out of the lab, but you couldn't take the lab out of the geek. "Don't know. I had a dog that was a beagle. I wasn't going to go with Peanut for my boat's name. No one would want to fish on a boat named *Peanut*."

"Mmm-hmm," Jess said, taking his hand as he helped her aboard. She looked good, but then she'd always suited him with her long limbs and wild curls. Both Becky and Morgan wore bikini tops paired with athletic shorts and flip-flops. Conversely, Jess wore a T-shirt, tennis skirt, and sneakers. Her sex appeal wasn't the blown-up obvious type. She dressed like a lady who didn't like to show the goods, which of course made Ryan want very much to see those goods. Some girls knew how to build anticipation. "I brought some beer and chips. Not much of a cook, but I can use my credit card."

"Come with me, and we'll put them in the galley." He turned to Becky and Morgan. "Ladies, make yourselves comfortable. I have a few of my friends from the marina coming, too. Oh, and my friends Francine and Max . . . if they can get a sitter for their four-year-old. We'll shove off in half an hour or so."

He headed back to the galley. Jess followed, setting the chips and six-pack of craft beer on the small counter. Looking around, she said, "I like your boat."

And I like everything about you, Jess Culpepper.

But he didn't say that. Because he'd spooked her a bit a few nights ago at the diner by flat-out asking if he had a shot with her. He should have remembered how Jess had always been. Back in high school, she'd been a measure twice, pour once chemistry partner. Jess was confident, but it took her a while to get there. Once she made a decision, she held on with both hands, which was why letting go of that jackass Benton Mason seemed to be hard for her. So Ryan wouldn't push anything between them. He preferred an organic approach. If something happened, it happened. He'd be more than happy to scratch any itches she had. But if they never progressed past friendship, he'd live. But he didn't want to. Because he wanted her . . . in his arms, on his lips, in his bed, enveloping all his senses.

But if he had any shot of making it a reality, he'd have to be patient. Practice being a friend. That had been in chapter fifteen of *How to Get Girls Without Even Trying*, one of the books he'd studied when he'd decided to become the cool version of Ryan. The writer implied a modern man had to know when to press a woman for more and when to pull back and give space. With Jess, he'd definitely employ the pullback philosophy.

"Thank you. She's a good boat," he said, opening the small fridge and nestling the six-pack inside. "Want one now?"

"Not yet. Morgan made to-go margaritas, and I had one on the way over."

"She makes good margaritas. She was a bartender once."

"Well, it *was* good," she said, turning and watching as Morgan and Becky slathered themselves with suntan oil. "Are they actually putting oil on themselves? Becky should know better. She's a nurse."

"Knowing better doesn't seem to stop people. I saw three nurses standing outside the hospital smoking."

"I know. What's with that? And really, I'm acting like an old mawmaw. And I sound like my mother. God help me." Jess walked over and whisked the hulls of the used limes into the small bag he had tied to the drawer handle. "What kind of boat is this? Can you sleep on this thing? Or is it just for fishing?"

"It's a forty-six-foot Newton, customized specifically for charter fishing, but we have a few bunks down there"—he jabbed his thumb behind him—"for overnight fishing trips."

"You go out overnight?"

He nodded, pleased she was interested. He'd had a few girls on the boat before, but none had ever seemed interested in the boat. They liked the sunsets, the sunbathing, and the sex on the deck with no one but God and a few seagulls watching. But none had asked about his boat. "For tuna trips and whatnot. Have to get at least sixty miles out to catch them. I went out to a few platforms yesterday and caught this. Well, a few bankers caught this. I kept one."

"That's interesting. Must have a big engine."

The way she said it made it sound sexy. Or maybe he was reading too much into everything, because once again, like that skinny thirteen-year-old kid, he was crushing on her. "It's decent. I can get it up to twenty-eight knots."

"I don't even know what that means. I'll assume that's fast. Can I help you do anything? I can chop or peel."

"No, enjoy yourself. I actually like cooking. I like the monotonous rhythm of chopping onions and"—he lifted a small basket of grape tomatoes—"these babies." Lord, he was being weird, talking about fruit, calling them babies. Good Lord.

Morgan poked her head inside, saving him from any other asinine comments. "Some dudes just parked in the shell lot. Think they could be your friends. Thought you'd want to know."

"Thanks. I'll be right out." He'd invited Logan Yount, an accountant and avid fisherman, and Marcus Geyer, another boat captain, to join them for fish tacos and a sunset cruise. Probably a little OCD of him, but he liked round numbers of people. Made sense.

"Wait, this isn't a setup, is it?" Jess asked, rising and looking unsettled.

"No. I thought Becky might like Marcus. He's funny and very flirty. Seems her type." Ryan covered the tuna he'd rubbed with garlic and ran water over his hands.

"Is the accountant for me?"

Ryan jerked his gaze to Jess. "God, I hope not."

Jess's hair was in a ponytail and big hoop earrings hung at her earlobes. She wore very little makeup—a little gloss and maybe some mascara. She looked naturally gorgeous in a Jennifer Lopez sort of way. He'd be damned if he let Logan lay one pale, number-crunching finger on her.

Jealousy was a junkyard dog that sank its teeth into him.

Ryan shook off the ridiculous urge to shove everyone off his boat and jet away with just Jess. Patience. That's what he needed, so he pasted on a casual smile and stuck his head out to find Marcus and Logan stepping onto the boat. "Hey, guys. This is Morgan and Becky." He pointed to each of the now glistening women.

Marcus and Logan both wore shades, but he could see the approval in the way they said hello to the ladies.

His phone vibrated, and he looked down at the text before glancing back up at his friends. "Drop your beer in the ice chest. Marc, if you'll untie us, I'll fire up the boat. Just got a text that Frannie and Max can't make it. No sitter."

Jess appeared at his elbow and gave a wave to the newcomers. "Hi, guys. I'm Jess. I work with Becky and live next door to Morgan."

After all the how-do-you-dos were said, Jess followed him back to the galley, which pleased him. He wanted her to want to be with him.

"So how come you didn't want me to put my beer in the cooler?" she asked.

"Because I knew you'd bring the good stuff, and Logan is an accountant."

"And?"

Ryan grinned. "He brings cheap beer. Have you ever met an extravagant accountant?"

Jess tilted her head. "Actually, no."

"It's because they don't exist." Ryan waved his hand like a magician in front of Jess's face, making her giggle. Which was something he'd never seen before. The Jess he remembered—and the sad one who'd walked with him on the beach over a week ago—didn't giggle.

"You're a funny guy, Ryan. How come I never knew this?" Jess said, sliding by him, obviously planning on going back outside with the rest of the party. Her body brushed against his back, and he almost stepped back, pinning her against the side of the cabinet just so he could feel her fully against him . . . so she wouldn't leave him.

Which was insanity.

"Because I was too busy trying to be invisible? And being around you made me extra nervous," he said.

"But no longer, huh?" Jess said, slipping out onto the boat deck with the others. Ryan headed for the captain's chair, trying to affirm her words within himself. Fading into the background, while often comfortable, wouldn't get him what he wanted—a life. So, yeah, he no longer tried to be invisible, and he was no longer nervous around women.

Five minutes later he pulled the *Beagle* away from the marina and motored out into the bay. Behind him, his guests sprawled on the cushioned benches, sipping cold beer and enjoying the wind on their faces and the sun on their shoulders. And this pleased Ryan. He liked having people with him. Sometimes. Like on days like this when he moved his boat across the still waters bathed gold by the sun. The salty tang on his tongue harkened to olden times when sailors found respite in the swish of the waters against a hull. Days like today scrubbed away any residual doubt he'd made the right decision when he stood in his apartment and declared himself done with being Dr. Ryan Reyes, researcher, scientist, and Comic-Con annual pass holder. The boat skimming the waters, racing along the infinite horizon, was like poetry, giving him something he'd lacked in his life.

Clarity.

After twenty minutes of cruising along Santa Rosa Sound, he entered the pass into the Intracoastal Waterway and motored into

Big Lagoon. When he neared Redfish Point, he killed the engines and dropped the anchor. It was the perfect place to bob on the Gulf and use the grill he'd installed in the galley.

"It's so pretty out here," Becky said, crossing her legs and tossing back her shoulders, giving her best Playboy Bunny impression. Jess sat with her legs pulled to her, long arms looped around her knees. The guys sprawled, tanned legs stretched, visors shielding their faces. Morgan lay on one bench seat and looked asleep.

"Morgan?" he called.

She stirred and yawned. "Out too late last night."

The sun was a good hour and a half away from sinking into the waters. "I'm going to cook the tuna and set out the chips and salsa. Y'all want to swim?" he asked.

The girls shook their heads. The guys kicked off their flip-flops and dived overboard.

"You can swim over to the dunes. Beach is on the other side," Ryan said to the girls.

"We'll just hang here and watch those morons get eaten by a shark or something," Becky drawled, cracking open another Coors Light. Obviously Marcus had been classy enough to buy Coors. Last time he'd brought Natty Light.

Just after Becky said the word *shark*, a fin appeared. Jess's eyes widened, and she pointed. "Oh my God," she breathed.

"Dolphins," Ryan said, smiling.

"Oh yeah. Of course." Jess looked embarrassed. Which was cute.

Marcus and Logan tried to swim out to play with the squeaking sea friends, but the dolphins were having none of it. Ryan went back into the galley and started heating the corn tortillas in the microwave. He could hear the girls chatting, a soft, higher-pitched pleasantness that was sweet accompaniment to his preparations. He wished Jess would come back inside and talk to him, but he'd given her no real reason to do so.

He was giving her space. Even if he wanted to crowd her, gather her to him, kiss the hell out of her.

A few days ago, she'd made it clear she wasn't ready to go where he wanted to go. Yet. So he'd backed off, and they'd spent a pleasant evening talking about her friend Rosemary, who'd recently become engaged to a guy who was opening a pizza place in Morning Glory. They chatted about their ten-year reunion. She had been a committee member; he'd not bothered to attend. Wasn't like anyone missed him. Then they'd talked about *Dr. Who*, Celtic music, and his work at Caltech. With Jess, he didn't have to guard against his inner nerd showing. He could talk passionately about his comic book collection, and she could mention people from back home without have to explain their neuroses or give background. It had been the easiest nondate he'd ever been on.

They'd driven back to Del Luna with the top down, stars twinkling above them, and all he could think of as they blew past condos, beach restaurants, and the state park was how much he wanted to taste her. Her hair blew back, whipping, occasionally brushing his cheek. She smelled like summer—coconut and vanilla. Her sundress moved up and down her firm thighs and the soft cotton molded her breasts. A necklace with a silver turtle charm hung down, brushing the neckline, teasing his thoughts. Her wide mouth curved when he turned up "Peaceful Easy Feeling" by the Eagles and started singing along. It should have been foreplay.

It wasn't.

They said good-bye in the driveway of her condo with a quick hug. He might or might not have huffed her hair like teenage glue addict. And then he'd gone home alone. Alooooone.

He wanted to kiss her, tell her to let go, to not worry, to be in the moment. With him. But chapter fifteen held him back. *Give her space. Be her friend.*

"Hey," Jess said from the open doorway.

Inside he did a happy dance though outside he remained cool. Sliding the jalapeño he'd diced onto a saucer, he quickly wiped the counter. The small cuts burning on his fingertips were hazards of being a fisherman. "Everyone ready to eat?"

"I think so," she said, taking in the food. "Uh, that guy Logan just asked me out."

Ryan froze. "He did?"

"Yeah, out of the blue. We were talking about dolphins, and he asked me if I wanted to go on a dolphin cruise tomorrow afternoon. It was odd."

Not so odd. Jess was naturally gorgeous and didn't try as hard as Morgan and Becky. Logan was the kind of guy who liked cool chicks. Logan also liked big breasts, which was why he'd hoped Morgan's pendulous attributes might hypnotize him . . . or Marcus. Either way, as long as one of them took her focus off Ryan. Obviously, he'd underestimated how much Jess would appeal to his friend. "So are you going to go? I thought you weren't ready for . . . dating."

"I kind of have to. I already admitted to having no plans for tomorrow. Besides, turning him down would have made tonight awkward." Jess frowned.

But she could turn Ryan down? Okay, so she hadn't actually turned him down. Merely implied she wasn't ready to move beyond where they were. But now she was going on a date with Logan the accountant? Perfect.

"You'll have fun. He's nice guy," Ryan said. 'Cause what was he going to say? *I invite assholes to my party. Don't get near him. And damn sure don't go dolphin watching with him?* Or maybe he should tell her he wanted to peel her clothes from her body, lick her stomach, move lower . . .

No. That's stalkerish. Control your impulses. Remember who you are—a seasoned pro who can control his desires, his mouth, and his need to watch Star Trek.

"Are you sure you didn't suggest he ask me out?" Jess asked, her eyes narrowing.

"Why would I do that?" His tone said it all. He didn't want any other man near her. Hadn't she gotten that from the other night? Or maybe she hadn't really known what he'd asked. Maybe she still thought of him as some kid.

"Because I'm new to town and you're being a good friend?"

Okay, she hadn't gotten the message. He'd read a lot of books on understanding women, but perhaps he needed to be more clear about what he wanted . . . without talking about licking her body. "I'm not that good of a friend."

Jess stared at him for a moment. "So I should probably go with him. It would embarrass him for me to back out of it even if I still feel like . . . ugh, I don't know what I'm supposed to do or who I am supposed to be anymore. This is so stupid."

Ryan didn't offer any words. Because at that moment, it occurred to him that maybe his plan to grow into something more with Jess wouldn't work because she was too screwed up. And it pissed him off that asshole Benton Mason was once again the reason Ryan couldn't have what he wanted. Back at Morning Glory High, Ryan's dream was to just be normal. Presently, his goal was to have Jess. But like a bad bean burrito, Benton's selfish, immature actions were stinking things up for Ryan. Jess's ex-husband had pushed Jess aside, but he'd hurt her so much in the process she couldn't find her way back to normal.

"Oh God," Jess said, slapping a hand against her forehead. "I'm that woman. Oh Christ, please don't let me be that woman. A whiny, pathetic loser. I mean, I ran in here and told you like you were going to tell me what to do. I've lost my goddamn mind. Sweet Jesus, who am I?" She spun to walk out of the galley, obviously disgusted with herself.

He caught her arm. "Hey, you just took the Lord's name in vain four times in ten seconds. Come on, Mississippi. Don't make me call your old Sunday school teacher."

"Seriously," she said, her eyes shining with disbelief. "That's your response?"

Oops. Try again, Ryan.

"I'm joking. Look, stop thinking so hard about everything. Chill," he said.

"Chill," she repeated. Then she curled her fingers over his. "I *should* just chill. You're right."

"Hey, it's been my motto for the last year, and it's working for me," he said. Her touch wasn't electrifying or erotic, but it was somehow profound. She'd never touched him intentionally before, and her fingers curled against his reminded him of eighteenth-century poetry, like Pope's "The Rape of the Lock," the ironic profundity of a simple gesture taken to new heights. To her it was no big deal, or perhaps it was; he didn't know. But to him, it confirmed only what he knew. Ryan Reyes hadn't lost any of what he'd felt for Jess Culpepper. She still had him in her hand, whether she knew it or not. He was poised to be her puppy. Embarrassing but true.

Whatever she wanted, he'd give her. Even if that meant watching her have it with another man.

Morgan entered the kitchen, her eyes riveting to his hand on Jess's forearm. "What are y'all doing? We're, like, starving out here."

Ryan pulled away from Jess, snapping out of the trance she'd put him under. She had him discombobulated with the whole vulnerability thing. Jess had never been weak; she'd never asked anyone for anything in all the time he'd known her. Something about rescuing her appealed to his machismo.

Maybe he needed to step away from Jess and look for the man he'd been for the past year . . . before he had to go out and find tampons for his vagina. The thought made him smile. "I'm putting the fish on the grill now. Won't take long. Morgan, you want to grab the plates?"

"Sure, babe," she said, sliding past Jess, giving her a possessive look. Then the younger woman slid an arm around his waist and gave it a squeeze. "Don't go getting the hots for our nurse friend here, Ry. Logan already asked her out. I told him we'd go with them to Perdido Key. A double date. Won't that be fun?"

Ryan slid his arm around Morgan and gave her a quick squeeze. Jess's gaze dropped to his hand on Morgan's naked waist. "I see dolphins every day, Morgan. I'm not sure I want to waste a day off watching them." He pulled away from her and occupied his hands with cleaning the knife he'd used earlier.

"No day is a waste when you're with me, honey," Morgan said, slapping him on his ass and grabbing the plates and napkins he sat on the table.

"You should come with us," Jess said, her tone even. But he knew she didn't want to go on a date with Logan alone. She wanted buffers. Had nothing to do with him, which sort of hurt. Why didn't she tell Logan no? Why didn't she put her arm around him and claim him . . . the way Morgan had been trying to do for the past month? If Jess was going to jump into the dating pool, why not do it with him?

He was afraid of that answer.

Maybe it was because he and Jess had history. He knew her past with Benton. But the biggest reason he feared she wouldn't give him a shot at romance was he'd been the Brain. Being who'd he'd been all those years wasn't something a guy got over easily. When he thought back to the boy he'd been, he winced. Horrible clothing—baggy parachute pants, ninja T-shirts, and Chucks—paired with thick glasses did nothing for him. He'd been painfully skinny, pale, and prone to forehead acne. His teeth had been yellowish, and he'd carried around a binder with Pokémon cards so he could easily trade at school with the other outcasts. When they'd finally found him in the storage closet in the gym, an ambulance had to be called. His reputation was hard to surmount. Then he'd made a thirty-six on the ACT and received the National Merit award . . . and gotten accepted into Mensa. With Jess, he couldn't hide who he was beneath the tan, bleached teeth, and gym-honed muscles. She knew the real Ryan. She'd already seen the locked door to his truth.

"You don't have a charter tomorrow. Marcus checked the marina log," Morgan said, sliding past Jess. "It will be fun, and I promise not to get wasted this time."

Jess's eyes pleaded with him.

Like he could turn her down . . . or leave her to a very handsy Logan. "Fine. I'll go."

"Yay," Morgan said, clapping her hands, leaving the galley.

Ryan shrugged and said in a sarcastic voice, "Yay."

∾

Jess was having a personality crisis.

That was the only explanation for why she acted the way she did. Who ran off to tattle when a guy asked her out? And to Ryan? Why was she treating him like the anchor he'd dropped in the Gulf half an hour ago?

Oh, Ryan, your friend asked me out. Should I? Or shouldn't I? Oh, let's do each other's hair.

Crap on a cracker. Why would she run to him like a silly little girl?

But deep down inside she knew why. She couldn't get Ryan out of her mind. Not the way he was years ago, but the way he was now. She'd never liked pushy people, Benton aside, so coming on strong like Logan had was an automatic turnoff. She much preferred Ryan's charming, nonpushy approach. She knew he liked her—after all, he'd asked about his chances. But she wasn't sure if that was merely his MO or if he'd been truly serious. After all, he'd pretty much admitted to being a guy who had been with a lot of women. And though she felt drawn to him, she wasn't sure it wasn't purely physical. When she'd touched his hand earlier, it had felt good. But she'd only touched his hand. She hadn't tested any other waters. So was that the first spark of physical

94

attraction? She knew he was very pretty to look at, but what would his lips feel like on hers? How unfamiliar would his hands be touching her arms, sliding lower?

It had been so long since she had to think about a relationship, she didn't trust her instincts. After all, she'd had sex with only one man in her life.

Yeah. Benton Mason had been her one and only. She'd thought it had always been good between them in bed. Now she wondered. Maybe she hadn't been adventurous enough, hadn't worn enough sexy lingerie or given him enough attention. Maybe she wasn't good in bed . . .

So as far as being an experienced woman of the world, Jess fell flat. But that was okay, because she was gathering new experiences. That word again. *Experiences.* And though Logan made her want to say no and disappear from the boat, she wouldn't, because at some point she had to go on a date. And Logan seemed safe. He was nice, attractive, and obviously had a thing for dolphins. It would be fine . . . and added bonus, Morgan and Ryan were tagging along. Conversation wouldn't lag, no chance for intimacy or an awkward good-bye kiss at the door. Going on a date with Logan would be easy.

"So, Jess, you work with Becky, huh?" Logan said, drying off with a towel. He had a farmer's tan—lily-white stomach and chest, tanned arms. He also had a goatee and shaved his head. Maybe because he had a receding hairline? She couldn't tell, because he seemed to be a blond. The gold hair sprinkled on his forearms spelled out as much. He had a nice smile and crinkly blue eyes that reminded her of her brother. In fact, he reminded her of her brother, Rob, a lot.

"Yes, I'm a contract nurse, and I'm filling in for two nurses on maternity leave. I'm from Mississippi."

"Oh, so you're only here for . . ."

"Three or four months. But I like the hospital. Becky has been good to me, helping me meet new people." There. That didn't sound too antisocial. She sounded like someone who liked people. Which she did, most of the time.

"So will you travel around to other places? Or go back home?"

Back home. She couldn't imagine not going back home. She loved Morning Glory because it was the perfect little town. Close enough to Jackson for decent shopping and good restaurants, far enough away to keep the small-town charm. And Morning Glory had small-town charm in spades—an old tiled bank with a broken clock out front, a town square with ancient oak trees, and a crumbling courthouse surrounded by magnolia trees and pretty crepe myrtles that bloomed a vivid pink in the heat of summer. There was a gazebo, a duck pond, old redbrick elementary schools, and exactly ten stoplights. There were festivals and parades and high school football on Friday nights. Why would she want to live anywhere else?

Because Benton lived there and currently dated all the twentysome-things arriving back home after college. That was a good reason to stay away for a little while. Until she was strong enough. Until the pain, hate, and sadness didn't burn inside her anymore.

"I'll eventually go home, but I'll also continue to work contract labor. Luckily I was able to lease my apartment to my friend's fiancé, but that's short-term. I'm finding it interesting working in a different city. I'm footloose and fancy free, so why not?" Hard to say those last words. She stared out at the gentle waters of the Gulf, letting their magic work on her.

"That's awesome," Logan said, sinking down beside her.

His thighs had freckles on them. Definitely a blond. Or he could have red hair.

Ryan emerged from inside with a small catering table. "I'm going to set this here and then bring out the fixings. It will be easier to serve out here rather than everyone crowding inside."

Jess studied Ryan as he competently set up the table. He'd taken off his shirt and wore a pair of board shorts that looked new. She gathered he'd never found the ones he'd lost the night of his birthday. That brought to mind his big, nude body sprawled in the sand. His body was amazing. Beat Marcus and Logan by a country mile. Ryan was hard, lean, and . . . very sexy. His ruffed hair looked suitably beachy, his Ray-Bans hid those green eyes, and his smile made her toes tingle.

And he wanted her.

What the hell was wrong with her?

Ryan Reyes had grown into the total package. He was gorgeous, fun, charming, understanding, silly, crazy smart, and sexy. Yeah. Very sexy. And she wanted to touch him. Feel his warmth. Indulge in him like he was a decadent piece of chocolate. Ryan made her laugh and feel herself again. Perhaps he was the perfect man to heal her wounds . . . perhaps he was the perfect man to jump into bed with. She longed to feel the excitement of a new romance—desire, joy, and crushing paranoia of wondering if it was all too good to be true. She'd felt it only once, but she remembered how horrible and beautiful it was at the same time. So was she really going to stick to friendship because it was safer?

"Here we go," Ryan said, pointing to several plates with chopped vegetables and slaw, drawing her thoughts away from the indecision that haunted her. For some reason indecision had become her shadow. She didn't like feeling that way.

"So impressive," Becky drawled, rising and giving Marcus an appraising look. Her gaze snagged on Jess's, and she smiled. Obviously, Ryan had been right about Becky liking Marcus. "I love a man who can cook."

"It's not so rare these days. I'm terrific on the grill myself," Marcus said, stepping beside Becky.

"And so humble about it," her friend teased Marcus.

Jess pulled her legs up again and stared out across the waters. The dolphins had disappeared, and the sun sagged toward the horizon, casting a golden glow. Everything looked soft, reminding Jess life wasn't so hard. She should focus on chilling. Not analyzing every glance and touch.

"Not hungry?" Ryan said, sitting down on the bench beside her. He handed her one of the beers she'd brought made by a local brewery that specialized in small batches.

She took a sip. "Good beer. No, I'm going to eat. Just letting everyone else go first."

"Ah, in your nature."

"What?"

"Being kind."

"No, it's not. I'm not all that kind. In fact, I can be super mean. Ask my brother, Rob. He loves to bring up my past role of torturous older sister." Jess smiled and thought about touching his arm again. "If you don't want to go on that dolphin-watching expedition, you don't have to. I didn't mean for you to get roped into it."

Ryan looked out at the sunset. "You didn't rope me into it. Morgan did."

"Do you like her?"

His gaze jerked back to hers. "Who? Morgan?"

God, why had she asked that? Of course, she knew why. She didn't want him to want any other woman, yet she'd told him a few days ago she wasn't ready for more than what they now had . . . which was still undefined. "It's just you spend a lot of time together."

"We're friends," he said, lifting a shoulder, "and neighbors."

"So are we."

Ryan's lips curved, and he moved his leg closer to hers. Not because he wanted to, but because Becky needed to squeeze by. "Yeah, but it's not the same."

"Why? Because we knew each other back in high school?" she asked, lowering her voice.

"No, because I don't want to be just your friend, Jess." She watched his hand as it brushed her inner knee, faint as butterfly wings. The soft friction shot straight to her belly, careening through her. The combination of his words and touch seared her.

"Ryan," she whispered.

"Just know that. Go on the date with Logan, but know I want you."

Jess swallowed hard and lifted her gaze to his, but he rose. He wasn't giving her time to respond.

"Let me get you a beer, Logan," Ryan said, scooting around Morgan, who once again had caught Jess in an intimate conversation with him. Morgan bit into a tortilla chip and chewed thoughtfully, her eyes resting on Jess.

The thrill she felt at Ryan's admission faded as unease crept inside. Morgan had been obvious in her pursuit of Ryan. From the birthday party to the implied statements on the way over to the marina, Morgan had plunged a flag into her territory, claiming Ryan as her own. Jess wanted to smack Morgan's hand and say *not so fast*. The other part of her wanted to pretend she hadn't heard Ryan's soft words, that she didn't feel tingly around him. It would make better sense to ignore the fireworks and focus on herself. She didn't need a man to heal her. She could heal herself. Anything more didn't make sense.

Ah, being sensible.

She'd done sensible. She'd set her course, bulldozing her way into the life she'd thought she should have because it was the way a person did things. Make a plan, follow the steps, keep focused. No stepping outside a comfort zone, no deviating, no second-guessing.

But that hadn't worked out, had it? So why should she back off the feeling she had for Ryan and do the sensible thing?

She rose, straightening her shoulders with conviction. If she wanted Ryan, and he wanted her, what was the problem? They were grown-up people who could do grown-up things. In fact, she should be doing very, very grown-up—and possibly downright dirty—things with Ryan.

Grabbing a plate, she waited behind Logan to try some of the fresh tuna Ryan had grilled. Morgan stood up suddenly and brushed against her. Very softly, her new neighbor said, "You're not right for him."

Jess jerked her eyes to Morgan's, shocked the younger woman had been so obvious. But then, standing on Ryan's boat, obliged to a date she didn't want with an accountant, Jess found the part of herself she'd shoved behind heartache and forgotten. That Jess didn't take shit from anyone. She smiled at Morgan and took a chip off the woman's plate. Sliding around her, she bit into the tortilla chip and said, "We'll see about that."

And that made her feel like her old self.

Chapter Eight

Ryan had just stepped out of the shower when his cell phone buzzed. He walked over to the nightstand, scrubbed his face, and stared down at the screen.

Martha Reyes.

His brain spun through all the possibilities in a nanosecond, landing on *something's wrong, so you better answer it.*

He picked up the phone, wrapped the towel around his waist, and pressed the button to answer the call. But of course, he had answered too late. Sighing, he flopped back on the bed, preparing for the worst. His father had high cholesterol, but he'd talked the man out of taking statins and into a better lifestyle. His father had dropped weight and lowered his triglycerides. His mother had back issues, but who knew at her age? Breast cancer had killed his maternal grandmother before he was old enough to know her. As his parents neared their seventies, a plethora of health problems awaited them. Today could be the start of a new one.

Dialing the number stamped in his memory, Ryan prepared for the worst.

"Ryan, thank goodness. I worried when you didn't answer," his mother said, breathless. Was that a symptom or merely her body's natural response to hurrying to the phone?

"I was in the shower."

"Oh good," she huffed.

Then his mother didn't say anything for a few seconds. Anxiety fluttered in his gut.

"Uh, so is everything okay?" he asked, sitting up, bracing for the news his grandmother, ensconced in Pleasant Acres Retirement Center, was in the hospital, or perhaps his mother might utter the *C* word. His grandmother had been the one person who'd made him feel normal. He wasn't ready to lose her . . . even though he knew he should have been visiting her. Guilt sledgehammered him.

"Everyone is fine," his mother said.

"Oh," he replied. So why had she called him? She never called. She and his father were still resentful over him leaving Caltech to "drive around a fishin' boat." "So you called for . . . ?"

"I haven't talked to you since March. Can't a mother call her child?"

"Sure. Oh, thank you for the birthday gift."

"That's the sunscreen they recommended in *Good Housekeeping*. It blocks the UV rays better or something like that. I guess you need something like that since you're out in the sun all day. Your father picked out the hat. Some kid at Loston's said it was a preferred hat by outdoorsmen. That's what you are now, I guess." She sounded quite sad about it, too.

"You can still call me Doc if you want to. My degrees didn't disappear the day I bought the *Beagle*." He used a light voice because he wasn't in the mood to argue with her . . . or rather, engage in passive-aggressive behavior where she pretended to be supportive of his decision but dropped not-so-subtle comments about him wasting his abilities.

"Ha-ha," his mother tittered. "Oh, I was calling to make sure you got your birthday gift, but also because I saw Donna Culpepper at yoga last week, and she told me that her daughter, Jessica, is working in Pensacola. Of course, Donna didn't know you live there, too."

"Because you allow everyone to think I'm still in California working on my speech for the Nobel Prize?"

"I don't let anyone think anything, Ryan James. But I don't know why I would tell anyone you're down there drivin' men around to catch fish half of them won't consume anyhow. But I don't want to talk about your new trade. Just wanted you to keep your eyes open for one of your old classmates."

It struck Ryan why his mother had called him. She didn't want anyone in Morning Glory to know her boy wonder now ran a fishing charter service. Not when she'd received so much recognition for his many accomplishments. The *Morning Glory Herald* had written several articles about his achievements, the last of which was selling his medical advancement to a major pharmaceutical company. He understood objectively that many parents received worth through the achievement of their children, so that didn't make his mother atypical. Perhaps shallow, but not abnormal. His mother had never been shallow, of course . . . not that she would admit.

"I don't have to keep my eyes open. She's renting a condo in my complex. We've already run into each other." Or rather, she'd tripped over him naked on the beach. He probably shouldn't tell his mother that, though. Not something she'd want to share with her Church of Christ knitting circle/Bible study.

"Does she know who you are?" His mother sounded worried.

"At first she didn't recognize me. I had to reintroduce myself." And try not to throw up on her or overly expose his junk . . . which he'd likely have done. He'd had a lot of tequila and rum that night. "Why are you so concerned?"

"No reason. How strange she's living in your complex. It's truly a small world," his mother said, clearing her throat. "So what did she think about your new career?"

"She said she liked my boat," Ryan said, unwinding the towel from his waist, sliding it from beneath him, and tossing it onto the leather bench at the foot of the bed. His skin itched to pick it up and toss it into the washer. But he quelled the urge. He forced himself to look at crumbs on the countertop and swore off organizing his canned goods according to daily vitamin allowance and seed type. He eyed an uneven toenail as he sat naked on his bedspread . . . another forced action.

"Oh," his mother responded.

"Actually, I'm going dolphin watching with her today."

"She's divorced," his mother said. She made it sound like Jess had gonorrhea or something.

"Thank God. Her husband was an asshole."

"Ryan James, watch your language," his mother said, her tone turning sharp. Martha Reyes had taught school for thirty-five years. She could freeze anyone with a mere look. "I must run now. I have to take a tuna salad to Mrs. Montgomery. She fell and broke her hip last month and is still having trouble getting around."

"Thanks for calling and wishing me a belated happy birthday," he said, eyeing his body in the mirror. He sucked in his stomach. Still flat, but he needed to watch the cheeseburgers. He'd worked so hard in the gym to perfect his body. No use in making more work for himself.

"'Bye, Ryan," she said, hanging up.

No *I love you* or *I miss you*. Just, "Bye, Ryan."

He set his cell phone on the bedside table, centering it on the *JAMA* he'd received in the mail last week. Then on second thought he bumped the phone so it slid halfway off the magazine. Then he walked away.

An hour later he pulled up at the Holiday Harbor Marina. Morgan sat beside him, smelling like coconut suntan oil and looking like the subject of a country song. Her bikini top looked like if he hit a big pothole, the stitching would pop. Her cutoff jean shorts were, well, short. He had a good shot of seeing her hoo-ha when she bent over. She also wore very impractical wedge sandals. Logan had texted he would pick up Jess, which didn't make much sense since she lived in the same complex as him and Morgan. Guess the man really thought this was a date.

And by the looks of Morgan, she did, too, which aggravated him. They'd had the conversation about being friends. Why couldn't Morgan accept what they had? She was like the swallows who built the nest on his deck—nothing would dissuade.

Jess stood by the huge ice machine wearing a tank sundress that skimmed her thighs and a pair of thong sandals. Her hair had been braided, and she wore lip gloss. Guess she thought it was a date, too.

Damn it.

"Hey," she said, donning a smile. "Logan went to talk to the guy who is taking us out."

Morgan said hello to Jess, but she was a bit cool about it. He'd never seen the happy brunette act standoffish with anyone. One of the reasons he liked Morgan was her sunny disposition and enthusiasm for everything . . . even grocery shopping. Ryan equated grocery shopping with the flames of eternal damnation. All that disarray, suspect smells emanating from the freezer section, and deli harboring pathogenic bacteria waiting to climb into his luncheon meat.

Logan came out of the marina. "Okay, folks, it's all set up. Captain Buddy's our guy. He knows where all the bottlenoses hang out."

"Didn't we just do this yesterday?" Ryan asked, trying to stanch the sour grapes in his tone.

"Yeah, but who cares?" Morgan said, studying her nails before blinding him with a smile. "This time it's a date, and Logan mentioned going to the beach afterward. We can play beach blanket bingo. It's my favorite game."

"It's the name of your beach house," Jess said.

Morgan rolled her eyes. "Duh, that's why it's my fave."

Captain Buddy, a guy Ryan had never met, came out and pointed out his boat, a flat-bottomed skiff. The man looked like Santa Claus and Jimmy Buffett had had a baby. He wore a bright Hawaiian shirt, baggy shorts, and deck shoes. His stomach hung over, and he had the habit of rubbing it while he talked. They all put on life jackets and climbed into the boat.

It was an hour of . . . watching dolphins.

Ryan liked dolphins well enough, but he saw them all the time. They frequently followed his boat, jumping in the wake. Not to mention Buddy took them back to Big Lagoon, where they'd docked the day before. Jess seemed to enjoy it, pointing out the rolling fins and beaming at Captain Buddy as he talked about dolphin adventures he'd had over the years. Logan watched Jess like a hawk searching a field for prey. Morgan played on her phone. Overall, Ryan would rate the date a C plus only because Jess smiled a lot. He remained silent, noting the way the captain piloted the boat more than watching the dolphins.

After an hour they motored back into the marina, bought some beer, and piled into Logan's jeep. Fifteen minutes later they walked along the white beaches of Perdido Key, which sat east of Orange Beach near the Florida state line.

"This is so gorgeous. No matter where you go on the Gulf Coast, it's paradise," Jess said, bending and scooping the crystal sand and letting it pour through her fingers. "I still can't believe I'm here and not looking at the muddy pond in the middle of Morning Glory."

"Morning Glory? Is that even a place?" Morgan asked.

Jess's forehead crinkled. "No, I'm making it up, Morgan."

Ryan tried to hide his smile, but Jess caught sight of it. Something in her eyes glowed triumphantly. The old Jess was somewhere inside the shell she seemed to have become. No, not shell, but the vulnerability Jess displayed was similar—luminescent and secretive—and so not what came to mind when he pictured her. He wanted that Jess back, the one who lifted her chin, argued when she knew she was right, and elbowed her way past the stragglers in life.

Morgan seemed oblivious to Jess's jab and pointed to an unoccupied pavilion on the state beach. "We can put our stuff over there. I brought a towel even though I didn't know we were going to the beach." She shot an annoyed look at Ryan.

How was he supposed to know? Wasn't like Logan had called him and they'd planned the day like a couple of adolescent boys on their first shebang. Ryan had been coerced into this double date . . . which he didn't consider a true double date. Not for him, anyway.

Logan headed over to the pavilion. "The day is too nice to go back home and do laundry. We're young. Let's play."

Morgan and Jess dumped their beach bags. One swish of her shapely hips and Morgan was beach ready in a matching bikini bottom. Jess watched as Morgan tiptoed out to the pounding surf. Then with a slight lift of her shoulder, she wrenched the tank dress overhead.

"Nice bikini," Logan said.

That was an understatement.

"Uh, thanks," Jess said, clasping her hands between breasts that were tastefully covered. Her bikini was not as revealing as Morgan's, having more substantial material and an almost modest cut, but her body was amazing.

He thought about the Jess he'd fantasized about all those years ago while lying in his twin bed staring up at the constellations that clustered on his ceiling—another educational Christmas gift from Santa Claus that he didn't have the heart to pull down. Her Morning Glory cheerleading uniform showed her long, tanned legs and clung perfectly to her breasts, nipping in at her slim waist. She had amazing collarbones, and her arms were somehow both elegant and athletic. He'd adored her then, dared to brush her arm whenever he added boric acid to the test tube. He'd breathed deeply when she was near, sucking in the scent of her perfume and shampoo. Jess had been his ideal girl.

And now she stood in front of him, no longer girlish, but splendidly woman.

"Okay, I'm heading into the water," she said with a smile that looked a bit forced.

"Me, too," Logan said, ripping off his shirt and following her toward the surf. The fool hadn't even put on sunscreen. He'd be a lobster tomorrow.

Ryan grabbed a beer and sank onto the bench, watching Jess cautiously step into the water. Her hands fluttered at the sides of her swim bottoms as if she were afraid the strong swell of waves might make short work of her suit. He'd seen plenty of boob and ass thanks to the ocean. But Ryan didn't want any cheap glimpses of Jess's no doubt extraordinary flesh. He wanted to earn his view the honest way. No cheating.

And right there as he sat on Perdido Beach watching Logan make an ass of himself trying to impress Jess by jumping waves, Ryan decided he was done with friendship. Screw chapter fifteen. His gut told him Jess was attracted to him. He didn't want to tread on what they had, but he was prepared to stomp all over that shit for a chance with Jess. He wanted her in and out of that bathing suit. No one-night stand. No one-week fling. As long as she stayed in Pensacola, he wanted her to be with him. And only him.

He still had a half year of debauchery in his plan for his new life, but Jess was worth smashing the plan into smithereens. Because she had always been his ideal.

And that was enough.

Jess stood in the surf and watched Morgan and Logan play in the water. Ryan remained on the beach under the pavilion, looking contemplative. Along the white sands, families frolicked. One little girl threw a Frisbee for a golden retriever. Another man scooped shells into a bright-orange bucket. All simple pleasures on a Sunday afternoon. And she stood on the edge, afraid her bathing suit might get compromised by the strong waves, struck by her inability to charge into the fray.

Oddly enough, back in Morning Glory, people hadn't really noticed how unsteady she was. To them, she was the same Jess they'd always known. Not even Rosemary had noticed her reticence, her lack of interest. Eden seemed to see how much she'd been rocked a bit more, but then again, Eden was sensitive to emotional undertow. It was easier for Jess to pretend she was okay. She sat on the same pew each Sunday with her family, balancing her niece on her knee. She went to Stitch and Bitch at Rosemary's shop on Thursday nights, shopped at the Piggly Wiggly on Mondays because Benton worked all day and had Rotary Club on Monday night. Less likely to run into him. She still went to baby showers, bridal showers, and dedications. She existed, pretending nothing had changed. She was good ol' Jess.

But standing in the Florida surf, wearing a red bikini while on a date with a guy she didn't want to be with, it became very obvious she was full of chickenshit.

She was tired of herself.

Women got divorced all the time. Their husbands cheated all the time. The scumbags came home and told them, divorced them, and took the dog all the time. Jess wasn't special. She was one of them. United by fear, hate, disgust, sadness, and loathing. Some of her kind got mad and got even. She'd read *The First Wives Club*. Some went crazy and slept with half a football team. She was sure there was a book about that, too, but she'd not found it yet. And others grew morose and started herb gardens and adopted stray cats. No one wanted to read about those women. So, no, Jess Culpepper wasn't special.

She had to stop sitting on the sidelines.

Glancing back at Ryan, she made a decision.

No more just friends with Ryan. He wanted her. He'd always wanted her, and now that they were both grown-up, single, healthy (okay, somewhat healthy) people, there was no reason to back off. She wasn't staying in Pensacola, and he rarely came home. Wasn't as if they would enter an awkward stage where for years down the road they'd not be able to meet each other's eyes. So why the hell not?

Why the hell not?

That should be her new mantra.

She unwrapped her arms from around her stomach and stiffened her back. Making her breasts stand out. They were nice breasts, the perfect C cup, still perky. Looking up to where Ryan sat, she called, "Come play with me."

And she meant every word.

Morgan didn't hear, and her date, Logan, seemed to be more interested in the buxom brunette than he did her at the moment, which made her feel better about yelling a totally suggestive thing to Ryan. And like the good puppy he was—no, strike that, there was nothing puppylike about Ryan any longer. He was a full-grown man . . . who stood up and shucked his shirt.

Which made her tummy flutter.

Dang, he looked good enough to sop up with a biscuit.

"How's the water?" he said, wading out into the crashing waves.

"Wet," she said.

His lips curved into a smile. She wished he weren't wearing sunglasses. She'd love to see the sparkle in his green eyes. Or maybe they'd smolder. She'd love to see them dilated with passion, half-lidded and focused on her. "You were always a keen observer."

"That's why I always kept the lab log in chemistry." She waded into the emerald water, dodging a few pieces of Sargassum seaweed that floated by. For a while she let the waves push her along, darting glances at Ryan, who bobbed along with the waters nearby. Morgan and Logan were farther out and seemed to be in deep conversation.

Ryan moved closer to her. "So what do you think about Logan?"

"He's nice."

"Just nice, huh?"

"I don't know him well enough to render another opinion. He seems to like dolphins a lot. And numbers. He said he likes being an accountant. Just the thought of staring at tax forms all day breaks me out in hives," she said, digging her toes into the sand so she stayed close to Ryan.

The former geek extraordinaire of Morning Glory High gave her a sexy smile that curled her toes deeper into the sand. "So you're saying he's boring?"

Jess darted a look toward Logan. "Shh. I didn't say that."

"You implied it," he said, moving closer still. He pulled his sunglasses off and let them fall to his chest, dangling by the glasses strap.

She could see the five o'clock shadow that somehow made his eyes even greener. Or maybe that was the water. Either way, those eyes looked like sea glass. "I didn't imply anything other than the fact I don't like doing taxes."

His hand brushed her side. "Who does?"

Her stomach leaped at the contact. She caught his hand underwater. "What are you doing?" She said it in a breathless Marilyn Monroe voice.

"Making sure you don't get knocked over by the waves," he said, lacing his fingers through hers.

Never had hand-holding seemed erotic, but his callused fingers sliding against the sensitive flesh of her palm was somehow unnerving. Yet she didn't pull away. Because Ryan made her feel warm and gooey inside. Like a chocolate chip cookie. Or perhaps a turned-on woman who needed to get laid in the worst possible way. No, the best possible way. With a guy who wasn't merely okay, but made her want to kiss the corner of his mouth . . . to slide her hands across his abs of steel . . . to grip his tight ass as he—

"Hey," Morgan trilled. "Y'all finally made it out here. Isn't the water nice?"

Jess wrenched her hand from Ryan's. Crap, she was on a date. With Logan the accountant. She had no business playing, uh, handsies under the water with Ryan.

Both Logan and Morgan moved their way.

"It's very nice. I like it in late summer. Like taking a bath," Ryan said, pressing his hand against her rib cage in a possessive manner. Or perhaps it was a message. One that said, *We'll get back to this later.*

A sweet ache of desire had awakened inside her. That feeling was something she craved. She needed to be loved again. She needed to feel the world fall away as a man touched her, stroked her, made her shatter against him. Yeah, she was horny, and it wasn't for the accountant. It was for the nerd who'd fashioned himself into an Abercrombie and Fitch model.

"I was telling Morgan that there's a place down the beach that sells the best piña coladas. You two want to walk down and get some with us?" Logan said, moving toward her.

"I'm actually going to towel off and sit in the sun a bit," Jess said, planting her feet under her and moving toward the beach. "I'm fine staying here."

"I can get you one," Logan said, offering her a gentlemanly smile. He truly was a nice guy, but not what she needed in her life. Of course, she wasn't sure if she actually needed Ryan, either. She glanced over at him, at the way droplets clung to his deeply tanned shoulders, the way his piercing gaze moved over the slopes of her breasts.

Yeah, she kinda needed him.

A lot.

"Ryan?" Morgan asked, dodging a wave, her big boobs bouncing as she giddyupped trying to avoid a wipeout. "You coming?"

His lips curled in a secret smile. "Not yet."

Morgan made a confused face.

"I mean, I don't want it right now. Maybe later." He slid a glance toward Jess.

She knew his words were sexy repartee, picking up where they'd left off. Flirting was wonderful, getting down to business even better. Nothing had to be spelled out—Ryan wanted her. She wanted him. Pregame warmups were over. Let the game commence. They'd waited long enough.

Logan looked at Morgan. "You still up for going?"

Morgan looked at Ryan and then looked at Jess. A little furrow gathered between her eyebrows, and then she looked back at Logan. Her gaze lowered, taking in the man's white—albeit flat—belly and long legs. Something flickered in her eyes. Jess liked to think it was acceptance and interest in a new conquest. "Yeah. I want to."

Both Logan and Morgan headed back to the pavilion, Logan grabbing the wallet he'd hidden in her bag. He held up a hand at the edge of the water. "You sure you don't want anything?"

Jess waved him off. "I'm good. Y'all have fun." It was her blessing to her date. *Go with Morgan. Flirt with Morgan. Feel free to make the next date with Morgan.*

Logan waved back, leaving her standing in the surf, waves crashing into the back of her knees.

"Aaaaand that's it. He's off the hook. I'm officially blown off," Jess said, turning back to Ryan, who splashed through the water toward her.

"Well, at least you didn't have to blow him . . . uh, off." Ryan's eyes danced.

"You have a dirty mind," Jess said, appreciating the raunchy comment. He'd been so kind to her that it was fun to see a different side of him.

"My mind has been called a lot of things, but you might be the first to call it dirty," he said, grabbing her elbow as they navigated the waves. The power of the surf churned the sand, turning over lots of tiny shells and some fragments of broken ones. Once they made it to the firm sand, he released her. Disappointment pinged inside her.

But what did she expect? After all, technically she was on a date with another man.

"So," Ryan said, turning back to her. Rivulets of water ran down his torso, drawing her eye to his etched stomach. The water weighed his suit down, making it dip lower than normal, showcasing a goodie trail flattened by the moisture. "What do you want to do?"

She almost said, *You*, but she managed to catch herself. "I don't know. Lie out in the sun? Not too long, of course, but enough to dry my suit."

"You look terrific in that suit," he said, shuffling around a kid trying to skim board across a flatter area where the water washed in.

Warmth that had nothing to do with the August sun curled around her. "I haven't worn a bikini in a while."

They stepped beneath the pavilion. He reached over and pulled out the towel she'd had the presence of mind to toss in at the last minute and handed it to her.

"Thank you," she said, wiping her face and drying her arms. He watched her, which made her skin prickle. There was no mistaking the current of electricity zipping between them. He might have routinely flirted with women, but he didn't look at a woman like she was Nana's banana pudding unless he wanted a serving. "You're staring."

"You're beautiful."

Jess felt the flush creep up her neck. "Ryan."

"What? I'm telling the truth. Benton Mason is a fucking idiot," he said, accepting the towel as she handed it to him.

There were a lot of things she could say at that moment. She could make like her mother and give him a chiding about his use of language in front of a lady. She could disagree with the fact she was beautiful and her ex was an idiot. She could ignore it. Pooh-pooh it. She could laugh and say, *Oh, you silly boy.* But she said none of those things. Instead she lifted her gaze to meet his and said, "Thank you."

The smile that tipped the corners of his mouth and lit his eyes told her everything she needed to know. Mutual attraction, mutual agreement. They wanted each other, and it would happen.

Jess lifted a hand and brushed errant sand off his shoulder. His skin was hot beneath the sun, mirroring the desire building inside her. "You want to come over tonight?"

"Like for dinner?"

Jess gave a light laugh. "If that's what you want to call it."

Chapter Nine

Rain settled in over Pensacola, turning the evening gray and making the bay unsettled. Droplets ran down the sliding glass door and plinked onto the tin roof that covered the beach condos. Ryan stood on the porch of Jess's rental carrying a bottle of expensive wine and a pie he'd bought at Publix. He had no idea if the pie was good, but by what Jess had implied, he wasn't there for the food.

Or at least he hoped that's what she'd meant.

Clearing his throat, he rang the doorbell. The door opened with a swoosh, and there stood Jess wearing an apron.

Okay, maybe he was there for the food.

"Hey," he said, holding up the pie. "I brought dessert."

"Oh good. That might be the only edible thing we have tonight. Oh, and wine." She grabbed the bottle from him. "That will work, too."

He followed her into the condo, turning to lock the door. The sound of the dead bolt sliding home made him want to turn and twirl the mustache he didn't have. "Then I brought the right thing."

"You brought yourself, and that's what I wanted. So, yes." She set the pie on the counter and then studied a long casserole dish. "Our dinner, however, is another story."

He peered at the dish. "There seems to be a lot of cheese." What he really wanted to ask was, *What did you mean by my being what you wanted?* But he stuck with commenting on cheese. It seemed easier.

Jess made a face. "I thought the cheese would help. Putting lots of it on stuff covers up disaster."

"What exactly is this disaster?"

"An enchilada casserole," Jess said, turned to him. "I suck at cooking. I'm great at calling for pizza or making something easy like nachos, but real cooking escapes me. I followed the recipe, but I put in a whole can of soup mix instead of four ounces. Why don't they say it's only half of a can instead of sliding those ounces into the recipe like we're supposed to realize there is twice the amount called for in the can? I think the soup people trick us on purpose."

Ryan laughed.

"Don't laugh."

"It's cute. You tried to make me dinner," he said, wanting to make her feel better. So he stepped behind her, wrapped his arms about her waist, and kissed her neck. Which smelled amazing.

But the snuggle caused Jess to go rigid.

"Jess?" he asked, lifting his head but not unwinding his arms.

"Mmm?"

"You okay?"

She patted his hand. "Yeah. I'm good."

"Is this too much too soon?"

Jess shook her head. "No. Maybe." She spun around, sliding her hands down his forearms to capture his hands. "I'm going to be totally honest, okay?"

A niggle of dread wobbled in his stomach. Did he want her to be honest? To admit she wasn't sure about him? That she was still hung up on dumb-ass Benton? Or maybe it was who he'd been before? He shut down those negative thoughts. She'd said she wanted him when he walked in the door. "I've always thought honesty a good policy. In fact, I think that's a saying."

Jess smiled. Then she released his hands and stepped away, staring out the kitchen window to the condo next door, which was, ironically, Morgan's place. Taking a deep sigh, she said, "The thing is, I've never been with another man."

The niggle dissolved as he processed her statement. She hadn't said she didn't want him. She'd said . . . "Oh."

Her pretty amber eyes lifted to his. Inside he could see why people often said the eyes were the windows to the soul. "I'm nervous and . . . I don't know. This all feels weird and exciting and scary. I don't want it to, but sex is sort of a big deal for me. I know that makes me so not a modern woman. I mean, Rosemary went to New York City and had sex with a virtual stranger. She did freaky things in a Central Park carriage and played a kinky strip game in the stairwell of her cousin's walkup. She got a tattoo on her ass."

"You're not Rosemary. You're you."

"I know, but I know you. I trust you. I want you. So this should be easy."

Ryan went to her, folding her into his arms, trying to show her he understood. After a few seconds, she relaxed against him. Then, with a sigh, she laid her head on his shoulder. He concentrated on how good she felt in his arms, not the thought he wasn't getting laid tonight. Hey, he was a guy. But he was a guy who cared about the woman he held. "I get this feels like a big step for you, but I'm not pushing you into anything. I want you to be comfortable with everything we do. So no expectations, okay? Not even from your casserole."

"Well, that's a relief. Uh, for the casserole."

"Hey, I'm happy to be with you, Jess. It's that simple."

"But I want to have sex. I mean, I need to go there. I have to get past, well, my past."

"Having sex is not like taking medicine, Jess. It should happen because you want it, not because you think it's a magic bullet that's going to fix things for you."

She gave a small laugh. "But you'd be good for me."

He pulled back and tilted her chin up. "We're good the way we are. Stop throwing up obstacles that aren't in front of us. We're two people who like each other who are having dinner together."

Jess nodded, and he studied her lips. He wanted to kiss her, but after the words they'd shared, he forced himself to step away. "How about some music?"

"That would be excellent."

"This rainy weather always makes me crave old standards. You have a dock?" He waggled his phone.

Jess pointed to the dock on the kitchen clock, and he set Spotify to his rainy-day playlist. Soon Etta James crooned "A Sunday Kind of Love." He unscrewed the bottle of sauvignon blanc he'd been saving and found the glasses while Jess cut up romaine for the salad. Then he sat down to chill and watch Jess make dinner. There was something so pleasing in the plink of the rain, the thunk of the knife against the cutting board, and the golden wine swirling around the goblet. A strange warmth settled over him, and he had the oddest belief that he was right where he was supposed to be.

Though he often experienced profound moments like this when he motored out into the Gulf, fully immersed in God's creation—or whatever one believed about creation—connected to who he was, connected to his new self, he'd never felt the way he felt right now. Leaning against the counter watching Jess in her calico-patched apron, slicing tomatoes and shredding cheese, made him feel . . . content. Had he ever truly felt content in this manner? He didn't think so.

"We may have to make the most of this salad," Jess said, picking up her glass and taking a sip. "Mmm, good."

"No, no. I think the cheese will do the job," he said, eyeing her casserole.

The track changed to Billy Paul's "Me and Mrs. Jones," and Ryan smiled. He loved this song and had always imagined the very pleasurable activities he could engage in while it played. With the rain sliding down the window, the wine warming his belly, and Jess's recent admission hovering above them, he'd have to settle for a dance. Setting his wine down, he tapped Jess on the shoulder. "Shall we?"

She set the knife down as an adorable crinkle appeared between her eyes. "Shall we what?"

He crooked an eyebrow and swept her into his arms, moving against her body.

"Oh," she sighed. "I haven't danced since May Claire's wedding almost a year ago."

"Then you're due," he said, moving them into the darkened living room. He took her hand and wrapped his other hand firmly about her waist and started moving.

"You're a good dancer," she said, resting her head once again on his shoulder. Her hair tickled his nose, and the scent of fresh apples filled his nose. Perfect.

"I took lessons."

"Really?" she murmured.

"When I decided to give up being a geek, I set about becoming Mr. *GQ*. I signed up for ballroom dancing and took a course on making cocktails. For the bedroom stuff, I read a dozen books. I mastered tantric sex. Or at least I think I did. As for learning about the habits of the red-blooded American male, like an anthropologist, I ventured into the field, otherwise known as Buffalo Wild Wings."

"Oh? What did you learn?"

"That the average male often lies in order to appear dominant, slaps fellow males on the back as a universal greeting, and wears too much cologne. They also have an extraordinary interest in girls with big breasts."

"Astute observation."

"Would you expect anything less?" he asked, taking that exact moment to turn them with a little dip. "When I set my mind to something, I don't half-ass it, Jess."

"Mmm," she said, and he could almost hear the smile in her voice. For the next few minutes they were content to sway against each other, the music cloaking them in intimacy. He sang the lyrics low in her ear, stroking her lower back, enjoying the feel of her breasts against his chest, the slide of her thighs.

The song ended, and they stood for a moment, still pressed together, totally still. He could feel her heart beat, hear her steady breath, and he savored the moment of having Jess in his arms.

"So do we have a thing going on?" she whispered.

"Oh, Mrs. Jones, we so have a thing going on," he said against the softness of her hair. He dropped her hand and wrapped both arms around her, holding her close as a new song came on.

"What's tantric sex?" she asked.

He should have known she wouldn't let that subject pass. "Maybe you'll get to find out."

"But not tonight," she sighed, her voice portraying a combination or regret and relief . . . if that were possible.

"I'll be content if I can get to first base," he joked, dropping a kiss against her temple.

"I thought you didn't like baseball."

"I don't. But the sexual euphemisms the sport provides are hard to resist. You know, sliding home, switch hitter—"

"Are you a switch hitter?" She pulled her head from his shoulder and stared at him with laughing eyes.

"No, I'm merely relaying the common euphemisms associated with the sport."

"God, you make me feel so good. How do you do that?"

Ryan shrugged. "I'd like to say it's because I've studied women, dating patterns, and the probability of getting laid. Or tell you I have all the right words and rehearsed moves, but that would be a lie. Truth is, Jessica Culpepper, you suckered me in a long time ago, and I'll do about anything to make you happy."

Her eyes glistened with sudden tears. "Holy shit," she whispered, lifting her hand to his cheek. "You really *are* good at this stuff."

Ryan traced the curve of her cheek with one finger. "So how about giving up first base?"

Using her finger, she swiped along her lower lashes, dashing away the moisture. "You can totally hit a single tonight. Maybe a double. I'd really like to see you score, but—"

"Shh," he said, lowering his head. Very gently, he slid a hand past the nape of her neck, through her hair, cupping her head and moving it so her mouth was in the perfect position. Jess had a wide mouth, and her lips were a yielding pink that beckoned like a siren. He'd been waiting a long time to taste her, so he wasn't about to rush the first time.

Counting off one, then two seconds, he lowered his head. Carefully, he brushed his lips against hers, but he didn't settle in. Instead he reversed directions and brushed against her mouth again, teasing her, drawing the pleasure out. He felt her breathing ratchet—a satisfactory signal his seduction worked. So he pressed his lips to her cheek, lowering his right hand, sliding past her waist to the firm globe of her ass. Slowly he brought her to him, fitting her pelvis against his, hoping she could feel the hardness stirring against her softness.

She sighed.

He began the journey to her mouth, moving millimeter by millimeter toward the prize.

When he reached her mouth, he twined her hair in his fingers and pulled her head back. Her mouth parted just as he intended. This time he didn't waste time. He swooped in and took possession.

Her body surged toward him, and her hands, which had lain inert, curled into his back. "Oh," she breathed.

"Mmm-hmm," he murmured, deepening the kiss.

She tasted like the carrots she'd been nibbling and some intoxicating elixir he had no name for. He broke the kiss and arched an eyebrow. "Did you sneak a carrot?"

Jess laughed. "Seriously?"

"Never mind," he said, hauling her against him again, resuming the kiss he'd dreamed of for years upon years. Her tongue met his as she opened herself to him like a flower greedy for rain. She pushed back, kissing him as hunger exploded. What was once tender and teasing turned urgent. He couldn't stop. She couldn't seem to stop.

Time stood still as they opened, accepted, embraced, and latched on to what existed between them. And it was perfect.

He couldn't have imagined anything better than kissing Jess.

After what felt like forever, they stepped away from each other.

"Wow," Jess said.

Ryan smiled and dropped another kiss on her forehead. "You see how easy that was? How right that was? All this might be easier than you think, babe."

He'd called her *babe.*

Benton had called her that, and she'd loved the intimacy, the implied stamp of *you're mine.* But she loved the way Ryan said it, too. Those words skipped along her spine, curled up in her belly, and burrowed deep.

And that kiss?

At the first touch of his lips, hot, furious desire had broken through and danced inside her. Right after Benton had left, she'd tried to imagine her future life. When she'd thought about kissing another man, letting him touch her the way her husband had, even make love to her, she'd always felt sick. How could she be with another man? She couldn't. Not when she'd given herself heart, body, and soul to the boy who'd copied her notes in Mrs. Farley's civics class. But months ago, lying alone beneath the sheets she'd borrowed from her mother in order to fit her new double bed, Jess couldn't have imagined Ryan Reyes. She couldn't have foreseen him holding her as they danced in the middle of a beach rental with rain sliding down the windows as someone crooned a sexy song she'd never heard before. She couldn't have imagined the sweet stirring of desire, the rightness of another man singing low and off-key in her ear. The old Jess couldn't ever imagine how good it could be.

How much easier it had been to let herself go with another man.

"Should we eat?" Ryan asked, brushing her hair behind her ear. Such a tender move. Everything about him was sexy and tender. Exactly what she needed.

"We could," she said, but she didn't move.

"Jess?" he asked softly.

"I don't want this moment to end," she said, curling her fingers into the back of his shirt.

His answer was to gather her against him, holding her, hands sliding along her back. His touch was both comforting and intoxicating. She could feel the hardness of his body, the scent that was Ryan's alone—a distinct, pleasant cologne mixed with a soapy clean and a salty sea breeze. His heart beat strong in his chest, and the skin at his throat where she burrowed her nose was so warm and alive.

They stayed still, holding each other for almost a full minute.

Finally, Jess released him and stepped back. "Thank you."

"You're welcome," he said.

"Guess we should try to at least taste that horrible casserole," she said, moving back toward the kitchen. She slid the casserole back into the oven to allow the cheese to melt and finished assembling the salad. Ryan poured more wine and slathered butter on a loaf of fresh-baked bread. After Logan had dropped her off without an offer of a follow-up date, she'd climbed into her car and gone to the store for dinner fixings even though she'd implied something altogether different to Ryan. She was glad she'd made the effort for him.

Poor Logan. She hadn't been the best date. Mostly because she'd been lusting after his friend. Of course, she hadn't been obvious about checking Ryan out, but perhaps the undercurrents had been there. Either way, the man had gotten the message she wasn't interested. Which made her feel like a heel. And then there was Morgan. Jess knew her next-door neighbor had picked up on attraction she and Ryan shared, because the woman kept narrowing her eyes and giving Jess *that* look—the one she'd already given a few times, the one that precluded the warning she'd given the day before.

He's not for you.

Jess gave a sidelong glance toward Ryan, who looked totally focused on covering every square inch of the split loaf with butter. Man on a mission. He was boyish, charming, hot, and as an added bonus, kind. Maybe he wasn't the right man for Jess, but did she want the right man? She was coming off a broken heart. Everyone knew the rebound relationship was temporary. Like a shooting star, it burned hot and bright before fading into nothingness. So how was he not for her? Exactly. He seemed perfect for her. They had two and a half months of temporary insanity before she went back to Morning Glory or another job, and he stayed here and played at being frat boy. They had a mutual past, a gratifying friendship, and the sexual chemistry was better than the actual chemistry they'd tried to make in high school years ago. Ryan would bring her back from the dead, and she'd be better off when she left Pensacola than when she'd arrived. She'd be almost whole again. That had to mean he was totally made for her . . . for a while, anyway.

"You want me to put this bread in with the casserole?" he asked, presenting her a tray of perfectly buttered bread.

"Sure. I almost have the salad ready."

Ryan slid the bread in and then leaned against the counter and watched her. He had slipped his shoes off when he came in earlier, and she noted he had nice feet—tanned, trimmed toenails, strong with crinkly hair atop. His shorts were khaki cutoffs, which made her wonder if the man had taken scissors to every pair of Dockers he'd owned. He was perfect for her. He was perfect for every woman. Morgan was a dumb ass.

She'd set the table, and they ate there, the sexy rainy-day music soft in the background. The wine was good, the salad average, and the buttered bread perfectly crusty and buttery. The casserole was . . . cheesy.

"I like this casserole," Ryan said, lifting his fork with the last bite.

"Liar."

"I ate the whole serving, didn't I?" he said.

"Because you're a nice guy."

"No, I'm not. I have you fooled."

"You probably could have bent me over the counter when you walked in, screwed me sideways, and walked back out the door. But you didn't. And you ate that subpar casserole. Face it. You're a nice guy."

He lifted his eyebrows. "Um, what kind of dates have you *been* on?"

She laughed. "Only one. With Logan earlier today."

He sobered. "You haven't gone on even one date since you and Benton split?"

"Well, the divorce was only final last month. Up until then, I concentrated on how to breathe."

Ryan set his fork down. "Was it that bad?"

How could she explain the loss? Were there words? "It wasn't good."

"That's not what I asked." His expression narrowed, focused on her. Gone was the boyish charm, the soft patience. In its place, a discerning clinician.

"You remember how crazy I was over him. The man had a lot of flaws—I knew that—but he was this guy I belonged to from the moment I saw him shooting hoops in the junior high gym."

Ryan folded his hands. He didn't respond but instead watched her.

Jess felt naked, and not in a good way. "I don't know why he stopped loving me. Maybe I got lazy; maybe I focused on all the wrong things in our life. I wanted a family, and I got a little fixated on babies and nurseries. Okay, my Pinterest board looked like Baby World upchucked on it. Maybe it wasn't even wanting a child. I'm a creature of habit, and perhaps my routines became so dull Benton stopped caring about me. Or maybe it was all him. I don't know. But the thing was, I never saw anything that would make me believe he'd changed. Not really. So when he came home and told me he was seeing someone else and didn't want what we had anymore, it was as if a wrecking ball smashed through the wall, taking out everything I thought I had. So, yeah, it was devastating."

Jess paused, not wanting to seem so pathetic, because she could see the sympathy in his eyes. She hated that look. "But my issues—or my inability to move forward with you or anyone else—really aren't about losing Benton. I lost myself during the marriage."

"How can you lose yourself?"

"Well, you forget you were once a person who had her own dreams, who existed before. You bury the person you are under expectations, plans, standards—all these things you think you're supposed to be— until one day they're gone. Then you lie on the floor, broken, realizing you'd built a castle out of air. Nothing was real."

"Do you still love him?"

Dreaded question. "A part of me always will love Benton, because he was part of my life. Part of my story." She paused for a moment. "I liked the life I had. It seemed easy, exactly what I had always wanted. Losing that was just as hard as losing him. But I'm no longer in love with Benton. Any leftover feelings I had for him died when I signed my name on the divorce papers. Those pages were cold, hard proof that what we once had was no more. I looked at him over the table, tapping on his phone as if being there was a bother, and my love shriveled up. I still hurt and felt the betrayal, but the active love . . . it turned to ash and blew away."

"I feel that way about my old life. I mean, it's not that strong of a comparison, but it's as if I cut off part of who I was. Sometimes I forget I got rid of that Ryan. It's like the phantom pain people say happens when they lose a limb. I forget and think that part of me is still there and then I remember and—"

"Regret?" she murmured.

A shutter closed on his face. "No. I don't regret my decision to leave who I was behind. That's not what I meant. That man who lived and breathed test results and bacteria cultures and getting papers published wasn't living. He had no friends, no adventures, no hope for love. That man had to go."

Was losing her marriage like losing her arm or leg? She didn't think so. One day she'd be fully functional again. Maybe it was more like experiencing a horrible catastrophe . . . or a drought. At the moment she was replanting her life, giving it water, sunlight, and nutrients. Spring was around the corner, and she'd be whole again soon. Ryan could give her that.

Her gaze landed on the wilted begonia Ryan had brought her over a week ago. Already with some liquid fertilizer and some culling, it had begun to grow again. "Maybe so, but the main thing I want you to know is I'm not hung up on my ex-husband. This reticence to jump into intimacy comes more from the quest to find myself again beneath the rubble. Not Benton."

"I can help with that. Say we leave these dishes here—which is very hard for someone like me with OCD issues to do—and try for a double over there on the couch?"

His charm was back. "Is water wet? Does a fish swim?"

"You realize there are species of fish that are ambulatory? Take the snakehead, an indigenous fish from Asia that can live out of water for three days. They've been found here in Florida."

"Guess that phantom limb comes back at the oddest times, huh?" she said, dropping her napkin next to her plate.

"I make my living by finding fish, so I have to study . . ." He clamped his mouth closed and pushed back his chair. "Come over here, and I'll show you just how nerdy I am."

"You promise?" she asked, smiling, glad to tuck the serious conversation away in favor of a little fertilization . . . for her garden. Her silly analogy made her laugh.

Then Ryan's arms were around her . . . and then the couch was beneath her . . . and then they worked really hard on perfecting that double.

And after a few minutes, Jess wondered why the man hadn't played baseball before. He seemed to have a knack for getting around the bases.

Chapter Ten

Ryan's vibrating phone woke him. He reached for the offending device, noting his neck was stiff, among other things. He pried open his eyes and wondered where in the hell he was. The light cast on the room poured in like thin milk, and something anchored him to a . . . couch?

Jess.

The memory of last night hurtled into him. Jess. Casserole. Binge watching *The Office*. They'd fallen asleep . . . and he'd never gotten close to third base. He carefully inched his arm from beneath Jess's head and paused for a moment to watch her sleeping in the faint early light. Her hair rioted around her relaxed face. Her mouth was open, hand tucked beneath her chin, and her ass cradled his morning erection nicely. Ryan didn't want to move, but his positioning was awkward, and if he allowed his little friend to stay nestled against Jess's ass, it could lead to a grand slam without the other team even being awake.

Yeah, he was totally geeked up for this girl.

Ever so carefully, he eased from between Jess and the couch, wincing as his knee cracked as he spider climbed over her. She never moved. Then he slid his vibrating phone from his pocket.

Late.

He had to get moving if he wanted to pick up a charter for the day. Mondays were typically slow, but since he'd avoided the marina yesterday, he needed to hustle some business.

Jess vaulted into sitting position with a gasp.

"Oh shit," she breathed, scrambling off the couch. Then she looked at him, eyes wide. He realized he'd surprised her by being there. "Ryan."

"We fell asleep."

She rubbed her face with both hands and started chanting, "Shit, shit, shit."

"Go shower. I'll make coffee," he said, not knowing if she even drank coffee but wanting to do something to help her. He had overslept, but his was not a shift job.

"No time. I have to go."

"You mean I have to go," he said, trying not to smile at how cute she looked when panicked. He figured she didn't appreciate his amusement, since she bolted for the darkened hallway. "I'll let myself out."

"Sorry," she called back, the light in the bathroom coming on followed by the shower starting up. "I'm beyond late. I should have been at the hospital thirty minutes ago."

"Call you later?"

The only answer was the sound of the bathroom door slamming shut.

"Or not," he said to the still-dark room. Stretching, he picked up the throw they'd snuggled under while watching TV and folded it. Switching on a lamp, he made his way to the kitchen, where he looked for coffee. Seeing none, he poured a glass of water, consoling himself with the thought of the french roast he'd have when he got back to his place. As he gulped the water, he realized he'd never spent the night with a woman before. Slept with someone? Sure. Slept over at her house? No. And the irony of it was he and Jess hadn't done anything more than have an old-fashioned make-out session on the couch. He hated irony most of the time. Sneaky bastard.

He heard the bathroom door bang open and the sound of feet scurrying down the hall. "I'm leaving, Jess."

"'Bye," she called. Another door shut.

With nothing left to do, Ryan scratched a *have a nice day* note on the pad by the cordless phone and let himself outside.

The beach highway was silent, and seagulls sailed overhead, swooping to capture breakfast. The sound of the waves on the beach made him itch to cross over and walk along the ocean, but since he, too, needed to make hay, he stuck to the concrete path that linked the units and skirted the tennis court. As he passed by the entrance to the pool, he saw someone approach the gate.

Morgan towel dried her hair, obviously having just finished her daily laps. "Walk of shame, huh?"

He stopped, dread pooling in his gut as she moved closer to him. The pain in her eyes plucked strings of guilt. Crap, he didn't want to hurt Morgan; after all, she'd been such a good friend to him. Here in Pensacola, friends were family. Morgan was his little sis . . . even if she wanted to be more to him. "Not a walk of shame. I fell asleep on Jess's couch last night."

"Right," she said wrapping the towel about her waist. This morning she wore a one-piece, similar to Olympic swimmers. The simple Lycra flattered her figure and made her look younger. "I could see the writing on the wall with that."

"What do you mean?" He played dumb. He wanted coffee, not confrontation.

"Oh, don't play stupid. You can't keep your eyes off the nurse. Dude, it's almost embarrassing." Morgan sounded disgusted. She relatched the gate and started down the path, heading back in the direction from which he'd come.

"Hey," he said, touching her arm as she passed. "I thought we'd talked about this."

Her brown eyes snapped. "You think highly of yourself, don't you? Like I'm so into you. Don't worry. I'm cool. Logan asked me out, and to be honest, I think he and I suit way better."

"Morgan."

"What? I told you . . . I'm cool. We're friends. You said that's what you wanted, and obviously I'm not your taste. And that's cool, too. I get it. She's temporary, and you have commitment issues."

"I don't have commitment issues." Or maybe he did.

Morgan arched an eyebrow. "Dude."

"I don't." But he didn't sound convincing. How could he tell her he'd made a plan well over a year ago that consisted of spending a set amount of time screwing around, playing at being . . . well, a player? When he'd decided to move here, engaging in casual sex seemed a no-brainer. He'd do all the things he'd never done. He'd make up for lost time. But for some reason, standing there as the world awoke to a new day, facing his friend and neighbor, the rationale sounded overly hedonistic. Infantile. Ridiculous. "Maybe I do. I don't know."

Morgan laughed, patting his arm in a sisterly fashion. "At least you're honest. I can respect that. I'll see you later."

"Yeah. Later," he said, moving in the opposite direction, preoccupied with the lightbulb moment he'd had. One question loomed large—had he been wrong to think casual sex made sense?

When he'd left the old drunk and the dog in front of his Pasadena apartment building, he'd grappled with a plan for how to find the life he should be living. The initial impulse was to jump in and get dirty fast, but because he didn't know much about the world outside academia, he'd first needed to ascertain exactly what normal people considered a good life. To do that, he consumed a steady diet of pop culture. Setting aside biochemistry journals, he bought copies of *Us*, *GQ*, and *Cosmopolitan* (and understood exactly why his lab partner had seemed so disappointed in the two minutes of sex in which they'd engaged). He forced himself to switch the seldom-watched television from National Geographic to channels that showed programs called *Teen Wolf* and *Gossip Girl*. Instead of spending late nights in the lab or playing chess with the chess heads, he went to bars. After a month, he created a spreadsheet with all the data he'd collected. By his calculations he'd missed 8.45 years of frolic, of which included drunkenness, flirting, promiscuity, and illegal pranks. Taking into consideration his advanced age, he'd projected engaging in two years of intensive frat boy lifestyle in order to catch up. Only after would he consider reevaluating his career choice and location.

But he hadn't taken his heart into consideration.

Not that he was falling in love with Jess. That would be illogical. Though he had history with her, he didn't know her well. Not really. So that wasn't the issue.

But the heart thing. That was an outlier he hadn't planned for. An unexpected variable that could destroy his experiment. Wait. Not experiment. His life.

Still, wasn't that what he'd wanted? On that walk he'd seen the messy, wonderful, hurtful, precarious aspects of living. He'd set forth a plan, but he'd not allowed for what it truly meant to plunge his hands into life. In other words, could a person plan what happened to his or her heart?

"Whoa," he said aloud, scaring a woman wearing hot-pink shorts, a fanny pack, and hair so stiff and mushroomlike she was likely solely responsible for the hole in the ozone. "Sorry."

"That's okay, young man," she said, heading for the sidewalk alongside the highway. Off to exercise.

And he needed to get some coffee. That could be the problem. Perhaps his plan for creating a better life for himself would be clearer once he was caffeinated. If not, he could hypothesize about modifications. Success in the scientific field came not from sheer determination but from a willingness to adjust, redirect, and pursue strange niggles. Gut feelings and specious inclinations often led to the greatest discoveries. So examining his plan was needed.

But first, the coffee.

❀

Jess should have known the day would be crap. Waking up late, running onto the floor with her hair looking like something out of a punk rock video, and seeing she had to work with a particularly difficult surgeon was only the beginning. She'd been unable to find an instrument needed for the cardiac procedure, had received a dressing-down from the charge nurse, and the ATM across the street didn't work, so she had no cash for lunch. Luckily Becky let her borrow ten dollars so she could buy a dry tuna sandwich and a Diet Coke. The Diet Coke had been the best part of her day.

Other than waking up in Ryan's arms.

Okay, so he'd already been up and staring at her, which was slightly weird, but she recalled the warmth, the scratch of his beard, and the way his body cradled hers. It was all so familiar yet newly exciting. And that the man hadn't pressed her to have sex last night when she probably would have made it all the more right for her.

She took her tuna sandwich out to the small garden courtyard and pulled out her cell phone. After scrolling through Facebook and Instagram and liking all the pictures of the dogs and babies, she dialed Eden, hoping she'd be on lunch break, too.

"Hey," Eden squealed, before saying, "hold on a minute."

In the background she could hear her friend tell someone she was taking a break and would be back on the floor in ten.

"Well, finally, stranger," Eden said. A door closed in the background, and Jess imagined her friend standing out behind Penny Pinchers where the loading guys smoked.

"I know. I haven't called like I should. But I did just like your picture of the pug grilling hot dogs on Instagram."

"He's so cute, isn't he? I so want a dog, but I can't afford the vet bills. And if I want to get out of Morning Glory and find a life, I can't have the complications of a dog in my life. So I pretend and post pics. So how are things in paradise? I saw the pics of the beach . . . because I got a new phone. It's a smartphone, so I can see pictures now. Looks like heaven, Jess."

Jess smiled at her friend's ramblings. "Welcome to 2016. Oh, the beach is a blessing. Pensacola is different, but good."

"And Rosemary said you were going on a boat to watch dolphins? Was that an official date?" Eden's voice held laughter.

"I guess. My first official post-divorce date," Jess said, frowning at the sandwich. She pulled a crust off and tossed it to a beady-eyed blackbird strutting nearby. The creature wasted no time swooping it up and making off with his bounty.

"Sooooo?"

"Eh, I'm not interested in him. He's nice, but there was no spark."

"Well, heck, Jess, you don't have to have spark to get a free meal."

"Eden," Jess chided.

"I'm kidding. Yeah, you don't need to mess around with a flatlined guy."

"While we're on that subject, there is someone." Jess hadn't been sure she would share the info about Ryan, but she'd been sharing all her thoughts on boys with both Eden and Rosemary for so long, why quit now?

"Really?" Eden sounded excited. It was almost like being back in junior high. The thought made Jess smile.

"And you'll never guess who."

Eden sighed. "How could I? I don't know anyone in Pensacola."

"Oh, you'd know him," Jess said smiling in anticipation. "Ryan Reyes?"

"Ryan Reyes, Ryan Reyes," Eden repeated before growing silent for a few seconds. "Is he related to the Reyeses who live here? The weird ones?"

"Their son."

"Wait . . . the Brain?" Eden's voice went down an octave. "What's he doing in Pensacola? I thought he was curing cancer in California. Didn't he win some award or something?"

"He's not in California anymore. He owns a boat. He fishes."

"Whaaaaat?" Eden's voice rose. "And, wait, you're interested in *him*? What have you been smoking, sister?"

Jess laughed. "You realize he was a kid when you last saw him, right?"

"Yeah, but he was so skinny and goofy. He was a stalker before we knew what stalkers were, Jess."

"Yeah, he had a crush on me and no social skills. He followed me around—"

"Like a puppy. Rosemary called him your puppy. He brought you presents, too. Remember that pink pencil with the fuzzy hair? He's totally a serial killer, Jess."

"No, he's not. He's normal now. Remember when you were four-teen? I had an altar to *NSYNC. We all grow up, and I must tell you, friend, Mr. Ryan Reyes grew up good."

"But . . . seriously?" Eden wasn't buying what Jess was selling.

"Let me prove it to you. I'm sending you a picture I took on the beach yesterday. Hold on a sec."

"Hurry. I have to teach yet another new employee how to manually enter a transaction. I hate to say we keep employing morons, but Douche Bag hires ones with big boobs and not much experience."

Jess found the picture of Ryan on the beach. She'd been snapping a few when they were waiting for Morgan and Logan. The background of waning sun and silken sands paled behind the roguishly handsome super nerd. His chiseled body, hard jawline, and sexy smile would give any woman the shivers. She pressed SEND. "Okay, you should get it in a sec. But you're going to die when you see what he looks like."

"OMG! That's not him. You're joking," Eden said, laughing as she said it. "The Brain turned into a total hottie. This can't be right. Holy shit."

"Eden."

"Oh, sorry, but he's cussworthy. And droolworthy. And . . . I'm running out of words."

"I know, right?" Jess said, smiling at the crow strutting back toward her. Greedy bird. She tore him off another crust and tossed it. He caught it in his beak and took flight. "But the best thing is he's so nice."

"He was always nice. Creepy, but nice. Have you sent this to Rosemary?"

"Not yet. I'm still on the fence about him."

"Why? If Mr. Brain–slash–eye candy can deliver the sexual healing, I would be all over that."

"You would not. You're a prude," Jess joked.

"I *am* not. I'm discerning. You've seen what Morning Glory has to offer. The best-looking man we've had move back in the last three years is gay. And if you're counting Sal, engaged. I'm not giving up the goods to any Tom, Dick, or Bubba around here. I'm still trying to live down my mama's reputation. But you, you need to take advantage of what the world has to offer in the way of good-looking guys. 'Cause

if you wait until you get back here, you'll have to go to one of the intimate parties Carla Minnis is talking about giving to buy a p substitute. Look at me—I'm practically a withered spinster. That's man's cup of tea."

Jess laughed. "What about Henry?"

"You and I both know that man's not interested in me."

"He mows your yard," Jess said, thinking about the handsome tractor who could often be found at the run-down Voorhees ho patching up the roof and shoring up the rickety wheelchair ramp.

"Not in the way it needs to be mowed. Besides, everyone kr he does things like that because he feels guilty about Sunny. That's for me."

Which made sense. Eden's older sister and Henry Todd Delm the Mississippi Delmars had once been the golden couple of Mo Glory . . . if there was such a thing. But bad choices and misplaced had conspired against them. The upside was Henry's guilt saved a lot of money. "I'm not staying in Pensacola, E. This is all temp so I'm not sure I should bust my divorcée cherry with Ryan. He's random dude. We share a hometown."

"So? Ryan never comes home."

"Maybe I'm using that excuse because I'm afraid I'll feel som more than just desire for him. He's really easy to be around. I don' to fall for him."

"Oh." So much to be read in Eden's simple response.

"I know they say women latch on to a rebound romance and they're in love again. I've read the relationship stuff. The rebour do the things your last boyfriend or husband wouldn't—he'll ro you, make you feel sexy and lovable and pretty again. And the v will read more into the relationship because she's vulnerable and being valued. But knowing what the articles say and living the are two different things."

"Dear Lord, who are you?" Eden asked.

"I know." Jess shook her head. "I'm being indecisive, and I'm never indecisive. It's embarrassing."

"No. It's okay to be confused, Jess. But I'm going to give you some advice I wouldn't take myself. Don't think so much. You're only there for a few months, and he's a hot guy who's interested in you. We're not talking marriage here, or even a relationship. Let it be about feeling good. You need that."

"I do," Jess said, staring at the half-eaten sandwich. "It's not about love. It's about sex and friendship. No strings."

"Exactly. Your whole life has been about wrapping yourself up in strings. Now you don't have any. Don't start pulling the yarn from the discount bin. Be happy to be unfettered. You can think about strings later."

"I'm so glad I talked to you. I feel better. And maybe I am ready to jump over into Ryan's yard for some grown-up playtime."

"Yeah, you should," Eden said with a laugh. "Just don't go falling in love with him."

"That's what I told Rosemary a few months ago, and look what happened to her."

Eden giggled. "Yep, she's marrying her fun."

"Yeah."

"Speaking of which, she's going to be calling you later today."

"What about?" Jess said, crumpling the sandwich into the napkin she'd spread on her lap minutes ago. Her mother would be proud she still remembered her manners like the good southern girl she'd been raised to be.

"It's hers to tell. Not mine," Eden said. In the background Jess heard the metal door open. They both needed to get back to work.

"She's not pregnant, is she?" Jess asked, half-thrilled at the idea, half-jealous . . . well, at least until she remembered she was no longer

married with a nursery freshly painted in the shade of Jack and the Beanstalk ready to go.

"No. I mean, I don't think so," Eden said as the phone went static. "Oops, sorry. I have to go. Call me later. And don't fall in love with him. Unless you want to. But whatever you do, stop thinking so much."

"'Bye, E." Jess clicked the button to end the call and finished off her Diet Coke. Fat chance of falling in love. Of course, she'd never truly dated anyone. She and Benton had grown up together, falling into a pattern of being a couple when they were in ninth grade. Benton had never asked her to a dance—he'd assumed she was going with him. They'd decided together what movies to see in Jackson, where to eat, and what steps they'd take toward S-E-X, which by the way happened their senior year after the Morning Glory Mavericks, led by quarterback Benton Mason, beat their longtime rivals in a playoff game. Jess and Benton had gone to college together, attended frat parties and football games together, and gotten married one month after they'd graduated from college. Nothing about their relationship had been typical. So when it came to dating, smart-mouthed, steely-confident Jess was a mass of indecisive nerve endings.

But she had to suck it up and stop trying to control every aspect. She normally wasn't a worrier—she left that to Rosemary—so she had to stop second-guessing everything.

"Hey, there you are," Becky said from the wheelchair ramp. "I heard about your morning."

Jess headed toward her new friend. "Yeah, not much fun getting called out in front of everyone. Not to mention I overslept. Fell asleep on the couch and slept there all night." She didn't add it had been with Ryan.

"That sucks. They have cupcakes for Nancy's birthday. Chocolate icing is the cure for almost anything."

"True enough," Jess said, holding the door open for Becky.

"I didn't eat any because I have a date on Saturday night and a gorgeous dress to get into," Becky said with a tone that begged to be questioned.

"Who?"

"Marcus. You know, the guy who went on the boat with us Saturday? Oh, I forgot. You went out with Logan yesterday. How did that go?"

"Fine. But I think he was more interested in Morgan than me."

Becky made a face. "You're better off. An accountant? *Please.* Besides, Morgan's assets"—Becky juggled pretend boobs in front of her own chest—"were on display. It's a wonder she can walk with those things. Wonder how much they cost?"

Jess laughed. "Maybe that's what I need—a chest expansion. Seems to work. But I do like Morgan. She's fun." And in love with Ryan. Another complication.

Stop thinking.

"You and me both, but something must have worked, because a florist just delivered flowers."

"For me?" Jess hadn't had anyone send her flowers since . . . well, her husband had brought some home and then dropped the divorce bombshell. She wasn't sure if she was thrilled to receive flowers or gun-shy about the intention.

When she got back to the nursing station, she pulled the note from the dozen stunningly gorgeous red roses.

"Didn't take you long," one of the other nurses teased.

Jess shrugged. "Life's short, right?"

The other nurses smiled as Jess ripped the small envelope from the prong. She slid the small card out.

Thinking of you today. Hope your new job is going well.

B

What the hell?

Jess blinked at the card, confused because she'd expected them to be from Ryan. Or, hell, even Logan as an apology for essentially abandoning her for Morgan on their double date. But her ex-husband?

She glanced up at the perfect, deep-hued red roses. The bouquet was splashy and expensive. So very Benton. And what did it mean? For nearly a year, he'd kept his distance. Their communications were perfunctory and polite. When he'd packed his things, he'd been mostly quiet, as if he were clearing out the effects of a departed friend. Solemn and solicitous. When they'd sold the house and Jess had been unable to stanch the tears that trickled down her cheeks during the signing, he'd retrieved a tissue and passed it to her. That was the only comfort he'd offered. And when Lacy had died, he'd worn his best suit and stood beside her in the church, never touching her, but there . . . and thankfully without a bimbo. He'd refrained from attending any events in which her family might participate, and he respectfully took his dates to Jackson. If anything could be said about Benton Mason, it was that the man tried to have class. *Tried* was a key word for a man who'd left his wife for a florist.

But why the flowers?

"So?" Becky asked, her eyes alight with questions.

Jess shrugged and then told a little lie. "Oh, they're from my family. Just a little something to lift me up."

"Oh," Becky said, obviously disappointed. "Well, they're pretty and thoughtful."

"Yeah. They are," Jess said, her mind still grappling with why Benton would do such a thing. Then the date struck her—August 19. Today was the anniversary of the day all those years ago, as they walked home from their first day at Morning Glory High School their freshman year, when Benton had asked her to be his girlfriend. For years they'd celebrated the day as their real anniversary with thoughtful little gifts. He'd remembered.

But she hadn't. That morning she'd woken up in the arms of another man, her world so different than the one she'd once shared with Benton.

He had no right to send her flowers, no right to shift her focus off her new life and back on to something so painful. It was selfish. Manipulative. It was almost as if he sensed she had found someone else to make her happy. So he'd swooped in with a reminder. But he'd failed. If anything, it made her even more determined to jump into something sexy with Ryan.

A lightning bolt of anger struck her, and she lifted the vase. "I'd love to share these with a patient. Anyone know of someone who hasn't had many visitors?"

Chapter Eleven

After Jess had showered the crappy day off and poured herself a glass of wine, she went to the ultimate advice giver, the person who'd inspired her to sign up for the contract labor nursing job and rent a place on the beach. As always, Lacy had the last word.

Opening her dresser drawer, she pulled out the paisley Vera Bradley ditty bag and tugged the strings apart. Tilting her hand, she allowed the silver charm bracelet to slip out. She caught it in her palm, closing her fist tight around it. Rosemary had passed the bracelet on to Jess when she said she was going to Florida for a few months. Jess had protested— she hadn't been ready to think about anything other than getting over Benton and resuming the normalcy of her life. What could possibly happen in Florida? But Eden had had a point when she said Jess had a better shot at adventure in Florida than she had working the day shift at Penny Pinchers in their hometown. So Jess had dutifully packed the bracelet in her suitcase.

So could coming to Florida and engaging in a healing affair with a hunk count as fulfilling a dream? It certainly counted as an adventure, something Lacy had hinted that Jess needed in the letter she'd left from the great beyond. The woman had meddled in their lives, and Jess often pictured the delight Lacy had, sitting in her hospital bed in her crooked blue wig, putting her last hold on her friends. She'd have had those bright-orange nails, insisting upon manicures and lipstick, telling everyone she'd go out looking better than when she came in this world. Lacy would have caught her tongue between her glossed lips as she used the last of her energy to write a letter to each of her closest friends.

Jess—

I know you're the Miranda (*Sex and the City* ref!) of our group, but your hard shell and no-nonsense toughness hide a tender heart. That bastard never deserved you. If I could get up from this damn bed, I'd tell Benton as much and probably kick his ass all the way to Jackson. (Don't tell Rosemary I cussed this much. Ha. Ha.) At times I can see how much you hurt, and it hurts me, friend. I know this whole bracelet thing is something you'll roll your eyes at in front of the girls, but I think deep down you'll like the challenge. You need something more than Morning Glory and the map you've drawn out for your life. In fact, crumple up that map and try to get lost instead. The unknown is so much more exciting. Look, having cancer makes me prophetic and way wiser than anyone else. It's like God's last gift to me, and since you can't really argue with me, I get to tell you what I see for you. I see a great love in your life. He won't be the man you've reasoned for yourself. He'll be unexpected, found off the path where he's been waiting for you. So do a favor for a dying girl—or in this case your new guardian angel—let go and find a high current to glide on. Go where the wind blows you, friend. Don't be afraid. Where it takes you, love will be waiting. Take care of Eden and Rose . . . but take care of you, too. I love you.

Hugs and ladybugs,

Lacy (Samantha) (I wasn't the Delta Chi sweetheart for nothin', sugar.)

Jess swiped the tears away so they wouldn't drip onto the handwritten words that were her last remembrance of a crazy, wonderful woman who made everyone laugh and feel better about living in this world. Jess missed her friend.

She could almost see Lacy's response to the crazy plan she'd concocted for seducing Ryan. Lacy would give her a high five and then help think of even more naughty things she could do. Yeah, Jess was certain the Delta Chi sweetheart would approve.

Glancing at her watch and giving a last swipe of her eyes, Jess refolded the note and tucked it and the bracelet back into the bag. After talking to Eden and reading the advice from her dear friend, she knew it was time to spread her wings and find a current to ride.

The current's name was Ryan.

No more cautious Jess. At least for a while.

Lacy had been right. Time to get lost.

∽

Ryan held his phone in his hand, contemplating exactly what to text Jess when the doorbell rang. He'd been debating whether he should invite her over or play it cool and join his friends at Cuesticks. He'd been studying up on how to perform a dead-ball shot and wanted to practice before the September Shootout tournament. But being with Jess, maybe even getting to that elusive third base, tugged at him. Holding her all night long had given him bigger fantasies . . . and an arm that had stayed numb for a good half hour.

When he opened the door, all thoughts of pool sticks and two-for-one beers flew from his mind.

Jess stood on his stoop wearing a pair of cat eye–styled glasses, a short lab coat that was buttoned from throat to mid-thigh, and a pair of high-heeled black pumps. She carried a clipboard, and her red lipstick smeared the eraser of the pencil she thumped against her lips.

"Jess?"

"Hello. I'm here to conduct a little experiment," she said, brushing back a tendril of hair that had escaped the loose bun gathered at the nape of her neck. She raked his body with a speculative gleam in her eyes.

"An experiment?" He grinned.

"I've heard you've spent much time in the lab and thus are sufficiently experienced for this potentially combustible endeavor," she said, a smile hovering at her lips as she scratched something on the clipboard. "May I come in?"

Ryan's heart did a little trippy thing when it registered she wore nearly sheer black hosiery beneath the lab coat. "Of course, Dr. . . ."

"Jessica. Jessica Anne Culpepper," she said, sliding by him and deliberately brushing her ass against the front of his shorts.

"It will be a pleasure to work with you, eh, professor?" Ryan said, closing the door and locking it for good measure. Just in case. They didn't want to be interrupted while engaging in kinky scientific role play. Please, sweet heaven, please let them be about to engage in kinky scientific role play. So he could hit a home run. He couldn't believe he was mixing baseball with kinky scientific role play, but he wasn't going to overthink it when Jess had showed up in heels with naughtiness on her mind.

"Exactly so," Jess said, pursing her lips. "Before we begin, I'm obliged to ask you if you have any objection to removing all or part of your clothing during the course of the experiment. For safety reasons, of course. Things could get volatile and messy."

"You're conducting an experiment that requires me to take off my clothes? I've never had to do that in a lab before."

She lifted an eyebrow. "Then you've had the wrong lab partner."

He laughed. "You do remember you were my lab partner once."

"Good point. But if I'm going to prove my current hypothesis, you might have to sacrifice your shorts," she said, walking toward him. She ringed a finger around his neckline. "You know, scientific pioneers must be willing to go where others haven't gone before."

"I thought that was *Star Trek*, but I'm up for exploring new frontiers," he said, capturing her hand and lifting it to his lips. Tenderly he kissed each knuckle while using his other hand to cup her waist. Was there clothing beneath the lab coat? Or was this naked waist he felt?

"Good," she whispered, pulling her hand away. "Let's get started."

"Okay," he said, following Jess as she entered his living room. He adjusted himself beneath his shorts, hoping she couldn't see the thickening erection.

But, shit, she was turning him on.

"Nice lab," she said, turning in a circle, checking out his place. Her movement gave him a nice view of long, lean legs clad in the silk hose. The lab coat brushed against her upper thighs, and he thought he glimpsed a garter. All he could think about was what she had on underneath the buttoned-up coat. He needed to get her out of that damn lab coat.

"Thank you. It has all the latest innovations. Should we go ahead and plug in the Bunsen burner?" he joked.

Jess smiled. "Is that a euphemism or do you really have a Bunsen burner somewhere?"

"I can get my chemistry set. There might be a Bunsen burner you can play with." Of course he made it sound dirty, because he had nary a test tube at his new place. When he left the lab back in California, he'd left everything, including his personal equipment. No need for anything like that on his fishing boat.

"We won't need it. We're about to indulge in chemical reactions that, while primitive in nature, are the basis for all mankind. Yes, I do believe we have everything we need right here," she said, unbuttoning the top button of her lab coat.

Ryan watched her walk over to the lamp next to his couch and switch it off. He jogged over and flipped it back on again. Jess arched a brow, so he said, "We need adequate lighting. Safety first. Oh, and I must be able to see everything we're doing. Makes it all valid."

She smiled and unbuttoned the next button. The swells of her breasts appeared. "So do you have protective suiting?"

"Uh, yeah. A whole box of protective suiting right in my bedside table."

"Of course you do. I remember you always being prepared. It will be a pleasure to—"

"—make all my nerd fantasies come true?" he finished for her, moving toward her.

Jess held out a hand to stop him. "I know lab coats are required for most experiments, but for this one, I believe it could pose a hazard. I think I should remove mine, don't you?" Her voice grew husky. He now knew he could no longer hide the result. It pressed against his athletic shorts, tenting them.

"I do. I would hate for anything to get in your way."

Jess gave a no-nonsense nod. "Right, then." With a quick flick of her wrist, she unbuttoned the rest of the lab coat and let it slide off her shoulders. It fluttered to the floor, landing on her stilettos. What remained took his breath away.

Her generous breasts were enclosed in a lacy black bra, and the tiny black satin and lace panties were partially covered by a see-through garter belt that held up silky stockings. Tiny black bows fastened the stockings to the garter, a mark of innocence adorning the dirty fantasy they presented. Her mile-high heels, smart glasses, and hair secured in a knot were so sexy he nearly lost his breath. If his fourteen-year-old self could have imagined this, he would have ejaculated on the spot. The grown-up sex goddess standing before him almost had him breaking a sweat just looking at her. "Holy cow."

"Umm-hmm," she said, taking the pencil she'd shoved from behind her ear and scratching something on the clipboard.

"What are you writing?" he asked, moving toward her, brushing a hand across the small of her back. He felt her response—the speeding of her breath, the tightening of her nipples through the peekaboo lace.

"Just the response of the subject to stimuli."

"Oh, 'cause that looks like you're writing lyrics from the SpongeBob SquarePants theme song," he said, trailing his hand down the globe of her bare ass, which was, by the way, spectacular.

"Merely code for an erection," she said with a smile.

"Pineapple under the sea? You're seriously making SpongeBob kinky?" he said, stepping so his body pressed against the back of hers. He put his hands flush against her stomach and leaned into her.

"I've always thought yellow sponges were sort of sexy. Sort of," she said, dropping the clipboard and leaning back. He nibbled on her earlobe and stroked her flat stomach, edging a finger beneath the lace garter belt low on her hips. She smelled amazing—something sultry and sweet at the same time. Like a woman should.

"Want to take this experiment to my bedro—uh, adjoining laboratory?"

"That seems wise, given the recent observations," she murmured, tilting her head so he could slide his lips along the column of her neck up to her jaw.

Ryan moved so she was in front of him. Taking the clipboard and tossing it onto the leather couch, he tilted her head back so he could stare into her eyes.

"Hey, babe, I appreciate this sexy role play. Ever since I was fourteen and had to stare at your gorgeousness across the lab table, I've been fantasizing about you in almost exactly what you're wearing. Okay, it was naked under the cheerleading uniform, but this is a very close second. But in lieu of our last conversation, are you ready for this?" He hated himself for asking. What man asked a woman looking the way Jess did, offering up what Jess offered, if she was serious about doing it?

Momentarily her eyes softened from the previous naughtiness to something gentle. "What a true gentleman you are, Ryan Reyes. Your mother would be proud."

"In this particular situation, I'm not sure we should mention my mother." He smiled, looking down at the breasts pushed up in her bra. "You weren't ready a few days ago. So why now?"

She licked her bottom lip, which nearly undid him. "I've been thinking too much."

"And you don't want to think anymore?"

"You of all people are asking me that?" she joked.

"Touché. Still, I care about you and I don't—"

Jess lifted onto her toes and kissed him. "Shh, I know this is right. I need you, Ryan. You are exactly what I want."

How could he argue with those words . . . especially when she kissed him so sweetly? Jess Culpepper needed to be held, touched, loved, and she wanted him. This wasn't him taking advantage of the brokenhearted or fulfilling a leftover fantasy from his high school days. This was about a woman and a man who needed something from each other. "Then we should proceed with our experiment, professor."

Ryan's room was tastefully utilitarian with a large king bed and soft gray coverlet that felt cold against her back when she sat down, crossed her legs, and leaned back onto her elbows. Ryan stood framed in the doorway, watching her with amused eyes.

She'd never done anything as wild as this.

Role playing.

After reading Lacy's letter, she'd visited a shop that carried sexy lingerie, looking for the perfect ensemble to seduce the former boy wonder of MGHS. When she thought about what his fantasy might be, she'd imagined a lonely scientist sitting behind a microscope in a laboratory. Somehow she knew he'd like the skimpy lingerie beneath the lab coat. What Ryan needed was a do-over on high school chemistry, replete with a fantasy science partner.

And by the results straining the front of his shorts, she'd say it had worked well.

"I'm assuming we'll conduct our experiment here," she said, smoothing the spot beside her. She felt naughty. And she liked that feeling. It had been so long since this sort of anticipation surged inside her, so long since she was soaking wet before she'd barely been touched.

"If that's what you want," he said, not moving from the doorway.

"Oh, so you want me to start without you?" she asked, sliding a hand over her stomach, inching down toward the miniscule panties. She uncrossed her legs and let them dangle off the side of the bed, giving him a small glimpse of her crotch barely covered in the skimpy panties.

His gaze never left her body. "What did you do with my practical Jess?"

"I gave her the night off," Jess said, dragging her fingers over her pubic bone. She'd never been one to be turned on by her own touch, but the sensation of her own fingers stroking so near the area that throbbed for release was an aphrodisiac that was heightened only by Ryan's gaze on her body.

She could tell he was turned on beyond the very obvious and hard indicator. His eyes were limpid pools, his breathing notched, and his hands fisted as if to keep him from grabbing her. It had been a long time since Jess had felt this sexy, so she embraced the desire coursing through her along with the knowledge that Ryan couldn't seem to get his fill of watching her.

"You know what you're doing, don't you?"

"Do you really have to ask?" Jess said, rolling over, planting her feet on the floor and presenting him with her ass. She stretched her arms far out, smoothing the wrinkles from the bed. "The experiment calls for putting the test subject through highly sexualized—ah!"

His hands slid up the backs of her thighs and cupped the behind she'd waggled high in the air. His touch made her nearly swoon with delight. She closed her eyes as he captured her waist and jerked her to him. Once again he stood behind her, his body pressed against hers, his hands wandering up and down. He took his time, touching, stroking, knowing how to drive her wild.

"You're bewitching," he murmured, kissing her neck. She sighed and allowed her head to fall back against his shoulder.

"That's not scientific," she managed to say.

"Ah, but it is," he said, cupping her aching breasts. Her nipples were so tight and her breasts so heavy and needy. He cradled them, murmuring indecipherable comments into that sensitive area where her shoulder and neck joined. She reached back and linked her arms about his neck while grinding her ass against his erection. "It's very much a biological reaction to stimuli, and, baby, you're good at stimuli."

"I try. For science's sake."

He laughed and spun her around, capturing her lips with his. His kiss was light at first, but then he nipped her lower lip. His hands returned to her ass, kneading her flesh. She slid her tongue over his bottom lip before plunging it into his mouth. He allowed her to take over, kiss him. And she did. God help her, she did. All the passion she'd been so afraid to let loose came roaring to the surface. And suddenly she couldn't get enough.

Ryan moved her so the backs of her knees hit the edge of the mattress. With a slight push, she fell back. He cradled her as they hit the mattress. He rolled to his side, not breaking the kiss. Jess lay mostly on her back, still in his arms.

Ryan lifted his head and looked down at her. She relaxed as his gaze moved down her body, the heat of his perusal almost its own caress. After a few seconds he lifted his gaze back to her face and said, "You're amazing. Sexy. Beautiful. I've never wanted a woman more."

She wanted to believe that. So she did. She knew words exchanged in the heat of passion were often words untrue. People got carried away, but at that moment she didn't care. She needed to believe that she was the most desirable woman Ryan had ever pleasured.

"Touch me," she said, lifting a hand to brush against his jaw. He was so gorgeous. So finely crafted and sexy. She tugged on the hem of his shirt. "And take this off, please."

He quickly divested himself of the shirt before tossing it somewhere on the floor. Then he turned his attention back to her, running a hand over her collarbone and down to rest beneath her breasts. The bra was a front clasp, and with one twist of his wrist, the cups parted, releasing her breasts.

"Nice," he breathed, cupping one, allowing his thumb to graze the nipple so tight with desire. "You're so pretty, Jess. I love the color of your nipples. Like pink peonies from a garden." He lowered his head and sucked the nearest nipple into his mouth.

Jess wanted to tease him about his poetry, but with his mouth hot on her breast she didn't have the words. "Oh, oh."

"Mmm-hmm," he groaned against her flesh. His hands moved over her stomach to her hip bone, turning her toward him, running back to cup her ass again. It registered in her mind that he was an ass man.

Jess explored his body, too, stroking his torso, loving the hard planes, the wide chest with the burnished brown hair. His abs were sculpted, his back lean, and that jaw was like rock. Everything about him was so sexy and hard and manly and—

"I don't know how to work this garter thing," he said, dropping kisses along her shoulder.

"Oh, here, let me," she said, unhooking the fasteners. The elastic straps bounced, and then she paused. "Should I take the whole thing off?"

"Hell, no," he said feathering his fingers over the crotch of the black satin panties that barely covered her. Last week she'd sprung for a bikini wax, since Becky said it was a must for a woman living on the beach. Tonight she was thankful she had. His touch felt hot even through the fabric. "Let me do the honors."

With the belt detached, he was able to slide his fingers beneath the G-string bikini and peel the satin panties from her body. She lifted her rear, and he cleared the tops of her thighs, pausing only to shift so he could pull them over the high heels. "You can leave these shoes on. You look so hot in them."

"Want my glasses on or off? Hair up or down? It's your fantasy," she said, stroking his shoulders as he tossed her panties aside.

His gaze zeroed in on the smoothly waxed juncture of her thighs. Her body felt flushed as he ran one finger over the trimmed hair there. She knew she was wet, but at his touch she felt herself grow even wetter.

"Oh, baby, you're so wet. That's so—" He didn't finish, because he leaned forward and caught her mouth in a kiss. His tongue thrust against hers as he covered her body with his. Her senses spun out of control. His hard hotness grinding into her, his mouth suddenly everywhere at once. "Jess, I want to go slow, but I'm, like, losing it over you. You're too damn hot, woman. Too hot. I need to be inside you, baby."

Jess wrapped her arms around his shoulders and kissed him hard. "Don't go slow. We can do slow later. Get the condom."

Ryan lifted himself from her and opened the drawer in the bedside table. "I really wanted the first time to be good for you."

Lifting onto her elbows, Jess said, "And you think it won't?"

He turned. "No. It will. I've studied all this stuff about delayed gratification, but with you, I can't seem to control myself." He struggled to open the box of condoms. "Damn it."

"Here. Give it to me," she said, shrugging out of her bra and holding out a hand. He ripped the box and tossed her a package. She ripped the foil wrapper and lifted an eyebrow. "Well . . ."

Ryan's cheeks flared red as he hooked his thumbs into the waistband of his shorts and tugged them off. He stood in a pair of tight black boxer briefs. Ryan Reyes in tight underwear was a fine sight indeed. "Nice."

"I'm suddenly nervous. I feel very much like that schoolboy you were playing a fantasy out for," he said, with a sheepish smile. "It's weird. I'm never nervous about this."

"Come here and let me take them off you," she said, beckoning him with a finger. She set the condom, still in the package, within arm's reach along with her fake glasses. Her body thrummed with excitement as she slipped back into the role of seducer. Never had she been so bold as to take the lead. She'd always enjoyed the more submissive position, but Ryan made her want to be naughty, to be modern, to take control of her own desires.

Ryan climbed back onto the big bed and inched close to her, staying on his knees. The black Lycra of his boxers outlined his erection, which looked fairly impressive. Jess rose on her knees and trailed little kisses along his collarbone, inhaling his scent of bay rum soap and that intangible maleness that couldn't be bottled. Maybe it was pheromones, who knew. But he smelled amazing. Her hands slid down to grasp his hard ass, and she gave it a light smack. She lifted her face to his, and he kissed her.

The kiss was less hurried, but very thorough. Jess tilted her head, letting him take it deeper as she slid a hand between their bodies and clasped him through his boxer briefs.

"Mmm," he groaned, moving his hips back so she could fully mold her hand to his length. He was weighty and thick, making her blood sing in anticipation. For a moment she was content to stroke him through the soft material. All the while his hands roamed over her ass, up her back, cupping a breast, squeezing a nipple. Until finally he made it to the place that ached for him. His fingers sliding against her clitoris took her breath away.

Jess hooked her fingers in his waistband and slid his underwear down, hanging slightly on the head of his shaft before dropping them down between his thighs on the bed. Capturing the bobbing length, she felt the full heat and breadth of the man. "Impressive," she said, nipping his bottom lip, fully aware that this was a huge first for her. She'd never wrapped her hand around any man other than her ex-husband. It was both exciting and somehow strange.

But his fingers worked their own magic, erasing any unease. He moved through her slick heat, ringing her entrance, teasing, tormenting, and practicing all the wicked things he'd no doubt read about in those manuals he'd admitted to studying. Three cheers for a man who took his sexual game seriously.

"I can't wait any longer," she whispered into his ear, nuzzling the scruff of his jaw. She reached over and grabbed the foil packet. "Let's suit up."

Ryan ducked his head and kissed her hard. "Like good scientists should."

Jess fit the circular latex over the head of his cock and rolled it down. Then she tipped him over. Like a felled tree, he went down easy.

Jess straddled him, rubbing herself against the hard ridge, anchoring her hands on either side of his face. She looked deep into his eyes. "I'm so glad you're the one."

There was no explanation needed, because she wasn't sure exactly what "the one" was. Was it the first man who'd seen her as a desirable woman after she'd felt anything but? The first man who made her feel something more than sadness again? The first man to screw her after her hurtful divorce? The first man to be a possibility for something more? She didn't know. And at that moment she didn't care. There was Ryan. There was Jess and there was . . .

She lifted herself and tilted her hips, sinking down on him.

"Yes," she sighed, holding herself still, feeling him stretch her, fill her. The sensation was more than physical.

"Oh shit, that's good," Ryan said, screwing his eyes closed and making that face—the hurt-so-good face—that caused her to hesitate for a millisecond. But then he grabbed her hips and pulled her down tight before reaching up to cup her breast. "You're so damn sexy, babe. I've never seen anything like you."

Jess started moving her hips, establishing a strong rhythm. Thirteen months. That's how long it had been since she'd had sex. The month before Benton had come home and dropped his shit bomb, they'd not had sex. He'd claimed stress, and she'd accepted it because he'd started a new position in his company. So the sensation of Ryan filling her, rolling her nipples between his finger and thumb, giving her honeyed words all combined to build quickly the delicious pressure of orgasm. Her body tightened; her mind went into that trancelike state where there was only him, her, and that ancient movement that brought dizzying pleasure. Blinding pleasure. Toe-curling pleasure.

And then his thumb parted her and found her clit. Like a huge wave rolling over a small boat, she broke apart, spasms of sheer, unadulterated pleasure washing over her. She screamed and leaned forward, fisting her hands in the softness of the quilt.

"Oh wow, that's . . . I can feel you coming," Ryan said, lifting his hips, turning her over. He slid his hands under her knees, tilting her back slightly so that he went even deeper inside her. The head of his cock rubbed the perfect spot over and over again until she fell to pieces again.

Jess slammed her hands down on either side of her. "Oh shit. I'm coming again."

Ryan's breathing was ragged in her ear. He dropped tender kisses against her neck. "Come again. And again. As much as you can, baby. Just let loose and give it all to me."

So she did. All thoughts other than stretching once again for that pinnacle fled as her body took over. She'd never felt anything like it, but she went with it.

Soon, Ryan's hoarse cry sounded in her ear, and the jerking of his hips signified he, too, had achieved that sweet crest. His body shuddered, and he gave a little shake, as if he had the chills, before slowing and collapsing on top of her. And even as he stopped moving, the muscles inside her clutched at him, demanding more. She didn't want to stop, but she couldn't take anymore. She'd lost track of the orgasms.

"Oh my God," she said, spitting her hair out of her mouth, breath coming hard as deep satisfaction ebbed and flowed inside her body.

Ryan laughed and kissed the side of her boob before withdrawing and rolling over. "Damn straight. That felt amazing."

Jess started laughing. "I may have set a record for the most orgasms ever."

"Let me get the clipboard," he said, making like he was about to get up. She grabbed his arm and jerked him back to her. He gave her a sweaty kiss and then collapsed back. "Doesn't matter. The hypothesis is proven. When Jess Culpepper, fantasy girl, shows up on dorky Ryan Reyes's doorstep wearing a black satin garter belt and a lab coat, something explosive will go down."

"We've got good chemistry," she said with another laugh. God, it felt so good to laugh, to have had amazing sex, to feel so sexy, sated, and . . . loved.

Of course, this wasn't love. At all. It was a post-coital glow. But still the feeling was much the same.

"You've got a nice set of test tubes," he joked, grinning like a fool. Jess rolled over to her side and stroked the sparse trail of hair on his belly. He still wore the spent condom.

"Pink peonies?" she said, smiling down at him.

He lifted a hand and tweaked her nipple. "I know. It was bad, but I couldn't think of a good comparison. My grandmother used to grow them in—"

"Ah, don't mention your grandmother! The woman would be appalled at what I just did with her grandson."

Ryan inhaled. "Actually, I think she'd be happy I was getting some. She worried a lot about me growing up. She kept telling my parents, 'The boy needs to be normal,' to which they'd reply, 'But he's not normal.' It was a constant debate. Ol' Granny Lou would probably high-five me. I haven't seen her in a while, so she hasn't seen my bid to be normal. But she'd be supportive of me claiming my own life . . . of me getting some from the head cheerleader." He wiggled his eyebrows.

"I'm thinking I should have worn my cheerleading uniform instead of the lab coat," Jess said, moving her hand up to his broad chest and nuzzling in close to him. "Maybe next time. Of course, it's in storage in Morning Glory, but maybe I can order something online."

"Will there be a next time?" he asked, stroking the piece of hair that had come down during their lovemaking.

Jess froze. She'd never thought this was a one-and-done sort of thing. But how stupid of her. Of course Ryan wasn't treating them as an exclusive thing. He had women swarming over him . . . or at least that's what Becky and Tanae had implied. Hadn't Morgan already tried to mark her territory?

The fact her hand had stopped on his chest and she hadn't responded must have alarmed Ryan, because he lifted his head. "Hey, I'll understand if you don't want to—"

"No, I just hadn't thought much beyond right now," Jess said, shaking her head. "I mean, I understand that you don't want to make this—"

"—a relationship?" he interrupted.

Jess pressed her lips together. "Maybe we shouldn't define anything. Maybe we go with it. I don't want to hem you into anything you're uncomfortable with, but to be honest, I'm not interested in doing this with anyone other than you. In fact, I turned a really cute oncologist down earlier today. But I don't want to—"

"No. I do," Ryan said, lifting upon his elbow. "I mean, I'm not interested in any other woman right now. You're all I can think about since I first saw you. I know I was bombed out of my mind, but still it registered that Jess was here, looking hotter than a . . . Bunsen burner. After that, there was only you in my mind, filling up all the spaces. So I want to do this thing, whatever it is, for as long as it's good for both of us."

"You do?" She couldn't keep the surprise out of her voice. She hadn't expected him to be so honest, but hadn't he been exactly that from the outset?

"Yeah," he said, smiling at her. "And I can't imagine this being the only time I touch you"—he brushed his hand across her rib cage, making her stomach tremble—"that I taste you"—he dipped his head toward her, capturing her lips against his in a soft kiss—"or that I'll feel your body tightening against mine. You're gorgeous when you come."

"Oh," she breathed, her body quickening once again with desire. "I think we're in agreement that our experiment must be carried out over the course of several months. We have much to touch, taste, and feel."

"Mmm-hmm," he said against her mouth as he kissed her once more. "Now let me take care of this used condom, and we'll start the next experiment. I think in this one we'll take off the stockings and garters so I can kiss every inch of your delicious body."

"And I'll start thinking of comparisons for your body parts while you're gone. Maybe the fleshy tuber of your love. Or perhaps the velvet steel sword," she joked.

Ryan slapped her ass. "That's right. Milton's got nothing on you."

Chapter Twelve

Two days later, Jess managed to get in touch with Rosemary. Her friend had called her several times, but it was always when Jess was on duty or rolling around in the sheets with Ryan. Then when Jess returned her call, Rosemary was busy helping her future husband at the restaurant . . . or rolling around in the sheets with Sal.

"Finally," Rosemary breathed with laughter in her voice. This was how her friend had sounded ever since Sal had crossed the town square of Morning Glory sweating buckets in order to propose to her. Jess had never seen her friend happier or more fulfilled. Jess remembered what that was like, that rosy glow. In fact, it was easier to recall now that she'd spent the past two nights having amazing sex with Ryan, pausing only to enjoy a pint of Ben and Jerry's before getting back to business. She was afraid if they didn't slow down, she'd end up with a bladder infection. But the hazy, wonderful feeling of having good sex paired with the laughter and waking up with someone there to make coffee—even though she didn't drink it—was something she'd been happy to wrap herself in.

"Sorry we've been playing phone tag," Jess said, sinking onto the hammock on the porch of the Dirty Heron, staring out at the bay gently lapping the sandy shore. "I've been working a lot."

"And according to Eden, you've been playing around with the Brain. She showed me the picture. Good God, he's like Adonis and Tom Cruise had a baby. Of course, I have no idea what Adonis looked like. Well, come to think of it, he wasn't even real, but you know what I mean."

"I do. And, yes, Ryan Reyes grew up to be a hottie. I almost feel dirty playing around with him. But not too dirty to stop," Jess said, feeling more like herself than she had in forever. Like she was getting back the part of herself that could joke and act nonchalant. The part of her that drawled naughty comebacks and drank gin martinis. The part of herself that wasn't a whiny bitch who got sad during Hallmark commercials and slept in an old shirt of her ex-husband's she'd found when she cleaned out her drawers. Yeah, the unpathetic part.

"Well, well, aren't you the cougar? Well, I guess technically you're not a cougar. But you know what I mean."

"I am a cougar. I think. I'm three years older than him, so does that make me one?"

Rosemary laughed. "I don't think so. Does it matter?"

"Nope. So what's going on? You don't have pregnancy brain, do you?" Jess asked. Rosemary sounded more scattered than usual.

"No! Good gravy, do not even suggest that. My mother would be planning the baby shower with gossamer ribbon and tiered petits fours. It's bad enough I have to deal with her and this wedding."

"You've picked a date?"

"That's what I wanted to talk to you about. We're actually getting married Labor Day weekend."

"Labor Day weekend? That's in, like, two weeks."

"I know, but for the past few weeks we've argued back and forth with my mom and Sal's mom and . . . it's just getting to be too much. Our families are driving us crazy. So since his parents are coming down here to meet my parents over Labor Day, we said to hell with it and booked the church. Luckily, his brothers and one of his sisters can come, too. Oh, and his grandmother Sophie. But I want you here. You have to be here for my wedding."

"I don't know, Rose. I can try to switch weekends with someone on another shift, but it's a holiday."

"I can't get married without you," Rosemary said, her voice suddenly quiet. Jess could almost hear her thoughts. *Lacy won't be here. I can't have you missing, too.* "You have to be a bridesmaid. Only you and Eden. I'm not even asking my cousin Mary Charlotte."

"And your mother knows this?"

"Not yet. It will cause another argument, but Mary Charlotte does not want to be in my wedding anyway. Sammi Jo Henry overheard her tell Marion Trask at Rio Grande that very thing when she stopped in for Taco Tuesday. Sammi Jo called me because she thought I ought to know when someone didn't have the decency to want to be in her own cousin's wedding. She said Mary Charlotte told Marion that if she had to wear one more ugly dress and paste a fake smile on her face, she was going to puke. So Mary Charlotte is out."

"Bloodthirsty, aren't you?"

"It's Sal's influence. The New Yorker in him cuts through the bullshit."

Jess laughed at her genteel friend rattling off "bullshit" like it was natural for her. Prim, prissy Rosemary rarely cursed. Her mother didn't deem it ladylike, so she'd stricken all swear words from her daughter's vocabulary. Once when they were sixteen, they'd spent the entire night calling each another "motherfucker" so they could practice getting ready for college. They'd also bought a pack of Virginia Slims and sat by the screened window blowing smoke out. Rosemary had managed to use *motherfucker* twice and puff on three cigarettes that she never inhaled. "I like when you talk tough."

"So will you ask your boss at the hospital? Beg them. Tell them I have to have my best friends with me."

"I'll see what I can do to get a shift change. I'll say pretty please and spring for lunch one day. That should to the trick. Nurses love free food," Jess said.

"Oh good. Let me know as soon as you can. Oh, and feel free to bring a guest," Rosemary said, her voice rising to an almost singsong trill.

"I don't have to, do I? Eden's not bringing anyone, is she?"

"Just Henry, but he was invited anyway. He's my cousin."

"I know. And Benton?"

There was a long pause. "I'm sorry, Jess, but I have to invite him. His family has been our family's friends forever. Lydia was in my mother's wedding, and they're still thick as thieves. Benton and I played in the sprinkler together when we were two years old. We vacationed together at Seaside for five years. And don't freak out, but Lydia is singing at the wedding. It was the one concession I made to my mother."

"Oh God," Jess groaned. "Tell me she's not doing 'Ave Maria.'"

"No. She's going to sing 'Loving You.'"

"Never heard of it."

Rosemary sighed. "It's an Elvis song, but that doesn't matter now. You have to understand, my mother is so pissed at me. I've already told her about serving Italian at the reception and having an open bar. She said it was profane. So I can only drop so many bombs on her each day."

"God," Jess groaned. "You're not making this sound attractive. Is Benton bringing a date?"

"Maybe. We're not asking for a RSVP. Too short of notice. Invites went out two days ago." Again, Jess could hear the apology in Rosemary's voice. Her friend's mother made Sherman's march through the South look like a freaking picnic. The woman rolled over anyone who got in her way . . . one of the reasons she'd never liked Jess. Of course, Patsy Reynolds didn't like Eden, either—wrong side of the tracks and all that.

Shit. Jess wasn't certain she could get off for her best friend's wedding, which would suck, but she wasn't certain it would suck more than showing up single at a wedding where her ex-husband would be sitting with some big-boobed plaything of the week. It would be humiliating. If Eden planned on going as a single, Jess wouldn't feel so bad. But that she'd asked Henry to be her date meant Jess needed a date, too. She just couldn't show up looking . . . lonely.

But she couldn't see Ryan agreeing to be her plus one. Labor Day weekend meant he'd be booked. And the biggest reason would be the hugest hurdle—the man hated Morning Glory.

But who else could she take as a date?

Maybe Chris Haven. He'd moved back to Morning Glory a few months back. Unfortunately, he did a disservice to most gay guys by having the fashion sense of Queen Elizabeth II. Still, the man loved a good wedding and wouldn't paw her on the dance floor. He could be a possibility. Or maybe she could hire a date? Like in one of those zany romantic comedies Debra Messing liked to star in. Or she could beg Ryan. Because the thought of Benton dancing with a Dixie Cream worker (rumored to be his newest conquest) made Jess want to barf. Besides, Ryan would look incredible in a suit. If he wore seersucker and a bow tie, he could make most of the Kappa Kappa Gammas who'd no doubt show up to watch their former vice president of pledge education get married spontaneously combust. He would be the perfect date . . . if she could talk him into it.

That was a big *if* and a tall order, since their relationship was very loose in structure.

"I'll get back with you tomorrow, Rose. I can't make promises, but God willing and the creek don't rise, I'll be there when you wed your sweetie."

"Thank you, Jess. Oh, and I'm making the bridesmaids' dresses. Vintage 1950s cocktail dresses. I bought the hot-pink satin years ago not knowing what I'd do with it, and it's going to make the smartest dresses. Thankfully, I already had your measurements from the Halloween costume I made last year, so no worries there."

Vintage satin cocktail dresses? So Rosemary. "Sounds pretty."

"I have this whole '50s theme I'm doing. Sal hired an Elvis impersonator for the reception. We saw him when we went to Memphis last weekend."

"Let me guess, you haven't told Patsy yet."

"God, no. And we're not telling her. She thinks Holly Bryson's quartet is playing, so don't breathe a word. Oh my God, I'm getting married in a few weeks. Can you believe?"

Jess smiled and rose, stretching on her toes, working the kink out of her neck. She'd banged it on the headboard the night before. Full-fledged sex injury. "Actually I can. You deserve this. I can't wait to wear pink satin and dance to 'Blue Suede Shoes.' Wait, we're not wearing those, are we?"

"No, silly. I am." Rosemary laughed. "See you soon. I pray."

"'Bye, Rose."

Jess hung up and walked back into the house, noting Morgan coming up the walk next door. She waved at the normally happy brunette. Morgan didn't wave back.

"Okay," Jess muttered and walked back into the condo.

Ryan had reported Morgan and his friend had gone out several times and seemed to be embarking on their own romance. Even if that were true, Morgan still hadn't forgiven her for stealing Ryan. Which was a shame, because Jess had liked Morgan when she wasn't being possessive. But it didn't matter if her neighbor didn't like her. Jess had only one more week at the Dirty Heron before she had to vacate. The realty company had found her another couple of places that might work, but

Jess had yet to choose one. None seemed as perfect as where she now lived. Of, course that could have to do with the fact Ryan lived a hop, skip, and jump away.

An hour and a half later, Jess had takeout from Little China on Ryan's table and wine chilling in the fridge, and she wore a pretty sundress that showed plenty of cleavage. After having talked Becky into covering for her, promising to bring her cupcakes and lunch for a week and take her shift for the following weekend, Jess was set to spend Labor Day weekend in Morning Glory. All that was left was to do was persuade her stud muffin to accompany her.

ᘒ

"No way," Ryan said, sipping the buttery chardonnay and setting the glass down. "I'd rather have my balls waxed than go to Morning Glory. And for a wedding?" He shivered and made a face.

"But it's for Rosemary. You always liked her, right?" Jess looked plaintive, but not plaintive enough to budge him.

"Sure. I guess. She never really talked to me other than to boss me around when doing the yearbook spread. I knew I shouldn't have joined that club. My mother insisted I needed to have at least one other activity other than chess club. I thought being a photographer would be interesting, studying the contrast in color and medium. I forgot I'd have to actually go to events and work under a very . . . uh, exacting editor. So if you want to call tolerating her liking her, then I guess I liked her even if she didn't appreciate artistry in photography."

Jess's eyes sparkled, reminding him of a honey tigereye stone he'd bought at a museum once. "You tried to bring artistry to taking the group picture of the Future Farmers of America?"

Ryan shrugged. "Even farmers deserve good bounce lighting."

Her laughter made his heart warm. "Bounce lighting? You actually brought a screen?"

"My mother's bedsheet."

Jess clutched her stomach and nearly choked on her lo mein. "Oh my gosh, I don't remember Rose saying anything about that. That's hilarious."

"And this is why I don't want to go back. I was weird. That's what people will remember."

Rosemary's eyes traveled over him. "Uh, dude. That's not what people are going to be thinking about when they see you. You're the quintessential nerd grown into a successful, gorgeous man. You can totally thumb your nose, give the bullies the comeuppance they deserve, and, bonus, you get to see your mom and dad."

"They don't want to see me." That much was obvious. They'd made a halfhearted plea for him to come home for the annual Easter egg hunt, which they rarely attended on account of it being a pagan ritual. Sometimes he wished his parents were just normal. That they insisted he come home or bundled up their practical holiday gifts and drove to see him. That they didn't make a point to be so . . . clinical.

Jess made a frowny face. "Uh, yeah, they do. All parents want to see their children. Well, most. Your parents may not understand your decision, but you're their child. Do you think they don't love you?"

Ryan felt something shut down inside him. He didn't want to talk about his parents and the way they made him feel. Which was pretty much like he was a freak of nature. They'd emphasized his exceptional abilities rather than helping him assimilate in a town that appreciated sameness. His father had hailed from Massachusetts, from a liberal family of researchers and educators, and thus wasn't versed in being southern. As such, Emilio pushed broader thinking and the exploration of intellectual capacity and experimented with alternative child rearing. Ryan had felt like something in a petri dish his entire life. Had his parents loved him when he was a child? He thought they had, but it had never been in the way the other kids had been loved, with their crustless sandwiches and T-ball shirts emblazoned with "Hunter's Mom."

"Of course they love me, but I'm not interested in going back to show off my abs and play nice with people who viewed me as an oddity. It's hard to explain how daunting that sounds. You wouldn't understand."

"I do. I know things were tough on you, but you've changed. You're a confident man. Please consider it," she said, not in a teasing way. But with quiet desperation in her voice. Her pretty tiger eyes deepened, and he could see exactly what she felt. Such a longing for him to be beside her, and that moved him a few inches toward agreeing. But not far enough.

"Jess," he said, sliding his hand across the table to capture hers. "I really, really would rather have my testicles waxed. I'd make the appointment right now if it meant I didn't have to go to a wedding with you in Morning Glory. It would be torturous for me."

"No. People won't even remember you. Not really. We all grow up and change."

"You didn't change. You're still the same. Beautiful."

"I changed. Or maybe I didn't, and that was the problem. But I feel different now," she said, caressing his hand. In her face he could see the honesty in her words.

"I'm glad you feel different, but I don't feel like I have anything to prove, and I have no good reason to go back there."

"Not even me?" she said softly.

Damn. She didn't pull punches. His heart or something inside him moved another few inches toward caving. "I'm sorry, Jess."

Jess curled her fingers around his. "It's okay. I respect the way you feel."

"Thank you." Relief flooded him. She understood how hard it was for him to go back to a place where he felt so diminished. This was what he loved—no, liked—about Jess. She was sensible and kind and—

"I'll go alone. I mean, I shouldn't be so insecure, right? It's pretty weak to feel like it would be easier to face Benton and whatever date he brings with you beside me."

"Is that what this is about? Benton?"

Jess set her fork down and looked out the double glass doors where the bay awaited twilight. "Maybe a little. For the past year I lived afraid to run into him around every corner. But even worse than running into him was running into the woman he left me for at places like the salon or at the grocery store. And you know what's the absolute worst? The pity in her eyes. She felt sorry for me even as she scurried away like a guilty rat. At times I felt like I couldn't breathe. So, yeah, taking you with me would help me feel less like a loser. You're pretty damn hot."

"So you want to use me?" he teased even as part of him wondered if that's all he was to her—just a good-looking guy to have sex with and prove to Benton and everyone else she was doing fine. Something inside him wanted to be more than arm candy. Didn't she feel anything for him other than desire?

William H. Macy, he was turning into a girl, wondering about feelings. He and Jess were exactly as advertised—they had fun in the sack. And they had fun out of it. They were friends and lovers. End of story. No complications need apply.

"No, I'm not using you. I *want* to use you, but you said no." She tried to smile, but the warmness didn't reach her eyes. They remained cloudy. Uncertain. Full of something he didn't want to see.

He watched her as she pushed the food around on her plate. For the past few days she'd been eating like a horse. She'd remarked once that she'd lost the taste for food after she and Benton split, but with Ryan she'd been making up for lost time devouring a couple of pints of ice cream, pizza, and homemade waffles. He'd had to cut back on indulging because he didn't want to spend extra time in the gym when going daily was already such a chore. Still, he'd noted the hollows of her hip bones and the outline of her bottom ribs. Jess needed to eat and not worry about silly things like what folks in Morning Glory thought of her. "Fine. I'll think about it."

Her gaze jerked up. "You will?"

"*Think* about it. I'm not saying yes."

"But you're not saying no."

"I am saying no, but I'm willing to play around with the idea of withdrawing my no and replacing it with an okay. A full-force yes is not an option."

"Thank you. Seriously, thank you."

"Don't thank me yet," he warned.

"Don't worry. Going home for a few days will be easier than you think. You don't have to attend anything you don't want to. Just the wedding and the reception," she said, picking up her fork again. Jess's eyes reflected relief and excitement. Damn it. She could probably talk him into hula-dancing lessons or getting a pedicure. Jess possessed remarkable power of persuasion in those expressive eyes . . . and in her delicious body.

"Wait, what else is there?" he asked.

"Let's see. I'm sure there'll be a bachelorette party, bridal tea, and rehearsal dinner. I, of course, will probably have to get my hair and makeup done, but you don't have to worry about all that. Do you have a suit?"

"Uh, no." He'd owned exactly one sports coat for interviews. It was brown corduroy with patches on the sleeves. His mother had picked it out. The day he'd cut off all his khaki pants and ordered a bunch of Hawaiian shirts, he'd bundled it and his striped dress shirts off to Goodwill, swearing he wouldn't wear a suit until he got married. In like ten or twenty years.

"That's okay. I saw an ad for an end-of-season clearance at Dillard's. They always have suits on sale. Oh, you know, you'd look amazing in seersucker . . . with a bow tie. Have you ever worn suspenders?" Now her eyes had an almost manic look. It reminded him of the way her friend Rosemary had been all those years ago as the yearbook editor. Very managing. "It will be so much fun to dress you, Ryan."

"Suspenders and a bow tie?" He tried to hide his repulsion. "You do realize I'm trying to shed the nerd image, so please tell me you're joking."

"Oh no. I was thinking southern gentleman, not Urkel."

Dear God. He hadn't even agreed to accompany her, and she was planning his wardrobe for the weekend. The whole idea made him itchy, like he needed to loosen a collar even though he was wearing a V-neck T-shirt.

He knew what he felt, because he'd read several books about relationships. Smothering was a common complaint for a lot of guys. The number-one reason most relationships failed was financial issues. The second was an imbalance of power and lack of communication. A man could take a bossy woman for only so long, and since Ryan wasn't officially in a relationship with Jess, he certainly didn't need her trying to take over his life. "I don't need you to dress me, Jess."

She stopped the mental shopping in her head. "What?"

"I'm not your husband."

She looked stricken. "Oh God. I know that. I wasn't trying to . . . I mean, I thought I could make it easier for you to come with me. You know, 'cause guys don't like shopping."

"I'm grateful you're excited about helping me pick out a suit for a wedding I might not attend, but I am capable of shopping for myself. I spend a good deal of time reading *GQ*." Which he secretly didn't care for, but if he wanted to keep up with current trends, it was a go-to guide.

"But *GQ* isn't exactly southern couture," she said her voice trailing off. "Oh crap, you're right. It's a fault of mine, getting super-focused on something. I'm sorry. I don't know what I was thinking."

He waved his hand and stared down at his beef and broccoli. He felt like an asshole and didn't know how to fix the sudden tension. "No worries."

She set her fork down and pushed her chair back. "I made brownies. You want one?"

Ryan felt the air thicken even more and wished he could erase the last few things he'd said. Why had he said he wasn't her husband? The words had flown past his lips before he could think better of it. Absolute wrong thing to say. Damn it. Relationships were hard. Caring about someone tossed a whole new ball into the game . . . a game he'd never played. This was why he had engaged in casual sex. No strings. No effing shopping for a suit for a wedding. He pushed back his chair and stood, meeting her as she headed toward the kitchen. "Look, I'm sorry."

She brushed his hands away. "No, you're right. I shouldn't have—"

"No, you were trying to help me out. I get it. And I shouldn't have read something into it. I'm not used to being in a relationship."

"Is that what we're doing?" she asked, lifting her eyes to meet his gaze.

God, that was what they were doing. Temporarily, but, yeah, what they had was the definition of being in a relationship.

"I think so." No way he could deny it. In a relationship. Perhaps he could put that on his Facebook status. If he ever checked it again. The only social media he bothered with was Instagram, 'cause that was as easy as taking a picture.

"I'm sorry for allowing my control issues to jump out of the gate with the suit thing, but I can't be sorry for wanting you to go with me. I need you there. This is me being vulnerable, something I've been too much of lately, but at least I'm honest. I don't want you to go with me merely because you're gorgeous and will get more than a few second looks. I want you beside me because even though I'm starting to feel more myself again, I'm still not the Jess I want to be. But something about you makes me steady." Jess caught his hands and held them firm. Maybe she hadn't meant it as coercion, but those last words and the way she squeezed his fingers in an innocuous plea worked.

He pulled her into his arms, recognizing as he did every time how nicely she fit him. "I like you the way you are."

She shook her head. "I still feel so . . . weak. Before that asshole pulled the rug from beneath me and sent me sprawling, I was secure in exactly who I was. I rolled my eyes at sad women who couldn't suck it up and move on. But now I'm one of them. Or at least I was. Coming to Florida and helping a drunk up the stairs opened a window in my life. But still—"

"I'll go."

"You haven't had a brownie yet. Or dessert," she said, looking up at him and fluttering her eyelids. "Don't leave yet."

"No. I mean I'll go to the wedding with you."

Her eyes filled with gratitude before she held up a hand. "No. I made you feel sorry for me. The thing is, I should have enough gumption to go home and not worry about what people think. No crutches allowed." She pressed a kiss on his chin. "No matter how gorgeous the crutch is."

"That's true. You could go back, and you'd be fine. But I want to be your crutch even if I have to sit through a wedding and drink kava tea with my mother." He stifled his inner cringe at the thought of both things, clinging to the way her eyes had looked when he'd surrendered. He could do it for her.

"Are you sure? Because kava tea sounds gross."

"It's horrible, but I'm going with you." He gave her a squeeze, finding satisfaction in being a good boyfriend. Wait . . . was he her boyfriend? No titles yet. "But I draw the line at wearing seersucker. Or a bow tie."

"Of course," she said, pulling back and giving him a tremulous smile. "But only if you're sure?"

"Yes. I've read that when women feel supported by the men in their lives, it makes for a stronger relationship. Makes sense to me. I think."

Jess issued a soft laugh then laid her head against his shoulder. "This thing between us is new for me, too, but thank you for sacrificing your abhorrence of Morning Glory and weddings for me."

He rested his head against the softness of her hair. "You're welcome. I guess it won't be too bad, right? I can do anything for two days."

"Three."

Sighing, he repeated, "Three."

Chapter Thirteen

Morning Glory, Mississippi, was a quintessential southern town. Fast food restaurants nestled beside places that had once hosted women in pillbox hats. The Ford car dealership sported a group of old men around the coffeepot every day while the Chevrolet dealership offered free doughnuts to the older ladies who came every Wednesday to do Bible study in the back room. One out of every two people on the street might be related to you . . . or have taught you in elementary school, Sunday school, or art class at the rec center. Parades left the Greater Galilee Baptist Church and wound around the square to celebrate the county fair, homecoming, Christmas, or the rodeo before ending in front of the First United Methodist Church. The favored pastimes were gossiping, talking high school football, and bass fishing.

When she and Ryan passed the Welcome to Morning Glory sign, Jess got a warm glow. Ryan looked more like he had indigestion.

"Congrats, you did it," she teased, glancing toward where he sat in the passenger's seat. He'd been quiet most of the way, content to listen to the Doobie Brothers and Slim Pickens, which was a weird combination, in her opinion. But whatever made him happy. She wanted him to be as comfortable as possible.

The past few weeks had been very good. She'd moved into a condo that was newer than the Dirty Heron but smaller and not so close to the beach. She didn't spend much time there, because she liked sleeping next to Ryan and he needed his orthopedic mattress for his back. They settled into a nice pattern of working, making love, and getting to know each other better. Like she learned he hated oatmeal, reggae, and spiders. She taught him how to make her mother's famous spaghetti and meatballs, one of the few dishes she'd mastered, and he taught her how to skim board. Well, sorta. She wasn't good at it. He took her fishing, which she didn't like so much because the smell of the bait paired with the bobbing boat equaled extreme nausea. She loaned him her Lee Child book collection. They talked about pop culture, how nicely the begonia thrived, and the upcoming football season. They did not talk about definitions of their relationship or the future.

Or going back to Morning Glory.

"My mom said she'd leave a key beneath the turtle planter in case my dad isn't home yet," he said as she wound around the town square, soaking in her hometown, enjoying a Thursday afternoon.

"Look, there's Sal's pizza place," Jess said, pointing to Sal's New York Pizza, with its red awning. Rosemary had done a good job of helping her fiancé select lettering that was both welcoming and somewhat upscale. Once it was complete, it would give the town something nicer than Dean's Diner for a date night.

"There are some new places since I was last here. Turn on Market Street then take a right on Cedar." He pointed toward the small park that held a swing set and several metal slides. "I loved that little park. Sometimes my father took me for free play."

"Free play?"

"He read the paper while I was free to play whatever I wanted. Would have been easier to join in with the other kids if I hadn't been wearing the play clothes my mother made for me. She got the fabric from a discount store. I looked like a van of hippies had decorated me. My parents went through a phase requiring specific clothing to signify social situations. That was the year I had to wear a dinner jacket at the dining table."

Okay, she'd known Ryan's parents were a bit odd, but good Lord. "Interesting."

"Isn't it?" he drawled, softening the sarcasm with a smile.

"Are you really upset at having to stay with your parents? I couldn't ask Sal to vacate my place, especially since his parents are staying in the guest room. And my parents feel terrible about not being able to host us. They weren't expecting me home, and the painters already started last week."

"I know all this."

"I know you do. Makes me feel better to repeat it, though. Like it's more legit. I called the owner, but Sal's brothers and Rosemary's cousins still have all the rooms reserved at Polk House. She said she'd call if there's a cancellation. If I had—"

"Jess, I can deal. They're my parents, not prisons guards. We'll be fine."

She quieted and focused on remembering which house was Ryan's parents'. Cedar Street was lined with beautiful Craftsman houses with lush lawns and sculpted flower beds . . . except for one. She headed for that driveway.

Ryan's parents, Emilio and Martha Reyes, owned a house that could only be described as neglected. The yard was a tangle of grasses and sad, spindly bushes, and the eaves on the Craftsman had been painted a strange olive green while the door was lavender. Jess pulled her car next to the covered parking area and killed the engine. Ryan looked over at her. "Why did you pull into the McGuires' drive? My parents live across the street."

Jess started laughing. "Oh, thank God. This place is a mess."

"I'm joking. This is it."

"Oh."

Ryan smiled. "You wanted to bring me. You could have stayed with Rosemary."

Way to remind her. "I know. But maybe you can be a good son and mow your parents' lawn while you're here."

"Why? My father will let it go back to its natural state. He refuses to use pesticides or herbicides because they poison us slowly. That's why it's hard for him to accept that his genius son runs a fishing charter. What I'm supposed to be I should be. And according to him I'm supposed to be discovering new elements or curing cancer." Ryan gave a snort and then opened the car door.

Jess followed suit, wincing at the heat that greeted her. September held on to summer with both hands . . . and wore a cloak of humidity. Cool fronts always seemed to stall as they crossed the plains, leaving Mississippi nice and toasty for most of the month.

Jess sighed and pulled the keys from the ignition. *Okay, you're sleeping here. That's it. And these are Ryan's parents, and you lo—*

No. She didn't love Ryan. She liked him a lot, but this wasn't love. Couldn't be, because Ryan was her rebound guy. She knew the rules about jumping back in with both feet when a gal got her heart broken. Of course, playing by the rules and having a game plan hadn't worked out too well for her with Benton.

Don't think. Uh, coast on the high windy current, like Lacy suggested.

"Found the key," Ryan said, dangling it from his fingers.

Jess hoped his mother didn't believe in not cleaning the house, because she could overlook a jungle outside her window as long as she could actually see out the window. She sighed in relief when she walked through the purple door to find the house clean, tidy, and smelling of lemons. The furniture looked functional and the parquet floors original. Decorating wasn't a priority in the Reyes house. Jess's mother would have hyperventilated over the ceramic chandelier with parrot heads on it and the . . . zero-gravity pool recliners in front of a really old TV?

"Ryan," someone said over her shoulder, making her jump with fright. She turned to find Ryan's father standing in what looked to be the kitchen doorway.

Emilio Reyes was a spare man of Hispanic descent who had dark skin and a high brow with bushy eyebrows. Neither handsome nor homely, he looked like the comedian from *Saturday Night Live* and *Portlandia* . . . uh, Fred Armisen. He wore tan trousers, a cream button-down short-sleeve shirt, and square tortoiseshell glasses. He wasn't nerdy chic in the least. Just nerdy.

"Hello, Father," Ryan said, donning a neutral expression. Gone was his boyish charm. In its place emerged a dutiful son.

"You're here early. I didn't expect you until after dinner sometime. Figured you get in some work this morning. I believe most fishing is done early. Oh, and is this your lover?" Emilio asked, turning his eyes on her.

Ryan's mouth twitched. She wanted to kick him for finding amusement in the situation.

"Hello, Mr. Reyes. I'm Ryan's *girlfriend*, Jess. You probably know my parents—the Culpeppers. My daddy's a dentist?"

"Oh, you're from here? Ryan didn't say that," his father said, blinking myopically at Ryan. "We use Dr. Hiedel."

"Well, he's a nice man, too." Not nearly as smart, pleasant, or accommodating as her father, but she'd try not to hold the Reyeses' choice in dentistry against them.

Ryan's father cleared his throat. "So you know, Ryan, your mother turned your room into a yoga studio last summer. Something about the position of the sun. Of course, she didn't stop paying for yoga classes over at the Church of Christ. The home yoga studio was supposed to save us money. You'll have to stay in the guest room. Or the use the old pullout in the den."

"Wait. A yoga studio? What did you do with all my stuff?" Ryan asked, his face growing panicked. "There were things in there I wanted to keep."

"In the attic, I guess. Or your mother donated them to the high school for their rummage sale. There seemed to be a lot of toys and things you've outgrown."

"Oh God. My comic books and Pokémon cards." Ryan lurched toward the dim hallway to their right, disappearing into the darkness and leaving her with his father. Mr. Reyes smiled at her and lifted his eyebrows in an *I don't know what's going on* gesture. Jess gave him an awkward smile and prayed for rescue from the uncomfortable situation.

"While Ryan's checking out his mother's studio, can I get you something to drink? Or if you want a sandwich, we have Vegemite. The lavatory's right over there if you need to make use of the facilities."

Jess shook her head and prayed Ryan would come back to save her. Instead her cell phone rang. She riffled through her bag and pulled it out. Eden.

Thank you, sweet merciful Jesus.

"Excuse me, Mr. Reyes, I need to take this," Jess said before stepping back toward the very brown foyer. "Hi, E."

"Oh my God, are you home yet?"

"Indeed I am," Jess said, pulling open the purple door and stepping out onto a porch that could have been stinkin' cute but instead held a pile of leaves in the corner and a few tenacious weeds creeping through the solid planking. "Where are you?"

"At work, but I'm about to get off. Want to meet me at the Lazy Frog?"

"A million times yes."

"You think your boy toy will want to come, too?"

Jess started at Eden's name for him, wondering if that's what everyone would think. She didn't want Ryan to feel like that's what he was. She glanced back at the front door. "Uh, I'll ask him, but I think he'll be too busy here." Finding his collectibles. You can take the boy out of nerddom, but you can't take the nerddom out of the boy. She'd found his Dr. Who collection, gamer magazines, and odd spreadsheets on sexual positions, pool shots, and volume of fish per square mile in the Gulf of Mexico hidden in his apartment. If she were a high-stakes gambler, she'd put a hundred on Ryan climbing into the attic within the hour.

"I can't wait to see you," Eden said with such warmth in her voice. "I mean, I love Rose, but it's been wedding this, Sal that. I've had enough pizza for a lifetime. She brings me a slice every time Sal tries a new specialty pie. I've gained five pounds."

"Pizza sounds good."

"No. We're not eating pizza tonight. For the love of God. I just can't."

Jess laughed. "I'll meet you in thirty minutes. Will that work?"

"Make it an hour. I have to close the register and run to the bank before it closes."

"See you soon."

Jess hung up and with a soft knock pushed back into the Reyes home. Emilio had settled onto the velvet couch with the *Morning Glory Herald* and the *Clarion-Ledger*. Ryan sat in an ancient green tweed chair, hands clasped between his knees. He didn't look happy. "There you are."

Jess held up her phone. "Eden. She wants to meet me at the Lazy Frog in about an hour. I haven't seen her in a month, so I told her I would. You're welcome to come with me."

His brow furrowed. "What's the Lazy Frog?"

"You don't know where the Lazy Frog is? It's been here since we were in elementary school. You didn't ever go for ice cream when you were a kid?"

"Too much sugar," Emilio Reyes said, licking his finger and turning the page. He didn't look up.

Jess mouthed, "Seriously?" to Ryan. He nodded. She shrugged and said, "You should come."

At that he wiggled his eyebrows and gave her a half-lidded stare. To which she mouthed, "Pervert." That made him smile and look like the sexy Ryan she knew, not the one who'd shit a brick when he found out his mother might have sold his collectibles in a rummage sale. His crocodile smile soothed her. It would be okay. He was the same guy who alphabetized his canned goods and made love to her under the walkway to the beach. Nothing was different. "I'll go, but my mother will be home soon. She always comes in the door at—"

"Four fifteen," his father finished, lowering the paper to smile at Ryan. "You can set the clock by that woman."

It was the first sense of easing Jess had. In the conspiratorial smile shared with his son, Jess saw all she needed to see regarding Emilio's affection for his son and wife. No matter how kooky and dysfunctional the Reyeses were, they loved each other . . . and they loved their son. Ryan might have hang-ups about their parenting style and overall oddness, but Jess hadn't missed the happiness in Emilio's eyes when he first saw Ryan.

So why didn't Ryan know this? His parents were as sore a subject as the town, but other than being . . . uh, different, Emilio seemed happy to have his son home. Hmm . . . she'd wait and see how the dynamics played out before questioning him. At the moment, she wanted to ease him into the environment.

"Eden can't be there for an hour, and I want to meet your mother before I go," Jess said, walking toward the front door. "Let's get our bags and get settled in."

"Dad?" Ryan asked, turning toward his father. "Is it okay if Jess and I share a room?"

Jess hadn't even thought about their sleeping arrangements. She'd assumed that since both she and Ryan were consenting adults they would share a bed, but the thoughtfulness and respect in Ryan's question made her heart warm.

"I don't see a problem. You're no longer a boy, and I'm assuming by your question that you and your lady friend frequently engage in sexual—"

"That's good, Dad," Ryan interrupted, his green eyes growing big. "No need to go into detail."

"Don't be embarrassed. Sexual attraction is a perfectly healthy inclination for individuals in your particular age group. Your mother and I celebrate your choice to engage in this natural—"

"Dad!" Ryan barked. "You're embarrassing Jess."

Jess wasn't embarrassed, merely uncomfortable at Ryan's father discussing their propensity to jump each other's bones regularly. Sure, it was natural and healthy . . . but she didn't want to discuss it with her *lover's* father. She'd probably need something stronger than coffee. Maybe she could talk Ryan into stopping by the Pak-n-Sak for a pint of whiskey. She glanced at her watch.

Four fifteen.

The kitchen door opened. "Yoo-hoo, I'm home!"

Yep, like clockwork.

⌘

Ryan shifted uncomfortably in the small wire chair in the middle of the ice cream-and-coffee shop. He should probably get used to it—lots of discomfort was headed his way if the last few hours were any indication.

His mother had sold his stuff. All of it. When she'd broken that news over kava tea and gingersnaps, he'd nearly exploded with fury. For years, his stuff had been his one source of pride. While other boys built their egos on catching footballs or driving a jacked-up truck, he'd ruled his own geeky world with a vast collection of rare comic books, mostly scored from his father, and collectible figures he'd purchased with the money given to him by his grandmother each birthday and Christmas. Other boys with the same propensity to collect *Star Wars* action figures and Spider-Man comics regarded Ryan as the balls. And his mother had sold it all. In a goddamn rummage sale to benefit the baseball team. The baseball team! She'd relayed the fact that Trent Mason, Benton's nephew, had bought most of them, as if that would be consolation for the loss. The little bastard probably sold them on eBay for a fortune.

"Rosemary just texted me. She's on her way down," Eden said, smiling at him with eyes that looked too violet to be real. "Do you remember Rosemary?"

Ryan blinked. "Prissy-Pants Reynolds?"

Jess laughed. "Ryan was on the yearbook staff. Photographer."

"Oh," Eden said, nodding as if she understood. "Rosemary really wanted to win that state award. It was her biggest goal that year. Well, second biggest." She and Jess exchanged a secret look, smiling.

"So what do you do, Eden?" Ryan asked, remembering to make conversation. Sometimes it was hard to remember the rules of society. Especially when he wanted to sulk about the enormous loss he'd experienced mere hours ago. His telescoping Darth Vader lightsaber circa 1978 was worth $6,000 alone. Made his stomach hurt.

Eden's pretty eyes shuttered. "I'm a manager at Penny Pinchers."

"That must be interesting," he said politely.

"Nope. Not at all."

He shouldn't have tried to make conversation with her. Here, he was out of his element. He felt stiff, like he wore a pair of new blue jeans that wouldn't bend when he sat down. The Ryan he'd been in Pensacola had vanished after only a few hours back in Morning Glory. He couldn't find the charm he'd conjured over the past few years, and his mojo was flat on the floor, pinned beneath the oppression that was Morning Glory. Why had he agreed to this?

Because of her.

He looked at Jess. She looked happy . . . thrilled . . . in her element.

The door to the Lazy Frog flew open. "Jess!"

Rosemary Reynolds tumbled inside, auburn hair bouncing, hands outstretched. "You're back home!"

Jess squealed. He hadn't known she was capable, but the high-pitched frequency probably had the dogs two counties over howling. Then she started singing, "Here Comes the Bride," and Ryan checked his arms for hives. Okay, not really, but he was taken aback by the exuberance.

"Oh my goodness," Rosemary said, unwinding her arms from around Jess's neck and setting her hands on her hips, gaze on him. "Look at you, Ryan Reyes."

He didn't know whether to smile like some greasy Casanova and say, "Yes, look at me, darling," or pretend he wasn't there. He went with the latter.

"Ryan," Jess chided, encouraging his response.

"Oh yes. Hi, Rosemary. Nice to see you again. Congratulations on your impending nuptials." He smiled and tried not to feel like the spaz he used to be.

"Thank you," she said with a laugh, giving Jess a look that said, *high five, my friend.*

The girls lapsed into another conversation that made him imagine being on the trading floor of the stock exchange. There were lots of exclamation points used, and they talked over one another as if there were so much to be said they couldn't wait their turn. And he didn't understand much of it, so he sipped his latte and studied the cartoon rendering of frogs jumping onto lily pads that had been painted on the wall. After a few minutes, he realized they were no longer talking. They were staring at him.

He felt like a cornered fox and darted his eyes back and forth. "What?"

"Tomorrow night," Rosemary said, trying to help him out, but he had no clue what they'd been talking about. His former yearbook editor had rounded out and grown softer in her look. Her hair was the same shade of reddish brown, and the light sprinkling of freckles gave her a mischievous look. Her eyes, however, had the same tenacity. He remembered how determined she could be. *I know you've worked hard, but all of these will have to be retaken. Sorry.*

"I'm sorry. I didn't hear the question," he said, folding his hands around the cup so he wouldn't fidget.

Rosemary's brow furrowed, and she said, "Tomorrow night after the rehearsal we're going to the Iron Bull. The girls wanted to give me a bachelorette party, so we're going dancing. I don't want anything risqué."

"Not until the wedding night." Eden snickered.

Ryan pulled at his T-shirt. He didn't want to be here. He should have stayed back at his parents', but he was so angry with his mother, he was afraid he might say something he couldn't take back. "That's fine. Jess doesn't have to check with me."

"I know," Rosemary said, tapping his arm lightly. "But the guys are going, too. Sal doesn't know a ton of people here in Morning Glory. He's only been here a little over a month, and during that time he's been working super hard on the restaurant. I'd love it if you'd come, too. Celebrate a little with him?"

"At the Iron Bull?" he repeated before catching himself. He sounded like a tool. Like a guy who hadn't spent a majority of his nights in various beachside bars for the last year and a half. The nightlife was his arena, a place where he bought drinks, danced with hot girls, and charmed them out of their too-tight jeans. Well, he had until Jess tripped over him on the beach. So why couldn't he hang at the local watering hole? "Sure. If it's okay with Sal."

"Speaking of the devil," Eden said, pointing out the clear swinging door to the man angling toward the Lazy Frog.

Sal Genovese was a big guy with broad shoulders, an Italian nose, and thick brows. He looked a bit like that *Friends* character—one of the shows Ryan had found fascinating when studying pop culture—with the toughness of Al Pacino. He wore a rock concert T-shirt and paint-stained shorts. The work boots weren't something Ryan would have worn, but they were probably practical in nature rather than a fashion statement.

"Well, I guess you're a happy girl," Sal said, dropping a kiss on her head before snagging a chair from a nearby table and sitting on it backward. He grinned and then noticed Ryan there. "Oh, man. Ryan, right? I'm Sal. Rosemary's ball and chain."

"Soon-to-be ball and chain," Rosemary said, tapping his arm.

Sal held his hand out to Ryan, and he took it. The man's grip was solid and warm, and the slight hint of yeast accompanied it. "It's good to meet you, guy."

"You, too. I'm Ryan Reyes."

"Yeah, I know. These girls have been talking about you like you're the second coming, you know." The man grinned, showing lots of white teeth. Ryan wondered if Sal had used whitening strips, too.

"Well, if you'd known Ryan when he went to school with us, you'd understand. Him turning out so delicious is . . . well, so delicious," Jess said, rubbing his thigh. Her touch felt good. It said, *You are one of us.*

But he wasn't.

At all.

"People change," Ryan said for lack of anything better.

"Do they really?" Eden asked, swirling her melting mint chocolate chip ice cream around in the cup. "I mean, physically sure. Look at Candy Simpson. She looks nothing like her eleventh-grade yearbook photo, but down deep we stay the same."

Jess glanced over at him, and he could read her look. Okay, so he'd freaked out about his mother selling his Super Geek Collection (as he'd dubbed it in his mind) and he tried to hide his intellect behind dude stuff. He knew he really didn't care anything about Tom Brady's reception percentage or whatever they called it in fantasy football. And he would much rather watch a documentary than *Sex and the City*, a show Jess seemed to have a fondness for. But he wasn't a dork.

Or was he?

The thing was, Jess knew his propensities to watch educational television and get lost in MMORPGs and still wanted to be with him. Hell, she'd begged him to come here with her. But if he were the same inside, what did that make Jess? When she'd been in school with him, she'd been this überconfident cool chick. Her only weakness had been Benton Mason. Whenever the star football player crooked his finger, she came running like a lapdog . . . much the way he'd done when she crooked her finger at him. Maybe the reason he had tossed his convictions about coming back to Morning Glory out the window was because he couldn't tell her no. Not all those years ago. And not now. Maybe she was his Achilles' heel. And maybe he was in love with the idea of having the ideal girl he'd built in his mind all those years ago more than he was with Jess. Of course, he wasn't in love. Not much. Perhaps infatuated, but love like his parents had? No.

So if all this was true, how would Jess react when she saw Benton again? What if the man who'd thrown his wife away crooked his finger again? Would she go? Because if people didn't change, how could Jess be truly free of Benton?

"Hey, man, you want to leave the girls here and come with me? I've been renovating an old bank here, turning it into my restaurant. You can come take a look. It's really cool. We just installed the awning and have a few more coats of paint to do in the bathroom, but it's almost ready to go. Besides, I've been working on the menu, and I have a Cajun pizza I designed today. I need taste testers." Sal looked like an eager dog. *Come play with me.*

Ryan looked at the three girls. Rosemary had pulled out her phone and was showing them pictures of the wedding cake with filigree frosting. "And look at this. These are the napkins I ordered. Do you think the gilded font is too much? My mother said it was, but I love how neutral metallics are now," she said, swiping her phone.

Ryan looked back at Sal. "Yes, please."

Sal slapped his hands together. "Okay, we're out. Later, ladies."

The three girls barely looked up as the two men rose. But the screech of Ryan's chair on the floor caused Jess to look up. Her amber eyes glowed with such tenderness. She reached out a hand and gave Ryan's arm a squeeze. She didn't say anything else, settling on a sweet smile before she turned her attention back to pictures of cocktail napkins.

Sal pushed out into the heat. "Jesus, I can't get used to the heat down here. I always thought the city was hotter than shit, but this place is soul sucking. The heat, that is. Actually, I like the rest of it."

Ryan fell into step beside Sal, liking the easy nature of the man. This man was likely comfortable in his own skin no matter where he went. Made friends easily. Probably had a big, noisy family and the ability to blend into whatever social situation. He'd probably never drunk kava tea or had play clothes with weird mushrooms on them. "You like it here?"

Sal shrugged. "Rosemary's here. And, yeah, I always wanted to live in a community like this. No taxis trying to mow you down, garbage in the street, and sirens twenty-four seven. We're going to have a yard. I'm looking forward to that."

Ryan nodded.

A mailman spotted Sal across the square and made a beeline for both men.

"Uh-oh, here comes Fred," Sal said, sounding a bit weary.

"Fred?"

"I thought you were from here? Fred Odom. Can't get away from the son of a gun once he gets to going. Better hurry. Once I'm inside the restaurant, he won't bother us. Step it up," Sal said, lengthening his stride and digging keys out of his pocket.

They'd just reached the locked door of Sal's New York Pizza when the chatty mailman Ryan didn't remember appeared, calling out, "Sal. Wait a minute. I have something to tell you."

"Shit," Sal whispered under his breath. Turning, he donned a big smile. "Yo, Mr. Odom, how's things?"

"Good, good." The mailman wiped his sweaty, bald head, noticing Ryan. "Oh, hey, I'm Fred Odom. You must be a friend of Sal's here for the wedding."

"No. I'm Ryan Reyes, and actually I used to—"

"Oh, of course, Martha's boy. The one who discovered stem cells! Well, I'll be."

"No, I didn't discover stem cells, merely a bio—"

"Same thing," Fred interrupted, giving a wave before wiping his bald head again. Then he smoothed down his bristly mustache. "I hear you came home with the Culpepper girl. Her mama told Stewart Wilson over at the Piggly Wiggly that you two have been seeing each other. Poor girl, after what Benton Mason did to her."

Ryan looked at Sal, who now stood behind Fred. Sal made talking hands . . . and a face that said, *Sorry we weren't fast enough, bud.*

"It's good running into you, Fred, but I have to help Sal hang something," Ryan said, lying like a dog. He'd forgotten how bad gossip could be in a small town, especially when there was a mailman who delivered juicy tidbits along with his mail. He pulled at the neck of his T-shirt again. Stifling.

"Sal, I came to tell you that while I was delivering mail over at the B and B—that's bed-and-breakfast, you know," Fred said, pausing so Sal could acknowledge the explanation. Sal nodded. "Well, anyway, while

I was there, your mama and the rest of your family arrived. Thought you'd want to know. Your mama's a right nice woman, and she looks a lot like you. Go on and get back to work. Everyone in Morning Glory is looking forward to sampling some real, legitimate New York pizza pie."

"Great. Thanks," Sal said, slapping the man on the back and darting into the now open restaurant door like squirrel escaping traffic. "Later."

With a nod to Fred, Ryan followed, and for the sixteenth time that day wondered why in the hell he'd agreed to come back to Morning Glory.

Chapter Fourteen

The hot-pink dress was too loose on Jess, but Rosemary whipped it off her and had the material under the foot of her sewing machine before Jess could refasten her bra.

Jess had spent Friday morning with her parents, touring the renovation they were doing on their 1920s Queen Anne house with its whimsical gingerbread trim and two turrets. Jess's bedroom had been in one of the turrets, and she'd curl up in the window seat reading *Sweet Valley High* books along with all Anne Rice's vampire novels. A fanciful house for a not-so-fanciful girl . . . on the surface. But Lacy had been right. Beneath Jess's no-nonsense demeanor beat the heart of a romantic. Her parents had been thrilled to see her. Her mother in particular had been ecstatic to see Ryan. She'd insisted on taking him to lunch at the Feedhouse, a barbecue place that had opened up near Lake Powhatan. Ryan had received more than a number of double takes. Jess would be willing to bet the town was already humming about the hunky former nerd . . . and how he'd shown up with poor Jess Culpepper. The thought of everyone gossiping about them made her uncomfortable, especially after last night's dinner with Ryan's parents. Ryan had relayed that Fred Odom, nosiest mailman in the whole state, had said something about her and the way Benton had dumped her. Yeah, they'd stolen some of Rosemary and Sal's spotlight. At least until the Elvis impersonator showed up.

"I can't believe how much weight you lost last year," Rosemary mumbled, pins clamped between her lips. "It's so not fair."

"Well, marry Sal and then in six years have him come in and tell you all this was a big mistake and see how your appetite is then," Jess said, wrapping up in the robe Rosemary kept in the dressing room of Parsley and Sage, her fabric and sewing shop. Often Rosemary did alterations or sewed costumes for the local high school productions, so she had a small tri-mirrored platform for fittings in the back of the shop. Several quilted pillows for her new venture with a New York City designer sat in piles along the mirrors.

"Point made," she said, narrowing her eyes as she took in the waist of the satin dress.

"But I've put on a few pounds since I hooked up with Ryan."

"Need plenty of nourishment, do you?" Rosemary asked, looking up and shooting her a half grin. The other side of her mouth still held the pins.

"Not just that, though that is really good, but he makes me happy," Jess said, sinking into the lone stuffed chair in the corner. Up front Lorraine worked the store as she hummed a Beatles tune. Eden had slipped off to give her mama the medicine she needed before the girls got dressed for the rehearsal that evening. They'd spent the afternoon helping Rosemary prepare small gifts for the wedding guests and oohing and ahhing over the vintage wedding dress Mimi had given to Rosemary. Her friend's older next-door neighbor had once lived in Chicago as the mistress to a railroad baron. When she'd married Ed Griggs and moved to Morning Glory, she'd stored all her fabulous clothing in her rambling antebellum house. The woman had no children, so she treated Rosemary as a granddaughter. Which meant Rosemary had played in Chanel and Dior as a teen.

The day had been nice, but still Jess felt so unsettled. She'd thought she'd be happy being back in Morning Glory, but instead she longed to hear the ocean crash on the beach and sip wine with Ryan while he gave her a foot rub. So odd to feel discomfort in the place she'd always thought she belonged. But everything felt so different.

"So I see," Rosemary said, turning the dress in order to take in the other side of the bodice. "And what about Benton?"

"What about him?"

"Are you prepared to see him again?"

"I don't want to, because I still want to kick him in the balls. But I suppose I must, so . . ."

"Are you still in love with him?"

"No."

Rosemary took her foot off the sewing machine pedal and looked up. Taking the pins from her mouth, she popped them into the giant tomato pincushion that had once been her nana's. "You said that very quickly."

"Because it's true."

"I'm not sure I could ever stop loving Sal." Rosemary pressed her hands against her worktable. Jess didn't like the way her friend looked at her. Like she knew so much about love. Sure, Rosemary couldn't imagine anything going sour with Sal. She stood on the cusp of the best two days of her life, deeply and profoundly in love with her New Yorker. But Jess had once been there. The day she'd walked down the aisle to Benton, she could never imagine a life different from waking up to him every morning, having his children, sitting out in their rockers as the grandkids hid Easter eggs. At that moment on her daddy's arm, not loving Benton was inconceivable.

But now, she knew, as her granny often said, "there's many a slip between the cup and the lip."

"Part of me will always love Benton. He was my first love, and we had a lot of good times. But sometimes life doesn't give us what we think we should have. Coming to terms with the anger over not getting what I thought I deserved has been half the battle. A relationship gives not just love but a sense of well-being. I missed that as much as I missed Benton."

Rosemary sighed. "I can't imagine what you've gone through. I mean, I know. I was there, but when I think about this past year, I can't grasp being you, Jess."

"I'm stronger now. I am. And I feel like I'm truly over it. I'll admit, I sorta begged Ryan to come with me. Somehow having him here with me when I face all that I was makes me feel more solid. Does that make sense?"

Rosemary nodded, flipping the dress right side out again. "It does. And I can see a change in you. Your eyes are clearer, and you smile a lot. That's a good thing."

"I can't help it. Ryan makes me smile. He's so funny and charming. He gets me and still gives me plenty of breathing room."

"Do you think you could fall in love with him?" Rosemary asked, holding the dress out to Jess.

Love. It was the word floating around above her. The last time she'd been in love it had been easy. Benton had always been there, filling up the spaces. He was a given in her life. But she'd chosen Ryan. And he'd chosen her. He had a lot of women to pick from—they swarmed him like honeybees—but he'd picked her. Something about having free choice in choosing to be with someone and not falling into something because it was comfortable seemed more legitimate. As for love, she wasn't sure. Maybe her definition of love had changed. Maybe love wasn't so much about the future as it was the now. Perhaps love wasn't as hard as everyone made it out to be.

Did she love Ryan?

That was the question.

"I think I could," she said finally.

Rosemary lifted an eyebrow. "You think?"

"I don't know. Love isn't like the chicken pox. You don't get symptoms that tell you what it is," Jess said, unwinding the robe and shimmying into the dress. The pink looked good against her tan, and thanks to the Florida sun, her brown hair had nice natural honey highlights.

"Yeah, you do," Rosemary said, eyeing her critically as she zipped the dress. "You can't think about anyone else. All you do is obsess about the way he smiles. The way he touches you. His kiss. The tight ass. The—"

"TMI," Jess said, holding up a hand and laughing.

"Okay, okay. But, hey, the dress looks perfect, and you look like one hot mama," Rosemary said, twisting one of Jess's curls. "Maybe it's not love if you have to think about it too much."

"It's *not* love. I don't want it to be love. Yeah, I do all those things you think about, hard ass included—but this is infatuation. It's a rebound. You don't fall in love with your rebound, no matter how awesome he is," Jess said, turning to admire the cut of the dress in the mirror. Cap sleeves, scooped neck, pleated cummerbund that nipped her waist before flaring out in a bell. Rosemary had bought fluffy slips to hold the dress form. It fell to tea length, as Rosemary deemed appropriate for her late-afternoon wedding.

"There aren't any rules, Jess," Rosemary said, adjusting the hem. "I know that disappoints a cut-and-dried girl like you. Love doesn't find you when you want it to. Nope, it slams into you and holds you hostage. Stop trying to put rules into place."

"You sound like Lacy," Jess snorted, unzipping the bridesmaid's dress.

Rosemary's eyes met her in the mirror. "Good."

Friday night at the Iron Bull meant a gal had to leave her sandals at home. Tons of cowboys and good ol' southern boys crowded into the local watering hole looking for cold beer and hot women. Which meant a lot of boots. Jess elected to wear a pair of pumps with a short dress that worked equally well for rehearsal dinner and navigating the nightlife at the honky-tonk.

"Looks hopping," Jess remarked, offering Big Jerry her hand for the stamp that would glow under the black light. "Let's get our crunk on."

"Does anybody say that anymore?" Eden laughed.

"Probably not. I'm not up on hip jargon. Don't be throwing shade on me," Jess said, wagging her head in a snappy way. Her hoop earrings hit her neck because she'd worn her hair up, letting tendrils fall sexily from the topknot.

"You're so weird," Rosemary said, her gaze searching the room, no doubt for Sal. The guys, Ryan included, had left earlier while the girls went back to change. Or rather, Rosemary went back to change. The bride-to-be wore a maxi dress she'd bought in SoHo and looked suitably glowing.

If things felt weird being back in Morning Glory, being with her girls felt right as rain. Jess had enjoyed being with Eden and Rosemary. Even the weird food Ryan's parents cooked hadn't dampened her spirits. She and Ryan had squeezed into the double bed in the guest bedroom, snuggled under the quilt his grandmother had made and had gratifying, quiet sex. Ryan had said he felt very naughty doing it under his parents' roof, but something about the subterfuge made it exciting. She'd had to cover her own mouth more than once as he whispered all his high school fantasies about what he wanted to do to her in her ear. They'd woken late, Ryan spooning her, and promptly had more whispery morning sex. She'd emerged from her morning shower feeling pretty damn good.

Even now, as her gaze snagged on him, leaning against the rough bar, talking to Sal, her heart got warm and gooey. He looked particularly yummy, too. He'd bought some plain-front khakis and wore a turquoise gingham shirt that made his eyes brighter against his tan. Next to Sal's rough-around-the-edges sexiness, Ryan looked together and polished. He made Jess long to mess him up a little.

"Jess."

She stiffened at the familiar voice. But there was no avoiding him. She turned to find Benton standing behind her, holding a beer. He'd grown a goatee, something she'd always hated on him, and smiled at her as if she were a long-lost friend and not the woman he'd divorced.

"Benton."

"I figured I'd see you here," he said, his gaze dropping to take in her dress. She'd worn the dress she'd bought the first week in Pensacola, the one that was a bit short and showed off her legs. She could see the appreciation in Benton's eyes, which made her angry. He didn't have the right to appreciate her assets any more. "You look good."

"Thank you." She didn't say anything more. Wasn't making it easy for him. That was the problem—she'd always made life easier for Benton. She filled in awkward conversations, gave him way too many passes, and buttered his toast each morning. Jess had let Benton get away with being a lazy-assed husband who glommed everything she had and gave little in return.

"How is Florida?"

"Very nice. I'm really enjoying the work again," she said, catching Eden's eye. Both Rosemary and Eden had stopped in their progress toward the rest of the wedding party. "I have to go."

Benton nodded, and she noted he needed a haircut. His hair curled at the neckline, and his cowlick stuck up. His shirt wasn't ironed, either, something she'd always done for him. He'd lost weight but still looked like the man she'd once loved. "It was good seeing you, Jess. Did you get my flowers?"

She nodded. "Mrs. Giambi in Room 323 really enjoyed them."

Jess walked away, even after seeing the flash of pain in Benton's eyes. *That's right, buddy. I didn't keep your fucking flowers celebrating the tender innocence of our budding love in the ninth grade. Not when you brought me more fucking flowers put together by the woman you were screwing to tell me you didn't love me anymore. You don't get to bring me flowers anymore, asshole.*

"Crap," Eden breathed, "you were cold as ice. That was awesome."

Jess found Ryan with her gaze again. He'd been watching her. She smiled at him, telling her with her eyes that he was her focal point. Ryan was the man who'd picked her up, brushed her off, and made her totally whole again. Okay, he hadn't done it all. Wasn't like she had to have a man to feel her worth, but having Ryan helped.

"You made it," Sal said, pulling Rosemary to him and giving her a sweet kiss. "You want a drink? It's your bachelorette party, and you should get bombed."

Rosemary pinched him, but rose on her tiptoes to give him another kiss. "Do you know what I look like after I've gotten bombed?"

"Yeah. I remember. Sorta pasty and green about the gills."

"Exactly," she said with a smile. "I'm having two drinks tonight. No more. I want to look my best when I marry you tomorrow."

Jess pretended to stick her finger down her throat.

Eden giggled then said, "Uh, I'm the only single one here. Why don't you have any single brothers, Sal? They're all so cute and taken."

"My mom pairs us up as newborns. I got lucky and got away," Sal said, giving Rosemary a soft smile. Jess almost made the gagging motion again, but both she and Eden knew about Sal's mother and the woman she'd tried to marry him off to.

Sal's brothers arrived along with several of Rosemary's cousins. Her mother had tried to horn in on the outing, but Rosemary had put her foot down. Jess's once reticent friend did that more frequently now. Sal had a positive effect on Rose.

Ryan caressed her waist, and she leaned in to him.

"Drink?" he asked in a low voice.

"Sure. I'll take a tequila shot," she said.

Ryan raised his eyebrows and then turned toward the bartender.

"I'm joking. Just get me a beer. You know what I like," she said, enjoying that he did indeed know what she liked. Over the course of the last three hours of rehearsal and dinner, Ryan had had to field lots of questions regarding his transformation into stud muffin, leaving the scientific world, and, from all the men present, the species of fish he most often caught in the Gulf. Once they made it to fishing, he relaxed into the charming, carefree man she'd first met. But still, she could feel the tightness in his body. Coming to Morning Glory had been harder on him than she'd thought. At times she could sense him shutting down, and it made her wonder who he truly was beneath his carefully designed facade. How much baggage did he carry about his past? She'd been so focused on her own healing, they'd not talked much about his feelings about growing up in a world that wasn't forgiving of being different.

Ryan ordered them both a beer, and then the others arrived. For the next half hour, they chatted with the wedding party, some people breaking off to dance when the band struck up a fun song. Eventually, Sal and his brothers eyed the pool tables in the back of the bar. Ryan looked at her questioningly, and she said, "Go kick some ass and make a little money."

"The hell he will," Sal laughed, slapping Ryan on the back as he followed his brothers to the tables. "I can shoot a combo with my eyes closed."

Ryan glanced back at Jess with a gleam in his eyes. She'd seen his spreadsheet and watched him study shots on an Internet forum for billiard enthusiasts. Ryan was a scientist who calculated every shot. Sal would likely eat his words.

"I really like Ryan," Rosemary said, watching the guys as they disappeared into the throng of Friday night revelers.

"Me, too," Eden said, sipping her white zinfandel. Her cute dark pageboy framed her dramatic eyes with their too-long lashes. She looked like an advertisement for mascara. "I still can't get over how gorgeous he is. I want to ask him to take his shirt off . . ."

Jess made a face at Rosemary, who smiled.

Eden blinked. "Did I say that out loud?"

Jess laughed. "You want me to ask him to take it off for you?"

Her friend looked alarmed. "No. Oh, I really didn't mean to say that. Oh crap. Damn. It's Gary! Hide me."

"Gary your boss?" Rosemary asked, craning her head and spotting the balding man who liked to stare at Eden's boobs and sometimes say inappropriate things like, "It's so hot in here," while he stared at Eden's butt. "Ugh, he looks even grosser than he did in high school. And bald. And what the heck is he wearing?"

"A black leather jacket," Eden said, giving a little shiver. "He bought it on eBay. Said it's a motorcycle jacket. He got a Harley in July, and now he's thinking of getting a tattoo. Wanted to know if I would help him pick one out that was badass."

"Oh God," Jess said, wrinkling her nose. Gary was the bane of Eden's existence, but her friend couldn't quit her job because of the benefits and flexibility with her schedule. Until Eden's sister moved back, she was stuck at Penny Pinchers.

"Ladies," Benton said, swooping into the open spot where they were viewing Gary trying to put the vibe out to the soccer moms at the end of the bar who looked to be having a girls' night.

Jess drew back in horror. Like in a movie when a spider dropped onto someone.

"Hey, Benton," Rosemary said, not looking happy to be interrupted by him. None of the girls had said much of anything to Jess's ex-husband. They stood in solidarity even if it looked rude to everyone else. Her friends knew the heartbreak Jess had endured.

"What do you want?" Eden asked, her blue eyes growing ice chips.

"I'm just saying hello to some of my favorite girls in town," Benton said, donning his good-old-boy smile. It had gotten him a lot of stuff in life—job interviews, free tickets to State games, and women.

"We're your favorite?" Rosemary asked, her lips flattening. "I hear differently. Who are you on now, Benton? Mallory Simon? Thought that was your latest. Hope you're getting tested monthly."

Jess choked on her beer, and it went up her nose. She started coughing as fire burned her nostrils.

"Here," Benton said, lifting a napkin to her mouth. "Breathe, babe, breathe."

Jess pushed his hand away and took the napkin. *Babe?* What the hell was he doing? "I'm fine. Stop."

He pulled his hands away and looked concerned. Then he turned to Rosemary. "I'm not dating anyone right now, Rosemary, but I do appreciate you looking out for my health."

Rosemary didn't say anything. Just glared at him. Jess took a moment to admire the new sass in her friend. She had always known Rose had a wicked side. It was nice to see her unleash it in public.

"Again," Eden said, "what do you want?"

Benton ignored Eden and looked at Jess. "Can we talk?"

"I don't think so. I'm spending tonight with Rosemary. It's her night." Jess gave her friend a smile.

"Please. I have some things I want to say to you, and I want to do that face-to-face. How about a dance? I can do it over a dance," he said, gesturing to the crowded dance floor.

Jess didn't want him to touch her, but she knew Benton. He was like a dog wanting to be fed. He'd nip and yip and bounce until he got what he wanted. Better to deal with him now than have him ruin her night by constantly popping up demanding attention. She sighed. "Fine. I'll be right back, girls."

Benton tried to take her elbow, but she shrugged away from him. She nodded toward the dance floor and then followed him. The band had been playing a rousing rendition of a Tim McGraw song, and as she and Benton stepped onto the weathered dance floor, they rolled into a cover of Zac Brown Band's "Sweet Annie." Made Jess want to mutter, "Shit."

"I love this song," Benton said as he set his hands at her waist. He knew she loved it, too. Had he tipped the band to play it before he came to ask her to dance? Probably. Whatever Benton Mason wanted . . .

Jess's heart contracted as he pulled her to him and the words washed over them. She had so much anger. So much. But he felt so familiar, and the tender words of the song written for a wedding with the apology for past wrongs also in the lyrics made her soften. She didn't want to feel so . . . hurt, so achy for what she'd lost, but those feelings came flooding back. As they moved for a few seconds—her hand set on the shoulder where she'd lain her head many a night, her other hand clasped in his familiar one—she felt the devastation that lay between them so sharply it nearly took her breath away.

She swallowed the scratchiness in her throat and managed to say, "What did you want to say to me?"

Benton looked down, his face once so dear to her, now like a stranger's. "I needed to tell you I was wrong to do what I did."

Not *I'm sorry*, but close. He'd said he was sorry over and over those weeks after he'd packed his clothes and moved in with the florist. But he'd never said he was wrong. "Why?"

"Because I was. I thought I wanted a different life. Like my daddy told me—the grass is greener on the other side of the fence, but you still gotta mow it. He's right. He'd love me saying that, right?"

Jess wasn't sure where Benton was going with all this, but the flowers he'd sent, the fact he had come tonight when he knew the wedding party would be here, all added up toward something that made her want to stamp her foot in frustration. She knew this man, and he wanted something . . . and it wasn't merely forgiveness for his transgression.

"I shouldn't have ever let you go, Jess," he said, softly, his eyes so sincere.

Jess stomped on his foot. "But you did."

"Ow," he said, wincing. "I know I did. I fucked up. All right? I wanted to tell you that."

"So you told me," she said, trying to pull her hand from his grasp.

"Hold on, okay? Just give me this dance," he said, holding fast to her hand and squeezing her waist with the other one.

"I don't want to."

"Why? Because you hate me?" He sounded incredulous, as if he hadn't actually thought about what she truly felt. Certainly to a man who'd always gotten what he wanted from Jess, this idea was ridiculous.

"You know I don't hate you, but I can't pretend what happened away. Not so you can be comfortable with how we ended. And I know that's what this is. Someone somewhere told you what a lowlife you are for leaving the good woman you had, and now you're looking for me to make it all better for you. Like I've always done. You want me to say it's okay and that I understand how you felt, but I can't do that. Because it wasn't okay, and I don't understand why you took the love we had and put it on the for-sale rack."

"That's not what I did." Benton moved her toward the edge of the dance floor, toward an area that wasn't so crowded. "I'm admitting how wrong I was. I didn't want to hurt you. It's just with you so focused on a baby, I got scared. I started thinking about—"

Jess pressed a hand against his chest. "Don't. I'm not rehashing all this. I know what you thought and what you wanted. You got it."

"But I don't want it," he said, looking down at her. His eyes begged her. "Don't you see what I'm saying? I was stupid, so fucking stupid. I know what I did, but I'm hoping you'll think about talking."

"Talking?"

He hesitated. "I've been thinking about communication and how if I had told you some of what I'd felt that maybe this wouldn't have happened between us."

"No, maybe if you hadn't stuck your dick in Brandy Robbins, this wouldn't have happened between us. I'm pretty sure that was the issue." Jess pushed against him. "At this point, I don't think talking will help."

"Please. Just think about it. I started seeing a therapist, and he's helping me see that I was scared."

"Or horny."

"No, it wasn't about sex, babe. It was about escaping because I couldn't cope with the idea of being like my father. It wasn't you. It was me."

"Seriously?" Jess asked, standing stock-still in the middle of the song. Part of her wanted to slap Benton silly, but even as she itched to lay a sting across his cheek, she acknowledged the truth in his words. She'd allowed herself to grow too focused on impending motherhood. She'd subscribed to parenting magazines, shopped for nursery furniture, and neurotically taken her basal temperature during ovulation. At first Benton had overlooked the obsession, passively giving her a "sure" or "yeah, that will be nice," but then he'd started shutting down. One month he'd refused to have sex with her, telling her he couldn't physically make it happen. In the corner of her thoughts, she'd known she'd pushed too hard, too fast. But she couldn't seem to help herself. She thought about their little boy or little girl all the time and the mommy-and-me groups they'd join and about which of her old smocked gowns the baby would wear for the christening.

Oh, she wasn't to blame for what Benton had done, but she knew she'd helped push him toward it with her baby mania.

"I'm not giving you a line. I'm being sincere. You didn't do anything wrong, Jess. It was me, and Dr. Williams is helping me see that. I had some issues with my father and the way he raised me and my brother.

It's stuff I never dealt with before, and it cropped up about two years ago when we were talking about starting a family. I didn't know how to deal with it, so I didn't. I looked for a way out so I wouldn't have to confront fatherhood. I'm being honest here."

And he was.

"Okay," she said,

"Okay, what?"

"I better understand your motivation. It doesn't excuse you having an affair and walking out on me, but it gives me a little bit of insight into what you were feeling. It somehow makes it . . . something." She couldn't give him a pass. She wouldn't. He'd made his choice. No going back.

"So can we talk about a future?"

Jess swallowed and gave him a little smile. "See, that's the thing, Benton. I moved on . . . and I did it without you. I get that you now have this new insight into yourself, but that has nothing to do with me. I'm happy now."

"Happier than when we were together?" he asked, swaying a bit and giving a smile to passing couples so they didn't look like two divorcés arguing.

Jess thought about that. "No, just different. I'm not the same woman."

"You're still Jess."

"But not your Jess," she said softly. She wasn't trying to hurt Benton needlessly, which was surprising, since for many months as she processed through grief over their failed marriage she'd wanted to make him cry in agony. "We can't go back, Benton."

"I know, but we can talk about what it could be like if we"—he paused, as if grappling for the right thing to say, the thing that wouldn't cause her to walk away—"were open to having a relationship again. I'm not talking about being who we were, but being a newer version of ourselves. We could date. Like real dating, not hanging out like we did in high school. I know it would take some time for you to trust me again. But maybe if you got to know me, the real Benton, not just the one you thought you knew, we could be better and stronger. I still love you, Jess."

"No, you don't. You like the fact I made your life easier. Like this shirt. It's not ironed. And I bet no one makes you oatmeal raisin cookies. Or can pick out a good watermelon. Or make the shower the perfect temperature after your morning runs."

Benton smiled. "All good things, but I'm not that shallow. I don't miss my assistant. I miss my wife."

Jess shook her head. "It's too late."

"Don't say that. Just say you'll think about it. You're coming home from Pensacola in a month or two, right? This is our town. It's where you belong. And I know you don't belong with Reyes. I don't care how fucking tight his abs are. He's a toy, nothing more."

Something inside Jess tightened at his words. Benton had laid out what she suspected everyone was saying. That Ryan was her boy toy, her bit of wildness after being dumped by Benton. They thought she was pathetic.

Or maybe even worse . . . what if she'd let them think that because it inflated her own ego?

She'd tried to convince herself that Ryan being her rebound fling was a perfect indulgence. Getting over the hurt was best done by chasing it away. Plenty of other divorcées had provided a cautionary tale when they jumped into something too soon and ended up divorced again in less than a year. Jess had watched many of her college friends lose weight or get a little work done. Then they hit the bars, drinking martinis and practicing their rusty flirting skills while wearing dresses too short for them. She looked down at her hem.

Right.

But had she marginalized what she felt for Ryan because she'd watched others fall on their faces when they tried to make a rebound work? After all, real love didn't happen that fast, and it certainly didn't happen for a sensible woman like herself. Yet what she'd had with Benton, something she thought was everlasting, had gone bad like pork in the August sun. Rosemary's words from that afternoon floated past her. *Love doesn't find you when you want it to. Nope, it slams into you and holds you hostage. Stop trying to put rules into place.*

But she wasn't falling in love with Ryan. And love couldn't hold her hostage if she didn't want it to. She had a say-so in her own life.

She turned from Benton and caught Ryan standing beside a pool table, cue stick clasped in his hand, alarm etched on his face. Her heart swelled at the worried body language. Then she looked back to her ex-husband, who looked so certain of himself. Some of what Benton had said made sense. She *would* be coming back to Morning Glory. Ryan would not. And, yeah, she'd played the part every newly divorced woman played. That knowledge made her feel so small. And to make it worse, she'd coerced Ryan back to a place he despised so she could feel better about herself. Shame burned inside her.

"I have to go," she said to Benton, pushing away from him.

"I understand. This is a lot to comprehend, but please think about it, Jess. We've always been a team. We could be an even better one. Stronger and better prepared for a future, for kids, because we now know who we both are. Just say you'll think about it."

Jess didn't say anything. Her words were caught in her throat, her heart clenched hard at the sudden onslaught of shame, doubt, and, oddly enough, tenderness. And she didn't know why that particular emotion was present, but it felt hard to swallow, hard to think with the music pounding and everyone looking at her. She shook her head and walked away from her ex-husband.

"Hey," Ryan said, taking her elbow. "You okay?"

"No, I'm not okay. I need to get outside. I need some air."

"Okay," he said, following her.

"No, stay here. Finish your game. I want to be alone for a few minutes."

His green eyes widened. "You sure?"

"Yeah, that's the one thing I'm sure about at the moment."

Chapter Fifteen

They hadn't made love last night.

It was the first thing that occurred to Ryan when he woke from troubled dreams, his body tense and his head achy. Jess lay beside him, still as a rock, curled away from him, her hand fisted beneath her chin. She looked so young, but her brow furrowed as if even in slumber she couldn't find peace.

Carefully, he slipped from the small bed and stretched, working out the kink in his neck. He stooped over and picked up the trousers he'd kicked off last night, exhausted from pretending to be just another good ol' boy out on the town. He'd shot pool, danced with Jess's friends, and bought drinks for a few other pretty girls who kept sending beers his way. He'd smiled, even flirted a bit, as he tried like hell to erase the geek he'd been from everyone's memory. For the most part, he'd succeeded. But it hadn't been a good night.

Damn Benton Mason.

He'd gotten a hold of Jess and said something that had caused her to pull away from Ryan. Oh, Jess had tried to play it off, but he could feel the ties they'd bound themselves with snapping one by one. When he'd questioned her about her need to take in some fresh air, she'd shrugged her cryptic response to his trying to accompany her, suggesting she was merely tired. She'd added she hadn't wanted to see Benton that night. She'd hated being coerced into dancing with him. And that was as forthcoming as she'd been.

When they arrived back at his parents' house, she'd claimed a headache and slipped into her pajamas. He'd tried to hold her, but she'd pulled away, saying she was hot. She'd given him an almost chaste kiss and then rolled over. He could feel her lying awake, feel her thoughts tumbling over and over, getting bigger and bigger. Conflicted and helpless, he'd not pressed her.

Because he was scared of the answer.

Thing was, even though he didn't want to admit it, he knew he'd probably fallen in love. Or maybe he'd never stopped loving her . . . even if that sounded implausible. Years ago, he'd been a kid, incapable of true romantic love. But still, something about her always pulled him like a magnet to a pole. He was helpless to resist the attraction because deep down, beneath his geeky T-shirts and plaid cargo shorts, the self-assured cheerleader had his heart in her hand. For the past month, he'd been so full of joy to have her back in his life again. Being with her, despite the unwritten rules he'd established for himself, had been the best idea he'd ever had . . . outside of the makeup of the polymer scaffolding he'd sold for a couple of million. And maybe even better than that. Because Jess didn't care that he liked dorky TV shows and read books about cell biology. She liked watching him play his online games, even trading insults with his online buddies. Jess liked him just the way he was. Or at least she had until Benton had twirled her onto the dance floor and filled her ear with what was no doubt a pile of bullshit.

His thoughts from the day before when Eden had asked if people ever really changed came tumbling back, smacking mockingly into him.

Softly opening the door, he stepped out and then pulled it closed again. Then he shrugged into a T-shirt he held in his hand before padding barefoot into the breakfast room. The table and chairs in the center of the nook were the same ugly brown they'd always been. Nothing changed here at his parents' much—the cutlery had been purchased at an outlet mall and the yellow coffee mugs were a grocery store promotional. He grabbed one, filled it with black coffee, and joined his father at the table. The headlines of the *Wall Street Journal* warned of dire economic times and bottomed-out gas prices. "Morning."

His father looked over the paper. "Oh, Ryan."

As if he'd forgotten his only child was in residence. "Still here."

"I know. I didn't expect you up so early. You went carousing last night."

Carousing? "Just a few drinks to celebrate the upcoming nuptials. No actual carousing involved." Ryan sipped the bitter brew. His father made it strong. Maxwell House. Good to the last drop.

"Ah, and today is the wedding, huh? We weren't invited, but I'm not surprised. We don't travel in those circles, thank God."

Ryan smiled at this. His parents didn't really have a social circle. They were too square. "Yes, I wish I didn't have to truss myself up like a Christmas goose, either."

"Do you?" His father sat the paper down. "Then why do it?"

"Because of Jess," Ryan said.

"You love this girl?"

Ryan shrugged. "I don't know. I'm going because she asked me to. She wanted me there."

"I never liked her first husband. That Mason boy. He once threw eggs at our house, remember? And rolled our trees in toilet paper."

"I remember." But he'd tried to forget. If people truly never changed, did that mean Benton Mason had never left his bullying ways behind?

Ryan had tried to chalk up Benton and his moronic friends' behavior to their age. Teens weren't fully developed cognitively, often making decisions based on obtaining power. But Ryan was a firm believer that people did change, or maybe they merely conformed to society's standards. After all, he'd changed. Sorta.

"And his father's not very nice, either. But you, you're a nice boy." His father picked up the paper and started reading again.

"Dad?"

"Yes?" Emilio lowered the paper again.

"When did you know you loved Mom?" The question had flown from his mouth before he could think better of asking. He'd never broached something so personal with his father. He knew next to nothing about his mother and father's courtship. He knew only that they'd met at Columbia when his father was on a lecture circuit and his mother was working on her master's. They'd tried to eschew the conventions of marriage, but Martha had been raised in a strict Catholic family and her father wouldn't pay for the remainder of her schooling if she "shacked up" with some Massachusetts weirdo. So they'd gotten married and had a nontraditional red-velvet wedding cake, rebels that they were.

"When she refused to change her thesis to reflect my belief that physical activity improves spatial perception and attention in adolescents. She said I hadn't proven it with hard evidence. I admired that about her, along with the fact she was willing to change her mind after we collected enough data. Your mother can't be moved when she believes in something, so I knew she was perfect for me. Oh, and her bottom looked incredible in the slacks she wore. That was persuasive, too."

Ryan laughed. "That's a good combo."

"Indeed it is. She still has a nice can. That's why I don't complain about the money she spends on yoga. So are you asking these questions because of Jessica?"

"Maybe." He wasn't sure why he wanted to know. "You haven't said anything about my career. Usually you have something to say. Why?"

"Because it's like beating a dead fish."

"Horse."

"Fish, horse, whatever. Still ugly when beaten. I don't understand you, but then again, you don't understand me. That is the human condition at times. I believe you were given a gift, something so rare and powerful. You believe you were cursed. Impasse." Emilio lifted the paper once again. "I cannot change the way you feel. I've learned to accept it. You're my son."

His father went back to reading.

Ryan stared at him for a few moments, grappling with this final words. *You're my son.* What power in three words. Inside he warmed, the flag of resentment he'd folded tightly years ago loosening. His father was correct—sometimes one had to learn to accept others exactly as they were.

Thinking to beat a dead fish, Ryan opened his mouth to ask his father exactly what he meant, but a knock on the door tore him from his intentions. "I'll get it. Probably someone delivering Jess's dress."

Ryan walked through the dim living room and unlocked the door. Pulling it open, he found Benton Mason standing on the front porch.

"Benton," he said, trying to cover his confusion with a cool demeanor.

"What's up, Brain? Solve any equations today?"

Ryan lifted one eyebrow, ignoring the dumb crack. "What are you doing here?"

"I was in the neighborhood and needed to talk to Jess. Can you get her for me?" Benton looked totally untroubled about standing on his ex-wife's boyfriend's parents' house's porch. Entitled jackass.

"She's asleep."

Benton ran a hand through his shaggy hair and tried on a smile. "She does like to sleep in."

"If you're trying to remind me of the intimacy you once shared with her, you can stop. It won't work." Ryan didn't want to feel prickly, but he did. Everything felt so unsettled, and now here was Slick Willie on his porch with his greasy smile and his mean pig eyes.

Benton's grin dissolved. "Oh, I get it. You think you're somebody now. Coming back here with your pretty boy shine and your new muscles. Like people didn't forget you wet your pants in the twelfth grade."

Ryan smiled a not-so-nice smile of his own. "You like to remind me of your glory days, don't you? Fine. I pissed myself, but only after spending five hours in the PE closet. I have claustrophobia, and I could hardly move, but you wouldn't have cared, would you? You shoved me in there and hid the key. You're a mean man, Benton. Just like your father." Ryan knew he shouldn't sink to the man's level, but damn if he couldn't help himself. The rage he'd tied down all those years ago broke loose, aided by Jess's withdrawal the night before. This man needed to come down a peg or two. Maybe three or four.

Benton's eyes flashed pain and bitterness. "You want to talk fathers? Really?"

"I'm not talking fathers. I'm merely reminded of how apples don't fall far from their trees. If you need to leave Jess a message, let me know. Otherwise, I'll thank you to find your way back to your vehicle and get the hell out of here."

Benton's smile was nasty. "No. I need to talk to Jess this morning. She's my wife. So do me a favor, bro, and go get her."

"Your wife? You tossed that privilege away over a year ago, *bro*. So I think I'll stand right here and watch you walk back to your big truck and drive away."

Benton stepped closer to Ryan. Ryan stepped closer to Benton, shutting the front door behind him with a snick. Years ago, Ryan was afraid of the larger upperclassman, but he wasn't anymore. He spent a couple of hours in the gym each day, and the black belt he'd earned in martial arts assured him he could face any particular threat with grace, power, and speed. No longer would anyone put him in a closet.

"You're asking to get your ass beat down, Reyes," Benton said, his voice low and threatening.

"I know your game, Ben," Ryan said, curling his hands, lifting himself on his toes, prepared for a strike. "You're playing with Jess's mind. She's over you, and you can't stand that, can you? You have a superiority complex with no real basis for it."

"Wait, you think *you* can make her happy?" Benton looked down at him. The older man had a few inches and a few pounds on Ryan, but it was obvious he'd traded physical fitness for an extra beer and slice of pizza. One strike to the throat and Benton would go down squealing like a stuck pig. Still, Ryan didn't want to collapse the man's windpipe. Much.

So he stared at him.

"I mean, what, you work out, get a tan, become a boat captain? You think that makes you a man? You're still a loser, Ryan. You established that long ago. You and your weirdo parents. You think Jess can't see through all this? It's so pathetic how hard you've worked to erase what you were. I liked you better when you were honest." Benton laughed and then slapped him on the shoulder.

Ryan didn't move. He stood his ground, outwardly stoic, inwardly reeling at the man's words. Was that how everyone saw him? Pathetic because he'd worked hard to change himself into what he thought a man should be? No. He'd been trying to claim what everyone else had in life. He'd not compromised himself for the approval of the world. Or maybe he had. Did he think a hundred crunches a day, teeth bleaching, and learning baseball stats made him more a man than what he was? Had he sacrificed his authenticity in order to present a man he thought would be admired? Using slang terms . . . wait, was he frontin'?

"Benton, what are you doing here?" Jess asked behind him.

Ryan turned to see her standing in the doorway, wearing a pair of slouchy shorts and a T-shirt. Her hair tangled around her face, and he could see the imprint of the sheets on her cheek.

"Hey, there you are," Benton said, his voice easing, sounding like a pediatrician addressing a reluctant child.

Ryan turned his attention back to Jess's ex-husband. The man's smile was all rainbows and lollipops.

Ryan didn't look back at Jess. Instead he said, "Benton was just leaving."

Jess ignored Ryan. "Benton, what are you doing here?"

"I'd rather not say in front of your boyfriend here," Benton said.

"Why not?" Ryan asked, crossing his arms. "You've caused her enough pain, so I think whatever you need to say you should say right now."

"She doesn't need your permission to talk to me, Reyes." Benton's tone held a warning.

"Of course she doesn't." Ryan finally looked back at Jess, afraid to see what he might find in her face. Yet she merely rubbed her face and stared at both men as if she couldn't grasp what was going on.

"Let me talk to my wife," Benton said.

"Ex-wife," Ryan and Jess said in unison.

"Fine, ex-wife." Benton held out his hand. "Come on, babe. I want to show you my new truck. Finally talked ol' Greg down on the price."

"No," she said, shaking her head. "All that needed to be said was done last night."

"Jess," Benton chided, tilting his head, looking as slick as a Bible salesman. "A lot of things were left unsaid between us. At least give us closure."

"Closure?" Jess repeated. "I think you better go, Benton."

Benton reached for Jess, but Ryan stepped in front of the man. "You heard the lady."

"Move, Reyes, before I shove you into another closet," Benton growled, feigning to the right before going to the left, heading for Jess.

Ryan grabbed Benton's forearm and jerked the man off balance just as Jess said, "*You're* the one who locked him in that closet?"

Benton lost his footing and fell back onto the railing of the porch. He righted himself and came back swinging. "You son of a bitch! That's my wife you're fucking!"

Jess screamed as Ryan ducked and then gave Benton a solid one-two punch. The first punch landed in Benton's gut. As the man doubled forward, Ryan gave him a left hook that snapped his head around. Benton staggered backward, grappling for leverage and finding it on the same rail he'd stumbled into earlier. When his gaze finally met Ryan's, it registered disbelief and then rage.

Benton pushed off the rail, starting back toward Ryan again. Jess screamed, "No!" and jumped in front of Ryan, holding her hands up. It registered in Ryan's mind that the crazy woman thought she was protecting him. He tried to pull her back so she didn't accidentally get hit, but thankfully Benton lowered his fist.

"Stop this right now!" Jess shouted, pushing against Benton's chest and darting a dazed look back at Ryan. "Have you both lost your ever-lovin' minds?"

Benton looked at her and said, "He started it."

Ryan started laughing at the asinine statement. What? Was the man a seven-year-old? He sobered quickly and muttered, "I did not."

And Ryan realized he was being just as infantile. What was it about a woman that drove two grown men into becoming scrapping little boys intent on one-upping the other?

"I can't believe you two. This is ridiculous. Like two dogs with a bone. Benton, I told you I don't want to talk to you. And, Ryan, did you really have to hit him?" Jess's eyes had lost the fogginess. The golden depths snapped with ire.

Ryan clenched his teeth, refusing to answer the question. He'd wanted to hit Benton Mason for as long as he could remember. The man had deserved everything Ryan had given him . . . and more. But he supposed he shouldn't have acted like some lowbrow Neanderthal fighting over a stick. It was a bit infantile, but the emotions roiling inside him had him reacting and not thinking logically.

She looked back and forth between the two men. "Ben, go home."

"But, Jess, I wanted—"

The woman clapped her hands under her ex-husband's nose and said firmly, "Go. Home. Now."

Benton tossed a glare at Ryan. "Fine. If I can find my way out of this fucking jungle. Freaking weirdos." Then he turned and stalked down the cracked path. Hitchhikers from the Bahia grass peppered his pant leg. Somehow that gave Ryan satisfaction.

"And you." Jess turned on him, jabbing a finger into his chest. "You hit him for the wrong reasons, and you know it. And anyway, I don't need you fighting my battles with Benton."

She spun on a socked foot and walked back into the house, slamming the front door for good measure. Ryan stood there, knuckles sore and stomach churning. He knew he'd been too hasty, but he couldn't bear the thought of Benton's hands on Jess. The man reached for her like some kind of crazy barbarian who had the right to touch her. And he didn't. Not anymore. But where did that leave Ryan?

Jess was mad at him for defending her.

No. She was mad because he'd indulged himself in hitting Benton. Perhaps she hadn't known the extent to which her ex-husband had tortured Ryan, but she'd had a suspicion. She'd said as much. But now she knew Mr. Morning Glory High had been the one who'd locked a boy in the closet, causing Ryan to pass out . . . and wet his pants. Ryan had never identified the person, though everyone knew (wink, wink) that some baseball boys had been horsing around, playing a silly prank.

That's how bullying was dealt with years ago. With a boys-will-be-boys explanation. Well, Benton had been a boy being a boy far too often in his life.

Ryan flexed his hand. He couldn't say it hadn't been satisfying. And he wasn't apologizing to Jess for punching Benton.

And at that moment, he didn't know what to say to her.

Everything felt upside down.

⁓

Jess sat in the guest room and tried not to cry. She felt so out of control. This weekend was supposed to be a chance for her and Ryan to be a couple. She'd introduce Ryan to her parents, everyone would see that she was over Benton, and she and Ryan would dance at the reception and look as happy as two pigs in the mud. Because they were happy. Or at least they had been. Now she was confused. Everything felt like it was coming apart just like the little pots she used to fashion out of the Mississippi mud when she was a child. Things not meant to be didn't hold together.

Ryan pushed into the bedroom and closed the door behind him. Tension filled all the spaces in between them, heavy and grim. For almost a month, they'd shared smiles, tender glances, and sheet-drenching sex, but never a disagreement.

Ripping her gaze from a hangnail, she looked up at him. "God, Ryan, what is wrong with you?"

He pressed his hands against his chest, his brow furrowing. "Me? What's wrong with you? You dance with that bozo last night, and all of a sudden you won't look at me. Won't let me touch you. We slept in that bed like strangers."

Jess swallowed the guilt. Dancing with Benton last night as he told her things she'd always believed had left her feeling mixed up. She had always wanted to live in Morning Glory, raise her babies here, and grow old rocking on the front porch of a cute house—the quintessential American dream. And the desire for that ultimate future hadn't faded. Those seductive words—*you belong here*—had rattled around inside her, making her doubt everything she'd found in Pensacola. Because splashing in the Gulf with cutie patootie Ryan wasn't what she wanted in a future, or at least she didn't think she did. Those words along with everyone hinting Ryan was her plaything had combined to make her wonder what the hell she was doing with the handsome fisherman. Not to mention she felt panicky about the strong feelings she had for him. Because inside, things felt real. Like she could be falling in love. But that's not what she was supposed to do. She wasn't supposed to fall into that rebound trap. Because she couldn't survive another crippling loss in her life. If she fell in love, she would get hurt. Because Ryan wasn't coming back to Morning Glory, that much was certain. Every hour spent here, he became less and less of the man she knew and more and more of the shadow he'd once been. She'd watched him pull at his shirt, look like he'd eaten a plate of wriggling worms, stare into space, employing diversionary tactics. Everything about him felt forced and nothing like the loose, chill guy who made her smile, who seemed so confident in being exactly who he was, who gave her a place to lay her head.

"This doesn't have anything to do with Benton," she said finally.

"So you're trying to use the ol' 'it's not you, it's me,' but we both know whatever is going on with you has something to do with that ass. Everything was good until that dance. So what? Has he changed his mind? Is he crooking his little finger and you're thinking about running back to him?" Ryan asked, his eyes glittering. Emeralds glinting anger. "Eden said it yesterday. We don't change. So is this you blowing me off because you're still the same perfect cheerleader whose big, dumb jock needs you by his side?"

"Ryan," Jess said, drawing back. Such anger in those words. Was that what he really thought about her? That she was that shallow? But then again, he had little reason to trust any of the people he'd gone to high school with. Back then everyone had a slot, and Ryan hadn't fit in any of them. He'd become a victim because of it. She recognized what he did because she dealt daily with hurting patients who lashed out not because they were nasty but because they couldn't tolerate the pain.

Jess straightened her shoulders. "Look, that's not what we're discussing. This is not about me and Benton. It's about you and Benton. You're pissed at him and this town for the way you were treated, and you hit him because of that. Not me."

"You're goddamn right I hit him for the way he treated me . . . and the way he treated you," he said, slamming a hand on the dresser. "You wouldn't understand what it was like having a group of guys hold you down and give you wedgies, the humiliation of having everything you wore picked apart in front of the lunchroom while everyone's laughing, or having to see the look in your parents' eyes when your house gets egged twice a month. My dad and I had to clean it up while I wondered why they hated me so much. He and his friends made my life miserable. So, yeah, I hit him. He probably deserved more, but I'll settle for what I just gave him."

"I'm sorry." Learning Benton had played a part in locking Ryan in that storage closet made her feel ill. She remembered hearing the ambulance arrive as she took her calculus test, and later overhearing people laughing over Ryan passing out and wetting his pants. She hadn't found much humor in belittling the boy who'd always shown her kindness. She, of course, knew Benton teased Ryan and some of the other nerdy kids, but she'd always thought it was good-natured. She'd never viewed Benton as a torturer. Just a guy who liked to clown around, a guy who liked to mark his territory.

"Now maybe you can see why I worked so hard to change and why I wasn't interested in coming back here this weekend. I'm not comfortable here." His words found their mark. He was implying all of this was her fault. Because she'd talked him into coming home with her.

"Christ, just have the balls to be who you are," she said, something ugly unraveling inside her. She wanted to hurt him. Strike at him. Put some of the blame on him. "You pretend to be someone you're not in Florida, and here you act like people still see you as a flippin' thirteen-year-old. You're grown, so let go of the past already."

Ryan stilled, his eyes shuttering. "You must be joking."

"No," she snapped. "You don't get it. You just said it. People don't change. You don't have to make yourself into some caricature of someone you think is cool. It's ridiculous. And when I come back here and remember who you were and compare that to who you've become, it's so obvious. You're living a lie." She leaped up from the bed, her emotions wrestling inside her. She was unable to stop herself from flinging knives at him.

Jess glanced up to see the disbelief in his eyes, the betrayal. And she hated herself for the words she said.

"I'm the liar?" Ryan said, his voice sounding like death—silent and heavy. "You brought me back here for selfish reasons. You're using me to thumb your nose at Benton. In fact, you've been using me the whole time so you could feel better about yourself. And I let you do it, just like I always did. Like your stupid fucking puppy."

Jess felt the cannon blast of his response. His words were true, but he didn't know that beneath the assumption of her vanity lay the fear she'd already started down the slippery slope of love. That thought scared the spit from her mouth. No, she wouldn't love Ryan. She'd push him away. Make him hate her. "Fuck you."

His eyes narrowed. "You already have."

Her heart shattered into a million pieces because she could see his disdain for her. Maybe they'd used each other. Him for his stupid adolescent fantasy of doing the head cheerleader and her to look better in front of the town. Maybe their romance had been a house of cards. One strong gust, and, poof, they were done. "I have to go."

"Where? Back to that asshole? Back to being what you think will make you happy? I do believe Lacy would be ashamed of you."

Jess stopped in midstride and looked at him. "You don't get to use her name, buster. She's nothing to you. And you didn't know her."

"I knew her well enough to know she didn't run from things because they were hard. That's what you're doing. You think there's some rule that says you have to be the Jess Culpepper you always were. Come back here and do whatever the hell people do here. Exist or wait to die or whatever. You're running from any other kind of future, for any chance to break out of being the perfect cheerleader, perfect wife, perfect daughter."

"I am not," she said, his words feeding the raging beast inside her. She looked at the hand reaching for the doorknob and dropped it.

Ryan thrust a hand in his hair. "Yeah, it's hard sometimes to let go of who you thought you were, but if you don't, you can't find the good stuff. I get that part of you wonders if it would just be easier to come back and fall into the life you thought you wanted. Because you know what you're getting. Rosemary ran from her safe world—that's what you told me—and you're trying to climb into the straitjacket she shed because you're afraid to be someone other than what you imagined for yourself. You're chicken."

Jess swallowed. Hard. And she thought about throwing something at him. "And this from the man who ran away from who he was. You're the pretender."

"Maybe so. But I'm willing to correct it. That's the scientist in me. I'm not afraid to fall down. I expect that to happen. I get back up again. I don't stay flat on the floor, accepting that's where I belong."

"You've never been in love. You don't know how I feel."

Ryan shrugged, the anger seeming to leave him. "Maybe I don't. But I'm not afraid of it. I thought I could plan my life, too, set up guidelines for the next few years, but I didn't plan on you. I was wrong. The heart doesn't play by rules."

Jess felt those words. The heart? No. This wasn't about the heart. This was about pretenses. This was about . . . she squeezed her eyes shut for a minute, trying to remember what this was about. Ryan hitting Benton. Jealousy. Revenge. Not love. "You don't know what you're talking about. Ever since we've come here, you've been sliding back into the past. I can feel it. You hide beneath a glossy veneer that you think erases who you truly are. You're the one who's afraid. So don't lecture me on who I am." She gathered up her purse and the bag she'd packed last night with her makeup and toiletries. "I have to go. I have to be at the brunch in an hour."

"Hey, Jess," he called. She turned and arched an eyebrow. Her heart thudded, and anger made her flushed. "Stop being such a pussy."

Jess walked out the bedroom door, her heart heavy, her throat scratchy, and her eyes aching. She wanted to hit Ryan for his cruel words even as she knew they held a lot of truth. She wanted to burst into tears and tell him she was sorry for saying such hurtful things. But she couldn't do either of those things. Maybe tomorrow she'd think about not being such a pussy. Today she had to be a bridesmaid.

Chapter Sixteen

Jess scooped a grape into her mouth and chewed the too-sour fruit. Across from her sat Mimi, Rosemary's next-door neighbor, along with Rosemary's cousin Mary Charlotte, who wasn't in the wedding but was invited to the bridal brunch. Eden sat too far away, between Rosemary and her grandmother on her father's side. The women in Sal's family filled in the rest of the places. Jess felt stuck.

"So you're dating Ryan Reyes, huh?" Mary Charlotte asked, eyeing her with speculation. Rosemary's cousin worked as a legal secretary and had the dirt on everyone in Morning Glory.

"Yeah," Jess said. Of course, they'd just hurled horrible accusations at each other, so that might no longer be true. Her heart sat heavy in her chest. She wanted to cry, but instead she took another bite of her chicken salad croissant and tried to chew. Her appetite had vanished over the morning's events. After they'd argued, she and Ryan had pretended to be pleasant throughout breakfast, though they hardly said a word to each other. His parents had noticed. A dead person would have noticed the tension. It had been awful, but she'd made it through by refusing to think of anything but getting through the day. For Rosemary.

Before she and Ryan had come back to Morning Glory, they'd been wrapped in a blanket of peace and happiness. But obviously it had been a blanket held together by wishes or butterfly wings or thin air.

God, how had everything had gone so wrong?

Thursday had been fine. They'd eaten dinner with his parents, he'd bonded with Sal over wainscoting and red leather booths, and they'd had giggly, hushed sex in the still hours of the night. But then Friday the questions came, the conjecture in the looks when people looked at them. She'd tried to ignore it, but deep down inside she suspected her fellow Morning Glorinians secretly shook their heads in disapproval of her bringing a hunk home just to prove a point. Or maybe she felt that way because she knew she'd wanted him there for that reason, too. And even though it was gender discrimination, because she doubted anyone had made Benton feel icky about sleeping with half the single women in town over the past year, she still felt the hidden censure of flaunting her hunk.

And then there was Benton. His words last night at the Iron Bull—

"Ryan certainly has changed." Mary Charlotte interrupted her thoughts. "Of course, I was two years ahead of y'all, but I remember him. I tell you, I wouldn't have recognized him if someone hadn't shown me his picture in the paper from a few years back. He was skinny then and wore glasses. But you could tell it was the same guy. But now, ooh-la-la, he's a hottie. Good for you, Jess."

"Mmm-hmm," Jess murmured, going back to her fruit salad.

"And who are we discussing, dear?" Mimi asked, leaning over and giving Jess a whiff of her Chanel No. 5 perfume.

"Jess's new man, Dr. Ryan Reyes." Mary Charlotte's eyes twinkled. "Ooh, I wonder if he makes house calls?"

"He's a physician, dear?" Mimi asked.

"No, ma'am. He has a doctorate in . . . something. He was a scientist, and now he owns a charter fishing service in Florida. He's Martha and Emilio's son." Jess gave an internal sigh. She was tired of doing this. And embarrassed to not know what his doctorate was in. Wasn't someone in a relationship supposed to know those sorts of basic things? Well, if they were still in a relationship. She'd left before anything more could be said on the matter. Before she could apologize for saying such awful things to the man she . . .

What? Loved? Slept with? Used? Yelled at? Sought revenge with? Who was Ryan anyway, and what was he to her?

Maybe that was part of the problem—they'd yet to declare to each other how they felt. She burned hot for his touch, loved his sense of humor, took pleasure in his hidden geekiness, and loved sitting beside him, his fingers twined in hers. What did those feelings mean, and could she trust them enough to change her vision for her future?

"Oh yes. A fine boy. He helped my husband do our taxes one year. Ed got mad at Wendell Edwards and refused to pay him one more cent to do our quarterlies. Emilio sent his boy over. Wasn't but twelve years old, but he did our taxes lickety-split with some newfangled computer program. It was amazing. Wouldn't take any money for it, either, but Ed forced him to put some in his savings. He's a genius, you know."

"I do," Jess said.

The striking of a fork against a crystal champagne glass drew their attention. Jess tried to tuck away the big ball of hurt inside her as she caught sight of Rosemary's face. Her friend glowed, positively vibrated with anticipation and joy. Rosemary's mother, Patsy, set the glass down and beamed at the ladies gathered round the large table in the Methodist church. "Thank you, friends, for being here with us on this day. I've dreamed about it for many years. Of course, I hadn't expected to have to pull together my daughter's wedding in less than a month." Patsy cast a patronizing look at Rosemary and someone giggled nervously. "But

I'm happy to say we've made it. Today is Rosemary's wedding day, and I'm so glad you're here to share it with us."

Rosemary clapped her hands and stood, effectively stealing the spotlight from her mother. Patsy frowned. "Yes, Sal and I are so excited to have our closest friends and family with us on this day. Our wedding is a reflection of who we are—two different people who chose each other over what made sense. So today will be a mixture of tradition and novelty, the expected and unexpected, but most of all it will be about choosing love." She sat down hard, refilled her champagne glass and lifted it, her eyes falling on Jess.

The message was clear: *Don't be confused about what is important.*

But unfortunately, Jess had thrown that baby out with the bathwater. Or something like that. She'd likely tossed away the best thing that had happened to her.

Because she was chicken. Or a pussy. Or a pussified chicken.

She shuffled the food on her plate around so it looked like she'd eaten enough not to be rude and then excused herself to the restroom. Except she didn't go to the restroom. She looked for a room to escape to for a moment. Pushing into a Sunday school room, she collapsed into a rocking chair and closed her eyes. Opening them, she looked around, noting she was in the preschool class. Large blocks and a patterned rug. Small chairs and the "Jesus Loves Me" song painted as a mural on the wall. All totally normal. All extremely sad to her.

Tears brimmed in her eyes, and she wiped them away, trying to tell herself to stop being such a crybaby. So she and Ryan had fought. So she felt out of place, discombobulated, angry, and small. She'd have to—

"Jess?"

She turned to see Eden standing in the doorway.

"Hey," Jess said, sniffing and wiping her eyes.

"You okay?"

"Sure."

"Really?"

Jess gave a little laugh. "No."

Eden eased into the room and pulled a small chair out and sat in it. Oddly enough, she fit. Jess would have looked like a giraffe in a clown car if she'd tried it. Eden looked up at her. "It's Benton, isn't it?"

"Yes and no. It's me," Jess said, sniffing so her nose didn't run. "And I shouldn't talk about it. It's Rosemary's big day, and I don't want to be the party pooper ruining it."

"What did he say to you?"

"Who? Benton?" Jess asked, her gaze finding Eden's concerned one. "He wants me back."

"Oh Christ," Eden muttered. "Of course he does. He likes to have all the toys."

"Yeah, people keep saying that, and I've realized it's true. I came back with a boyfriend, and he didn't like that. Suddenly he'd made a mistake. Funny, huh? For a good six months after he left, I would have believed him. I wanted him to get past whatever it was he was doing and come home."

Eden stared at her.

"I know," Jess said, hating the woman she used to be . . . hating the woman she still was. "But he didn't come back to me. And I got over him. But last night when he said all the right things, part of me wanted to believe him. And I don't know why."

"Because you loved him once. You had a nice life, and you want it back. I understand that," Eden said with a shrug. "The thing is, society tells us it's all about the heart, but in a practical sense, it's all about security. Look, I live in Grover's Park, where sometimes people don't marry for love. They marry for a steady Social Security check."

"That's horrible."

"Yeah," Eden said with a shrug, "but that's life for some people. And Benton is like a Social Security check. He has money, a good job, a respected family, and though he can be a total asshole, you know what you're getting with him."

"That's . . . true," Jess said, looking at her friend in a new light. Eden didn't have much in the way of financial security. Perhaps the particular glasses Eden wore changed the light she saw the world in. And they surely weren't the rosy designer pair Jess was viewing the world through.

"Yeah," Eden said, folding her hands and staring off toward the easel holding a large picture of Zachariah climbing the sycamore tree. "But I'm not like that. I believe in love."

For a moment silence sat between them, pregnant with reflection, accepting of life's unpredictability.

"You know what I think bothers me the most, E," Jess said.

Her friend turned her eyes back to Jess.

"I hurt Ryan," Jess said. She waited a few seconds for Eden to respond, but her friend remained silent, waiting on her to explain. "I'm scared of getting hurt, and, well, Ryan's acting crazy. He punched Benton this morning—"

"He punched Benton? Why?"

"Benton came by while I was sleeping, and they exchanged some words. Benton wanted to talk to me again, and Ryan was all crazy protective. When Benton tried to go around Ryan, he punched him. Twice."

"Oh my," Eden breathed, her eyes sparkling even in the dimness. "What did Benton do?"

"He fell down."

Eden laughed, and that made Jess laugh. "He was shocked. I don't think anyone has ever hit him before," Jess said.

"The man spent too much time around people who see only one way—theirs. People who don't ask, just take. If anyone needed a come-uppance, it's Benton. And he was awful to Ryan growing up. Bet Ryan didn't hold anything back," Eden said.

"No, he hit him pretty good." Jess smiled at the memory of Benton's face. She didn't condone violence, of course, but the incredulous look had been amusing. "He was one of the guys who locked Ryan into that PE closet."

"I know," Eden said.

"But you never told me."

"You never wanted to believe anything bad about Benton. You saw him as the perfect guy. You never saw the chinks in his armor."

Jess frowned. "Yes, I did. I lived with the man for years. I saw plenty of chinks and cracks," Jess said, rubbing her hands along the worn rocker arms. "I don't think I can live here anymore. I think that's why I'm so conflicted."

"Why can't you live here? You love Morning Glory."

Jess stilled for a moment, almost unbelieving of her own words. Not live in Morning Glory? Golly gee willikers. How could that be? "I do love Morning Glory, and it will always be my home, but this year has changed me. I don't want Benton back, and he's not running me off or anything. But coming back here after having been gone a month feels like pulling on shoes that are too small. Or maybe trying to go back into the cocoon. I just don't think I can come home and be the same woman I was."

"No one expects you to."

"Maybe not, but I think I need something different for a while. You understand?"

Eden laughed. "Oh, I understand. As soon as Alan gets through with this tour, he'll be getting out of the marines. He and my sister will come back here, and I'll spread my little wings. No more cocoon for me, either."

Jess smiled at that thought.

"And Ryan?" Eden asked softly.

"I'm scared to love him."

"That's probably a natural reaction, but if you let Benton's cheating on you, leaving you, driving you out of your hometown stop you from loving again, I'm going to kick your ass." Eden stood up and slid off her ballet flats. "Seriously, I'm ready to do it right now. Because Benton doesn't get to win. He doesn't get to put you in a corner and have the satisfaction of knowing you can't be happy because of him. So if you're going to run from Ryan and being happy, I'm going to have to beat some sense into you."

Jess looked up at Eden with her eyes shining in defiance. "You think you can take me?"

"I'm stronger than I look, and you know where I grew up," Eden said, curling her fists. "Don't let him win, Jess."

"I'm not," Jess said, though she didn't say it with much conviction. Things felt too overwhelming.

"Get up," Eden said, tugging Jess's wrist.

"Stop," Jess said, shaking her off.

"Do you love Ryan?" Eden asked.

"I don't know."

"Do you love Ryan?" Eden said, her voice harder. "It's not a hard question. You either do or you don't."

"Eden, stop acting crazy."

"No. You're leaving me in this shitty town, and I want it to be for a good reason. Do you love him? Does he make you happy? Can you imagine your world without him in it? Does he make your heart skip a beat? Does he make you ache for him? Do. You. Love. Him?"

"Yes. Okay, yes." Jess threw her hands up and burst into tears. "I love him. And that's so stupid, because I'm not supposed to. He's my rebound."

"You are an idiot. Would you stop following the shit you read in magazines or on Facebook? No one knows you or your heart. Stop pussyfooting around, flip-flopping and hemhawing. Life is short, sister, and you have a man who loves you. If you're holding back because you're scared or because you think people will think you're doing the wrong thing, then you're stupid. And I've never taken you for stupid."

Jess felt something inside her break loose. Everywhere she'd turned, the people she'd trusted had told her to let go of her reservations and reach for happiness. She hadn't wanted to listen because she thought she could control her life. But she couldn't. All that had happened to her over the past year had nothing to do with her. Not Benton leaving. Not the divorce. Not falling in love with Ryan. Things happened, and she had to learn how to . . .

. . . find a high current to glide on, far above the madding crowd of guilt, conventions, and doubt.

Lacy had known exactly what to say.

Digging the letter out of her pocket, she unfolded it. Eden stepped back, her gaze finding the letter. Her friend's eyes widened. "Is that Lacy's letter?"

Jess nodded. "It's silly, but I wanted her with us today.

Eden's expression deepened, and sudden tears sheened her eyes. Slowly she reached into the pocket of her dress and pulled out a folded sheet. "Me, too."

For a moment they looked at each other, tears brimming in their eyes. Jess found the lines Lacy had written to her and read them out loud. "'Go where the wind blows you, friend. Don't be afraid. Where it takes you, love will be waiting.'"

Eden sniffed and wiped the tears from her eyes. "She was pretty smart, huh?"

"Yeah, and so are you. I'm the idiot, remember?"

"No, you just wanted a happy ending, but your prince turned out to be a toad."

"And my puppy turned out to be a prince," Jess joked, wiping her eyes. "And now, after I've said some truly horrible things to him, I have to get Ryan back."

Eden reached into her other pocket and pulled out her new smartphone. It was lit up. "After we get our hair and makeup done. Rosemary's panicking because we're supposed to be at House of Beauty in five minutes." Eden grabbed Jess's hand and pulled her up.

Jess refolded the letter and slid it into her pocket. "I need a plan."

"We can discuss it over the manicures. How bad did you screw things up with Ryan?"

"I called him a pretender, and I screamed"—she looked around at her surroundings and lowered her voice—"'eff you' at him."

Eden's eyes grew big. "Wow. Okay, I'm thinking this is going to have to be a grand gesture. We might be able to incorporate the Elvis impersonator. Does Ryan like Elvis?"

Jess shook her head. "I don't know. I wish I didn't have to get my hair done. My gut is churning, and I feel like if I could talk to Ryan, I could make everything better."

"He's not going anywhere. He doesn't have a car. Now, let's go get prettied up. You want to look good when you get your prince."

Jess followed Eden out of the pre-K Sunday school room still feeling unsettled but knowing what she had to do. The words Lacy had written were true. She had found a current, and now she was ready to spread those wings. She could only hope that Ryan would want to soar with her.

Ryan pulled up to the church and killed the engine of his parents' tiny Smart car. He couldn't believe his father had bought something so ridiculous, and when he'd said as much, his father had launched into a long narrative about the effects of automobile emissions on the planet. Once his eyes had unglazed, Ryan nodded, grabbed the key, and got out before his dad started talking about greenhouse gases and ozone layers. Ryan was more than happy to leave less of a footprint. He only wished to hell the Smart car was bigger than the go-kart he'd yearned for as a kid.

All morning he'd alternated between being angry at Jess and feeling stupid that he'd let her walk out. Once he got past the anger and hurt, he'd tried to call her, but she didn't answer her phone. No doubt it was on vibrate since she had a brunch to attend and then an appointment at a salon. He consoled himself with the thought that once she saw his calls, she'd return them. But she hadn't.

That worried him.

So he got dressed in his new navy-blue suit and wore the stupid pink bow tie he'd bought, learning how to tie it from a YouTube video, and vacillated between throwing himself at her feet or playing it cool. He still wasn't sure what to do until he killed the engine on the Smart car . . . or rather, pushed the button to turn it off.

The Morning Glory First United Methodist Church was a light beige brick with a large stained-glass window of Christ on the cross. Crepe myrtles still dressed in showy white blossoms decorated the brick path to the double front doors. A pair of ferns sat to either side of the entrance bedecked with fluffy white bows. A steady stream of trussed-up wedding guests made their way up the path, looking eager to see the impending nuptials. It was an afternoon for happiness. Not the horrible accusations he'd thrown at Jess earlier.

Ryan needed to find her.

He had to tell her that the anger and inferiority he'd locked up for years had come tearing from inside him, rampaging like a wounded boar with little regard for her feelings. He'd said some hard things. Some were true. Some would have better been left unsaid. Either way, he needed to apologize and tell her how much better his life was with her in it. He didn't want her to throw away what they had . . . and he damn sure didn't want her to ever think about going back to Benton. Sure, she'd come back to Morning Glory in a few months, but she didn't have to settle for a man who didn't deserve her.

And Benton did not deserve Jessica Anne Culpepper.

He opened the car door and contemplated how to actually get out of the vehicle. He wasn't huge, but the thing didn't seem to be made for anyone over five feet tall. He grasped the frame and hefted himself out. No way to look cool unfolding out of one of these.

"Ryan," someone called. He turned to find Jess's mother hurrying over to him. Donna Culpepper was as tall as Jess, and still trim and stylish in her late sixties. "Hello, honey. You look very nice. Why don't you come sit with me and Jim?"

Her earrings winked at him, and her smile was brighter thanks to a vivid red lipstick. Jess's father toddled up behind his wife and extended his hand to Ryan.

Ryan took it, remembering his manners, even as he wanted to tear off through the church, calling for their daughter. An image from *A Streetcar Named Desire* flitted through his mind.

"Thank you," he said, managing a smile at both her parents. "But I need to talk to Jess before the wedding. She's not responding to my texts."

"Oh, that's funny. She just texted me and told me to look for Connie Guthrie. This wedding is going to be hard for Lacy's mom. Those four girls were like peas and carrots, and the thought of Lacy not being here, well . . ." Donna's face flashed sudden grief. "Doesn't seem fair, does it?"

"No, it doesn't. Uh, do you know where Jess might be? Do they have a place to wait?"

Donna Culpepper smiled. "Of course they do, dear. The church just redecorated our bridal suite a few years back. It's very nice. I helped pick the fabrics myself."

"That's nice," he said, trying not to look too anxious. He wanted to fix things with Jess. Or at least apologize. Let her know he'd been an idiot.

"Sure. You can slip on back there. Just go through that door over there and listen for all the chatter. You'll find the girls, but you better make it quick. The wedding starts in fifteen minutes. You want me to save you a seat with us?"

He nodded his thanks and took off toward the door Jess's mother had pointed to. A minute later he ran into Eden. Like, literally ran into her when he turned a corner.

"Oh," Eden said, taking a few steps back. Ryan reached out a hand and steadied her.

"Sorry. You okay?" he asked, trying to look past her to see if he could spot Jess.

"I'm fine," she said, running a hand over her shiny hair. "What are you doing back here?"

He ignored her question. What in the hell did she think? To get his makeup done? To pose for photos? "Have you seen Jess?"

"Of course I've seen her. We're in the wedding together. But don't go in there." Eden jabbed a finger at the door marked Bridal Suite. "Rosemary ripped her hem when she tripped over a duffel bag. Her mother found out about the Elvis impersonator, and there was a huge argument with her mother. That's when Rose tripped. It's not pretty right now. Running mascara and lots o' drama. I'm personally going to hide in a bathroom stall for the next ten minutes. I think Jess is still in the courtyard."

"Thanks," he called as Eden pushed into the ladies' room, leaving him alone in the hallway. Through the door to the bridal suite, he heard someone crying. Sounded like Patsy Reynolds. The doorknob turned, and he jumped into action, pushing out the heavy door into the church courtyard. He breathed a sigh of relief and turned, adjusting his jacket.

Across the stone pavers, Jess sat on a bench . . . next to Benton.

And they were holding hands.

And smiling.

He felt like something slammed into him. His chest hurt so that he clutched it. Blinking his eyes rapidly at the sight in front of him, he tried to make sense of Jess and Benton holding hands, looking somehow . . . content. For a moment he thought it was a joke, but then the neurons in his brain connected and the sight in front of him became clear.

She belongs to Benton now.

Ryan took a step back and groped for the handle to the door just as Jess's gaze made contact with his. Her eyes grew wide, and her mouth fell open. She shook her hand away from Benton's, looking as if she would rise from the bench.

Ryan stood there for a second—fight or flight? Would he leave them to their reconciliation or confront them?

Shaking his head in disgust, he turned away and yanked the door behind him open wide. An older woman who he belatedly realized was Rosemary's mother gasped, clasping her hands against her bosom. He couldn't even manage an apology. The words pounding against his skull drove him forth. *Get the hell outta here.*

"Ryan," Jess called out behind him, her voice full of panic.

But he didn't stop. He pushed past the older woman and headed back the way he came, not running, but moving at a good clip. Blood roared in his ears, and his heart pounded a jolting rhythm. He didn't want to see anyone he knew. He just wanted to get into that clown car of his father's and get the hell away from Jess Culpepper.

He'd been so wrong.

Until yesterday, he'd thought she might be falling in love with him. Stupid, stupid, stupid. Jess had always belonged to Benton Mason. Weirdo Ryan Reyes had been deceiving himself if he thought any differently.

God, he was such a fool.

Bursting out the door he'd entered minutes ago, Ryan hustled down the walkway, his face set in such a furious manner that several people sidestepped him when he passed them on the way back to his father's car. No way could he let her catch up, because he'd say some more really ugly things, things that people who were streaming into a church didn't need to hear. He riffled through his pockets for the key, feeling the anger settle inside him, sending out grappling hooks, pulling his chest tight. Pride had never been a vice, but at that moment the shame burned in him. He wanted to punch something, and if Benton Mason had been handy, the man would have a black eye to match his suit coat.

Ryan had been suckered. He'd lost his heart to love like a true dumb ass.

Well, you wanted to get dirty, have fights, fall in love. Living that life means you take the good with the bad, bud. Welcome to the short end of the stick.

He wrenched the door open, and from the corner of his eye he saw Jess doing a walk/jog toward him. Her pink dress fluffed out around her, and a piece of her hair had come down from whatever fancy do she'd received at the salon. Her face reflected worry; her bottom lip was caught between her teeth. People turned and stared as she made a beeline for him. He started the car as she grew nearer.

"Ryan," she called, waving her hands. "Stop. It wasn't what you thought."

He pressed the START button on the car and shifted into gear. He wasn't going to talk to her right now. Maybe not for a while. Pulling away, he kept his gaze straight ahead. If he stopped, he'd ruin Rosemary's wedding with a crazy altercation outside the church. No need to do that to either her or Sal. So he did what he'd accused Jess of doing that morning.

He ran.

And he'd called *her* a pussy.

Chapter Seventeen

Jess dropped the arm she was waving, stopping short of hammering on the rear window of the odd little car as Ryan pulled away. A clump of hair that had been painstakingly battened down with hairspray a few hours ago came loose and fell into her eyes.

Shit.

"Jess," Eden called, skidding to a halt a few feet behind her.

Jess turned and shook her head. "It wasn't what he thought."

Several wedding attendees had stopped to watch Jess chase Ryan down the church walkway. Now they stood, craning their heads, watching Eden take Jess's hand. More gossip for the reception.

"Come on. We have to go. Time to line up," Eden said.

Jess felt her heart tremble in her chest. She wanted to cry, but couldn't because it would make her mascara run and ruin the nice job Sadie at the House of Beauty had done on her makeup. "This is so screwed up. He thinks I'm back with Benton, but I'm not. That was just . . . and look at my hair."

Eden tucked the huge hunk of hair behind Jess's ear. "We'll get a bobby pin. That will hold it."

Jess pressed a hand down the shiny satin of the dress and tried to think about puppies frolicking or little kittens curled into balls sunning in a window, because if she thought about Ryan and the look on his face, she was going to cry. She wiped the moisture from her lashes and sniffed before pulling her shoulders back. In four minutes she had to walk down the aisle and watch her dear friend marry the man of her dreams. No time to fix the catastrophe that had just occurred. Ryan's timing was epic and shitty . . . and if she disassociated herself and put herself in his shoes, she knew she'd have felt the same way.

But it was not what it looked like.

After she and Eden left the salon, they'd gone to the church to get dressed and take pictures. The wedding started at four o'clock, and she figured after she'd fulfilled her obligations, she could spend some time with Ryan. She'd make him understand the silly fears she had, and she'd tell him she wasn't going to run from love anymore. She wanted to be with him . . . not merely for the next few months, but for longer. She'd look for a job in Pensacola so she could be close to him, so they could build a new future together. No planning. Just taking one day at a time. After her conversation with Eden in the preschool room, calmness had settled inside her. She knew her decision to let go and enjoy the current she glided on had been the right one. All she had to do was convince Ryan that she loved him and wouldn't be so stupid again.

But when Rosemary's mother received a call from the caterer about where to set up the Elvis impersonator's speakers, all hell had broken loose. The reception was to be held on the grounds of the Reynoldses' antebellum estate and surrounding rose gardens, and obviously the idea of a man in a rhinestone romper crooning "Love Me Tender" made Patsy's hair curl. She and Rosemary had started in on each other, and then there was a torn hem, tears, and more accusations. Jess had slipped out to sit in the garden in the courtyard, because she couldn't handle any more drama that day. Between the fistfight and the horrible argument with Ryan, she was done.

The courtyard of the First United Methodist Church looked a little tired, but since a long hot summer was drawing to a close, Jess couldn't fault them for not tending the weary flower beds. She knew in the fall chrysanthemums and pansies would give the walkways a cheerful border. As validation of the thought, a cool breeze wafted through. Jess sank on a bench beneath a shady crepe myrtle and pulled out her phone. Ryan had called twice. She wanted to call him back but knew what she had to say to him would be better said face-to-face. If he could see in her eyes how much she wanted him, he'd believe her. She hoped.

"Jess."

Lowering her phone, she looked up to find Benton walking toward her. He wore his charcoal-gray suit that fit him nicely and a tie she'd bought him a few Christmases ago. He'd shaved the goatee and gotten a haircut. The Rolex his father had bought him when he got his MBA peeked out beneath the perfectly tailored sleeve. He was both familiar and a stranger.

"You're a determined man," she said with a sigh.

"I need to talk to you."

"So you said."

"Can I sit?" He gestured to the bench.

Jess didn't want him to, but to be petty seemed, well, petty. She deserved to be petty, but she scooted over and left a large spot beside her. "Go ahead."

Benton sat down and clasped his hands, staring out at the bedraggled petunias in the concrete planter across the way. "I know I come on too strong. It's a fault of mine, but then you know that."

She nodded but remained silent.

"I meant what I said the other night, you know." Benton paused for a few seconds.

"Benton, I gave you an answer. Don't let your persistent nature convince you that I'll change my mind. I won't."

"I thought you'd see things differently in the light of day," he said, smiling like it was a joke. "No, seriously, I know you don't have a good reason to agree to see me again when you move back, but I hope you'll at least think about it. This is not about me needing you to make my life easy. Sure, I took you for granted. I can't deny that. But I truly believe we could find our way back again, Jess."

"But that's the thing, Benton. We can't."

"No," he said, picking up her hand. His grasp felt so familiar—the callus on his thumb from playing golf, the warmth of his touch. "What we had isn't gone, babe. It's been beat up and bruised and wounded, but love doesn't just go away. I know it didn't for me."

She looked down at their linked hands. How many times had they held hands over the years? Too many times to count. Benton had left his wedding band sitting on the dresser the day he moved out, like some token he couldn't bear to have. How odd it looked to see his hand naked, tanned from a summer without a band. "Benton, I can't. It took me a long time to get over you. For fifteen years I spent every hour of every day believing we were meant to be. When you came home that day and told me I was wrong, it killed me. Part of me will always love you, Ben. You were my first love, my first everything, but I'm not in love with you anymore."

"Don't say that," he said, his voice breaking. "I deserve the hurt. I do. But don't say there's not a chance. I love you, Jess. I screwed up, but I know that now."

Jess took a deep breath and blinked away the tears that seemed to appear if the wind blew right that day. "I'm glad you realized it, but I've made some decisions this weekend. One of them is I'm not coming back to Morning Glory. At least not for a while."

"Why?" he said, his gaze jerking to meet hers. She had always loved his eyes with those thick eyelashes and crinkles on the edges. The pain in the depths of his eyes was sincere.

"I'm happy where I am. I'm happy with Ryan."

Benton's expression changed, aggravation flashing. "He's not for you, Jess. He's too young, and he's . . . the Brain. You can't be serious with this guy."

"But I am."

"You've only known him a month."

"I've actually known him longer, but even so, I love him."

Benton dropped her hand and looked at her like a horn had sprouted in the middle of her forehead. "You're crazy. He's . . . not even your type. He's kinda girly and . . . weird. Come on, Jess. Don't be confused by your first lay after me."

Jess almost slapped Benton. How damn full of himself could a man be? "I'm not confused. I was. But not anymore. I don't care what you or anyone else in this town thinks. Ryan Reyes makes me happy."

"Why, because he does whatever you want? Follows you around like a dog in heat begging for a crumb of Jess. If you want a pussy-whipped man, then yeah, he's probably the right guy for you." Benton shook his head in disbelief. "This is un-freaking-believable."

"That pussy-whipped man sure beat your ass today," she retorted, curling her hand in her lap. "Look, you let me go. Don't be angry if I'm happy where I am. I've found a new me, and she's stronger than I thought she was. Beneath the bluster and bullshit, I'm strong, and I'm worth loving. And if Ryan loving me makes him weak in your eyes, then I feel sorry for you. Because love doesn't make a person weak, Benton."

"I didn't say that. I just don't get your fascination with him."

"You don't have to. You don't have a say-so in my life anymore. You forfeited that when you chose 'experiences' over sustaining and growing what we had. I get you were scared. Life is pretty damn scary sometimes. But you and I . . . we're over."

"I can't believe this shit." Benton sighed, running a hand over his face. "I thought you loved me. Everyone's been telling me that I broke your heart, and I was going to fix it. I wanted you to come home to me."

The old saying "Want in one hand and spit in the other" came to mind. "We don't always get what we want."

He stared out at the wilted flowers. "Are you doing this to punish me?"

Jess didn't even have to think about that. "No. I'm not. There was a time I wanted to hurt you, but I'm over that. I want you to be happy, Benton." She picked up his hand and gave it a squeeze.

"Don't," he said, trying to pull away.

She held fast. "Benton, you don't want me. If you had, you would have never left me. I understand that you've had a year of dating, and I'm pretty sure you found some toads. But that's no reason to want me back."

"I wasn't doing that," he said like a petulant boy.

"You remember that Christmas when you wanted a new shotgun."

He nodded. "A Benelli Super Black Eagle."

"And you loved it, but then—"

"I lost it in Reelfoot Lake."

"You came home mad but said you didn't care because you could use your old gun. That you liked it better anyway. But thing was, you didn't. You convinced yourself it was good enough because you'd killed a lot of ducks with it. This situation is sort of like that."

"Are you comparing yourself to a Remington 870?"

"I guess."

Benton laughed and gave her hand a squeeze. "See? This is what I miss."

"But this isn't being in love. This is me doing what I always do— making it better for you. But you never thought about making it better for me. And here's the thing, Ben—I'm worth someone wanting to make things better for me, and that's what Ryan does."

Benton nodded, and for a moment they sat quietly, hands still linked. After a minute of silence, her ex-husband gave her hand another squeeze. "I hope he'll make you happy. You're right. You deserve that, and I'm sorry if I made things harder on you."

She nodded. "Thank you for saying that."

And as she looked up, she saw Ryan standing across the courtyard, his expression going from confusion to disbelief to disgust. Jess shook her hand from Benton's right as Ryan yanked open the courtyard door and bolted back inside.

"Ryan," she yelled, hiking up her hot-pink bridesmaid dress.

But he was gone.

"A real man doesn't run. He stays and fights for a woman," Benton said, standing and crossing his arms.

Jess whirled and jabbed a finger at her ex. "No, a real man doesn't screw our florist."

Then she turned and ran after Ryan. But she hadn't been able to stop him from driving away, hurt evident in his posture, anger flaring in his stormy eyes.

"Cheer up. All this can be fixed," Eden said, jarring Jess from going over the events of the last few minutes in her mind. "I think."

"Maybe. I don't know. Today has been such a colossal disaster. From the moment I woke up until this." She jerked a thumb over her shoulder. "And it's all my fault."

"No, it's not. You're entitled to be messed up when it comes to love," Eden said, giving her a smile. "Now let's go fix your hair and put on some lipstick. Rosemary needs us there with her. And I hope you weren't depending on the Elvis impersonator to pull off the grand gesture. Patsy fired him. Rosemary's pissed."

"What a mess," Jess said.

"Nah, this is life, right? Rosemary will be right as rain as soon as she's standing beside Sal, and you'll be okay, too. Because Ryan loves you."

Jess pressed her lips together before saying, "Grand gesture?"

Eden smiled and shrugged. "It was just a suggestion. But I have no clue what you can do."

Jess glanced over at the limo waiting out in front of the church. "I have an idea."

~9~

The Smart car ran out of juice right outside Morning Glory on Highway 121. Ryan unfurled from the depths of the bright-blue clown car and slammed the door. For good measure he kicked the tire, which didn't even register any pain in his foot, because the tires were so damn small. "Shit."

He didn't know what to do. Did he have to plug the car in or would it take gas? He thought his father had said something about it being dual but needing gas. He circled the car, spying a gas tank.

Thank God for something going right today.

Shielding his eyes, he looked up the road and spied a sign for a gas station about a mile or so away. He got out his phone and called his parents' house. But, of course, no one answered.

"Perfect," he said to the roadside grasses waving in the late-afternoon breeze. The September sun pressed down on his suit jacket, making sweat run down his back. He shrugged out of the navy jacket, folded it and placed it on the passenger's seat. Then he unknotted the stupid bow tie and tossed it inside, too. It fell on the floorboard. Gritting his teeth, he forced himself to leave it there. Rolling up his sleeves and unbuttoning the top buttons on the shirt, he locked the car and set off toward the gas station. Hopefully, he could buy a gas can there and figure out how to get gasoline into the small car.

As he walked, he cursed himself for even attempting to come back to Morning Glory. For buying a suit he'd never wear again. For choosing a pansy-assed pink bow tie to try to please Jess's vision of a southern preppy gentleman. For falling in love with a woman he knew . . . KNEW . . . didn't belong with him.

He should have left that dumb pink-and-green beach towel folded up on her porch and forgotten about his former chemistry partner. She and that asshole Benton deserved each other. He hoped they made each other miserable. Maybe they'd have ugly kids. Stupid kids. Kids that ate their boogers. They deserved kids like that.

A truck roared by and honked.

Ryan raised a hand and flipped whoever it was off.

He hoped the bastard who drove the truck was offended and turned the big Tundra around. Ryan wanted a fight. He wanted to pound someone until the highway ran red with blood. He felt dangerous. Wild. Hurt. A wounded buffalo ready to charge.

The truck turned around and headed back his way.

Good.

The Tundra slowed as it reached him, and the tinted window rolled down. Ryan stopped and stared at . . . Elvis?

Ryan blinked once. Twice. And then he pinched his thigh for good measure. Just in case the heat had made him loopy.

"Did you flip me off?" Elvis asked, his mouth tight and the rhinestones on the white polyester bell sleeve catching in the afternoon sun. A pissed-off Elvis. Great.

Ryan nodded. "Sorry, King. It's been a shitty day. I ran out of gas in that joke of a car back there, and I caught my girlfriend cozied up with her ex-husband. So you blowing past with your smart-ass honk got me to the tipping point, you know?" Ryan started walking again, the bloodlust of kicking someone's ass dying when he thought about mopping the road with the King of Rock and Roll. That seemed a bit much. Better to keep walking.

Elvis pulled away and hooked a U-turn. Drawing up just ahead of Ryan, the driver put the truck in park. The passenger door opened.

When Ryan got even with the truck, Elvis said, "I've had a shit day, too. Get in, and I'll take you up to the gas station."

Ryan thought about sticking to his guns, but the sweat was pouring off his face now. Silently, he climbed into the cab. "I'm Ryan."

"Jason."

"Not Elvis?"

"Hell, no. Not now, anyhow. Just got fired from a reception gig. Drove all the way down from Memphis for that shit, too. Wish I'd brought a change of clothes."

"Genovese-Reynolds wedding?"

"That's the one. Crazy woman who owns the venue called me and told me to pack up and leave."

"I know the feeling," Ryan said, gesturing toward the Circle K. "Just let me off here. Appreciate you giving me a lift even after I acted like an asshole."

"Ah, hell, what's one little ol' bird flipped at me. I'm dressed like Elvis and stuck in Mississippi. That's easy livin', my friend," Jason joked, his rings flashing as he shifted into park. "Need me to give you a lift back to your . . . uh, car?"

"No, I'm good," Ryan said, climbing down. "Uh, thank you. Thank you very much."

Jason laughed. "Good one. Here's my card, in case you ever need the King again."

Ryan took his card and then waved as the King of Rock and Roll drove away. Ryan turned back to the Kuntry Kitchen.

Who spelled *country* like that? Rather than kitschy cute, it was annoying. But they had gas pumps, so he wasn't going to turn his nose up at the gas station/convenience store/restaurant. Sighing, he trudged across the oil-stained parking lot and pushed into the store. A bell rang, and the clerk looked up. "Welcome to the Kuntry Kitchen," he said in a monotone voice.

Ryan narrowed his eyes. "Kyle?"

The man looked up. "Yeah?"

"Kyle Stratton?"

The man looked annoyed. "Yeah?"

"It's Ryan," he said, pressing his hands against his chest. "Ryan Reyes."

The man made a weird face. "Ryan?"

Kyle Stratton had been as close a friend as Ryan had ever had. Kyle's parents had lived a street over from where Ryan grew up, and the two kids had played Xbox Live every weekend. Before Ryan skipped grades, he and Kyle had been in middle school together, both in accelerated classes. Four years after Ryan had graduated at the top of his class at MGHS, Kyle had been named valedictorian of his class and left Mississippi for a full ride at Tulane in New Orleans. So Ryan was baffled to find him behind the counter wearing a red button-down shirt with a chicken emblem.

"What are you doing here?" Ryan asked, gesturing to the register.

"Ah, long story, man. Let's just say it started with a girl named Beth and ended with a stint in rehab. Stay away from crack, dude."

Ryan nodded and wondered what to say to something like that. "I'm sorry to hear that." He pressed his hands against the tops of his thighs, wondering if he should offer his hand or not in this sort of social situation. Probably not.

"Yeah, well, that's life, you know. You think you're going to be one thing, and then you end up a crackhead," Kyle said, laughing. "But I'm back on track, dude. I'm enrolled over at the community college. But this makes ends meet. What about you? Saw the write-up in the paper last year. You're doing your thing, man."

"Uh, not anymore. I quit Caltech. I have a charter fishing boat down in Pensacola," Ryan said.

"Why?" Kyle asked, punching a few buttons and shutting the drawer of the register. Behind him a few ladies moved behind the deli counter, doing whatever people who cooked at these kind of places did.

An older gentleman shuffled from the back cooler holding a couple of forty-ounce cans of beer. "I mean, you were doing good stuff out there, right? Helping out the world."

"I like to fish."

Kyle laughed. "Sure. I get it. The stress get to you?"

"No."

"I mean, it happens. I get it. That's why I started smoking weed. The stress of all those damn classes. Being smart ain't a cakewalk."

"I didn't quit because it was hard."

His former friend scratched his greasy-looking blond hair. "Then why the hell, dude? I'm, like, confused. If I could go back and do things over, I sure as hell wouldn't be here."

"Hey," one of the ladies in the back shouted.

"Sorry, Mar, but it's true. This dude right here is, like, a genius, and he quit everything to fish." Kyle pointed toward Ryan, a silly grin on his face. "Can you believe that shit?"

"I like to fish, too," the older man said, shuffling toward the register, scratching his beard. The man wore a beat-up trucker's hat and pants that sagged because he had no butt. "I catch a mess of catfish near every Saturday. Fry 'em up good, too."

Kyle shook his head. "Man, you can never tell, huh? If anyone would have looked at us back in the day and then saw us now, they'd be shocked. I'm checking out old farts," he said, grabbing the beer and scanning it, "and you're running a fishing boat. We should be millionaires by now, a honey on each arm. Know what I mean?"

Something about hearing his life whittled down to such a state bothered Ryan. It wasn't like he couldn't be successful at Caltech. He'd chosen to leave. And he had millions. Well, now he had only $1.3 million, since he'd paid cash for the boat. He liked fishing and being his own captain. And while he certainly missed being on the cutting edge of science, he rather enjoyed drinking a beer and shooting a combo at Cuesticks.

What if you had both?

The question popped into his mind, another sudden epiphany similar to the one he'd had a year and a half ago. Why did he have to sacrifice any part of himself? Jess's words came tumbling back to him. *You're the pretender. You hide who you truly are.*

"Sure, that's right. Never can tell," Ryan said, walking down the aisle with the automotive offerings. He spied a three-gallon red gas can on the bottom shelf and snagged it. Even as he gave lip service to Kyle, his mind raced with the possibilities. What if he merged the nerd with the beach bum? What if he stopped hiding his OCD tendencies and still hung out at the bars? Perhaps he could even apply to teach something at the local university? Or he could go to a research hospital. It wasn't like he couldn't take his boat with him. And if he was so smart, why hadn't he already thought of this?

Jess had been right—he'd assumed a demeanor in order to be what he thought was the ideal guy. He hid much of the real Ryan.

"Ran out of gas?" Kyle asked when Ryan put the can and a bottle of water on the counter.

"Yeah. Go ahead and add two gallons of premium to the ticket," Ryan said, pulling his wallet out of his pocket. Kyle rang him up, and just as Ryan went to pay, a limo screeched into the parking lot.

"Whoa," Kyle said, craning his neck to look out the door. "We just saw Elvis and now this."

The two women behind the counter stopped working and came around, drying their hands on their soiled aprons. Everyone stared out the grimy glass at the limo idling, taking up three parking spots.

The driver door opened, and Jess stepped out, still wearing her hot-pink bridesmaid's dress.

"Hey, that's Jess Mason," Kyle said.

"Culpepper," Ryan said, taking his change from Kyle's hand and shoving it into his wallet. "She's divorced."

"I hated her husband. What an asshole, right?" Kyle said, tearing off the receipt and passing it to Ryan. "She's freakin' fine, though. I'd love a piece of that action right there."

Jess spied Ryan through the glass and stopped. Instead of coming inside, she parked her ass on the hood of the limo and waited.

"What's she doing, man?" Kyle said, his eyes narrowing in confusion.

"Waiting on me," Ryan said, grabbing his water and heading for the door.

Chapter Eighteen

Borrowing the limo from Barry Travis after he dropped a radiant and almost sickeningly happy Rosemary and Sal at the reception, Jess had kissed her friend and told her she had to go get her own happily ever after. She hoped. If she could find Ryan, who was not answering his phone.

The fact that she didn't have a class D driver's license and had never operated a limo before had not stopped her from pulling away from the reception. She'd almost taken out a small Honda during a turn, and she hadn't a clue as to where she was going, but she figured spotting a tiny car among the monster trucks that seemed to plague Morning Glory shouldn't be hard.

It was tougher than she thought, but eventually after ten minutes of driving around, praying when she took corners, she came upon the blue Smart car on the side of the road. Unfortunately, Ryan wasn't in it. Seeing no blown tire, she could only deduce the car had run out of gas or whatever fueled it and the man she loved had hiked down to Kuntry Kitchen for help.

Jess drove up the road and pulled into the parking lot, hoping like hell this was enough of a grand gesture even though she suspected Ryan wasn't the kind of guy who would need one. However, after the fight, the argument, him catching her in something that looked to be what it wasn't, and then running out of gas, she figured he needed something more than a text.

Spying him through the glass peppered with sales ads and beer signs, she killed the engine and climbed out. She didn't want to air her business in front of Mary and the rest of her workers, so she carefully slid onto the hood that thankfully wasn't too hot. A few seconds later, Ryan came out, carrying a red gas can and a bottle of water. He looked hot and tired and so damn sexy with his shirtsleeves rolled up revealing tanned forearms. The tail of his starched white shirt was out, and she could see the delicious skin at the base of his throat.

Her heart contracted in her chest when he lifted his gaze to hers.

"What are you doing?" he asked, his face expressionless. He clenched his jaw and stared at her, his eyes somehow cold in the heat of the afternoon.

"I heard you needed a ride," she said, because she didn't know what to say at that moment. He was angry, and she'd not seen him angry before today. If she were objective, she could say he was hot when perturbed, all hard angles, pulse throbbing in his temples. Not scary, but intimidating nonetheless. But she wasn't objective. She was very subjective with her emotions tangled into a pulsating ball.

"No, thanks," he said, angling toward the road, walking a few steps. Then he turned. "Where'd you leave Benton?"

"I don't know where Benton is, and I don't care."

He looked at her for a long time. "Right."

Then he started walking again, ignoring her.

"Ryan," she called, swinging her legs over the side so she could see him.

He stopped. "What?"

"It wasn't what it looked like."

His stare was uncomfortable.

"It was a good-bye. That's it."

He shook his head. "Look, I understand the score, Jess. You belong here. I don't. You and I, we're nothing but a hookup that spanned a few weeks and is dying a natural death because we don't belong together. No need to draw this out or try to spare my feelings."

"Is that what you believe?" she asked, her chest flooding with a sudden achiness. Surely he didn't believe they weren't made for each other? They were so good together, balancing each other out. When she was with him, she felt like a better version of herself, and though this weekend had shaken her a bit, she now knew where she belonged. Lacy had suggested she needed to get off the path, get lost. And Jess wanted to get lost in life with Ryan. "Truly?"

Ryan set the gas can near a stand holding free circular newspapers and came toward her. "What makes you think we belong together in any way other than having a good time?"

"I don't know." Other than the fact she felt it in her bones. In her gut. But most important, in her heart.

"See? Me neither. Because it's more and more evident to me each minute we're here in Morning Glory that we do not belong together. This is not my town. But it's yours. And it's Benton's. When I saw you together an hour ago, I knew that you belonged with him and I had been fooling myself thinking we could be anything more. Maybe it was that old daydream of mine. To have the cheerleader. To take something of Benton's. I'm sure a therapist would have a field day analyzing me."

"No. I don't belong to Benton. I don't belong—"

"Well, you and Benton sure looked chummy an hour or so ago," he interrupted, crossing his arms. "But it's okay. I'll survive without you, Jess. I was fine before you came into my life—a little too drunk, but fine—and I'll be okay without you. Can't say I won't miss you, but I'll deal."

She didn't know what to say, because he seemed to have already written them off. She prayed it was a pride thing. If he didn't want to be with her anymore, it would hurt. A lot. So she played the card she'd been holding. "I love you."

He actually flinched and then wrenched his gaze from hers. "Don't do that."

"No, Ryan. I do. I love you."

"No, you don't. I'm the guy who helped you get over heartbreak. I know my role. Don't patronize me by saying something you don't mean."

"I'm not," she said, sliding off the car. Her heels teetered a little, and she wanted to reach out and touch his arm. But she didn't, because he was still angry and resigned to letting her go. "What you saw back there at the church was me telling Benton that I'm not interested in getting back together with him. That I'm not coming back to Morning Glory."

He jerked his gaze back to hers. "Not coming back?"

She shook her head. "Part of my confusion this weekend is the way I feel being home. Thing is, I love this town, but I've changed. As crazy as it sounds in only a month's time, I've learned I'm more than the Jess Culpepper I've been for the past few years. I found a whole amazing world out there I truly like living in. Though working at the hospital has been challenging, I love being back in surgery. I like my new friends and the food from Little China and seeing the dolphins each morning. But most of all, I love being with you."

He swallowed, his eyes measuring her. "That's risky."

"I know. And I like the risk of telling you how I feel. I'm tired of playing by the rules."

Ryan lifted an eyebrow but didn't say anything.

"I never understood what Benton was talking about, you know. When he came to me that day and said he wanted out and he wanted experiences, I couldn't fathom him wanting anything more than me."

"I can't, either," Ryan said.

His words gave her hope. "But you know what? When I left the too-snug nest I'd built for myself here in Morning Glory, I found a way to breathe life into myself again. You breathed life into me. And it's been good being on this journey."

"Of course it is. You were in a bad place, and I was there to make you feel better about yourself. Like a good puppy should."

"You're not my puppy, Ryan. Just because you've always cared about me doesn't give you less power in our relationship," Jess said, moving a little closer to him. "But you are right. You made me feel better, and I convinced myself you were just a rebound. The rules said I shouldn't let myself love you. I shouldn't get attached."

"But I am your rebound."

"No, you're not. You're the three-pointer at the buzzer. You're the win."

He made a confused face. "Oh, a basketball reference."

Jess couldn't help herself. She smiled. "Ryan, I'm not giving up on you. My whole life has been about staying between the lines, following the path, sticking to the plan. I don't want to live that way any longer, so if that means I love you and you don't love me back, I'll deal. All I'm asking for is a chance to try out these new wings. To be with you."

"You're not coming back here?"

"Not if I can help it. I need to be away from here, to take risks, to find my new life. And I need to be with you . . . if you want me."

For a few seconds, Ryan looked off, shoving his hands into his pockets. His eyes ran over the gas pumps, the cars whizzing by on the highway, the scraggly grass in the ditch next to the gas station. "I want you."

The sudden moisture prickling in her eyes wasn't unexpected. She'd become a fountain over the weekend, dripping tears and emotion all over the place. Someone with a mop might need to follow her around. "Good."

"You hurt me. I didn't think that was possible. I mean, when I was a kid, all the mean taunts, them locking me in the closet, shoving me in a locker, and egging our house, that was rough, but nothing came close to seeing you with him today. It was like my heart had been ripped from my chest. I didn't want to love you, Jess. I didn't plan you, either."

"Oh, Ryan," she said, reaching for him. Her fingers brushed the back of his arm, and he withdrew his hand from his pocket and caught her hand in his.

She sighed. "I'm sorry for everything that happened. I shouldn't have asked you to come, but I'm so glad I did. I don't think I would have figured anything out had you not been here. I needed to know you better, and seeing you here helped me understand so much . . . about you . . . about me . . . about my ass of an ex-husband. I know it's hard to understand what I'm saying, but it was sort of like waking up."

"No. I've had those moments of clarity. Smacked me in the head," he said, his fingers caressing hers. "It can't be this easy, can it?"

"What?"

"Love."

"Love is never easy, but it's worth it. We can figure it all out together. I know what I feel when I'm with you, and it's better than anything I've ever felt. I feel loved, sexy, safe, excited, convicted. I just feel right when I'm with you."

"But what if—"

"That's the thing. We don't know. This is what you wanted that night when you walked home in California—a full life. It will be messy sometimes, and we don't know anything for certain, but I'm not running from this. Come do this with me. Let's—"

"I love you. I've always loved you," he said.

And then she was in his arms, and his lips were on hers.

Jess wrapped her arms about his neck and let all the feelings she'd been holding inside go. Ryan loved her. She loved him. They'd figure the rest out together.

His mouth grew more insistent as he clasped her waist and pulled her hard against him. She tripped a little and stumbled into him. He went back, but then spun so he landed on the hood of the limo. He fell back, taking her with him.

"Thank God," she muttered, kissing him again. And again. And again.

She didn't care that her skirt was likely hiked up or that the fluffy petticoat showed. She didn't care when one nude pump slipped off and clattered to the ground or that someone walked past to enter the store and stared at them. Because Ryan loved her.

Finally, he blinked up at her, his green eyes full of . . . love.

Sweet Jesus, he loved her, and this was right. So right.

"Yeah, man. That's what I'm talking about," someone called over her shoulder. She slid off Ryan and flipped into a sitting position. Ryan sat up and grinned at the man wearing a Kuntry Kitchen shirt standing in the door. He gave them a thumbs-up and then disappeared back into the store.

"Who was that?" she asked, laughing. They'd made quite a spectacle making out on the hood of a limo in front of a gas station.

"An old friend who helped give me my own lightbulb moment," Ryan said, sliding off the hood and fetching her escaped shoe. He carefully held it so she could put her foot in. Total Cinderella *I got the prince* moment. "Weird how people outside your life can give you perspective."

"Or people the closest to you can threaten to knock sense into you."

He crooked a questioning brow.

"Eden," she said, sliding her hand into his. "Hey, do you mind going back to the reception? I sort of have to take the car back."

"I'll go anywhere with you. Even to Morning Glory," he said with a smile. "But first I have to rescue my dad's clown car. For some reason he wants it back."

"I'll give you a lift," she said, sliding off the hood, opening the passenger door and plopping Barry's driver's cap on her head.

"You'll never believe who gave me a lift to the store," he said, the smile on his face mirroring hers.

"Who?"

"Elvis," he said, tapping the trunk. She popped the button so he could set the gasoline can inside.

"You're joking. The guy who was supposed to play Rosemary's reception?" Jess laughed.

Ryan walked around and got in the passenger side. Jess slid into the driver's seat and adjusted her cap. "Where to, Dr. Reyes?"

"Anywhere with you," he said.

Jess closed her eyes. "Those are the second best words I've heard today."

"The first ones?"

"I love you."

Ryan leaned over and pressed his lips to hers. His kiss tasted like a promise.

"You're going to love me even more for this," he said, lifting his cute buns to fish a hand into his pocket. He pulled out a business card. "How about we give Elvis a call and get him back for the reception? I didn't give Rosemary and Sal a wedding present, and something tells me this will be their favorite."

"I love you."

"I won't get tired of hearing that," he said as he grabbed his cell phone.

Epilogue

A month later Jess stood on the beach with Rosemary and Eden. They'd spent the pretty autumn day drinking piña coladas while lounging in beach chairs and reading magazines. That night they'd gone out for seafood and listened to Rosemary's account of her Vegas honeymoon with Sal. Jess never would have picked that location for her old-fashioned friend, but the pictures on Rosemary's phone showed a heart-shaped hot tub, Sal with a flamingo dancer, and Rosemary with, of course, an Elvis impersonator. They'd ridden roller coasters, played craps, and spent a lot of time in the Bellagio honeymoon suite.

"It's so beautiful here," Rosemary breathed, swiping a bare foot across the crystal sands. The sun lingered over their right shoulders, and children splashed in the rolling waves. Summer had gone, but the days were warm enough to swim, the night cool enough to make a walk pleasant. Jess started walking in the surf pushing onto the sand. Rosemary and Eden followed.

"I could live here," Eden said, kicking a wave.

"Not me," Rosemary said, smiling at her friend. "I like my small-town life, and so does Sal. He's now part of the Rotary Club."

"He'll be president by next year," Jess said with a smile. Coming up the beach, she saw Morgan with her new man. The brunette gave a wave. Jess waved back. Morgan had come around once Jess moved in with Ryan. They'd even had margaritas last week while Ryan and Logan repaired the railing on Morgan's condo.

"Probably," Rosemary said with a smile.

Jess had spent the last month moving all of her belongings to Pensacola. She and Ryan weren't engaged but instead had chosen to move in together. Her parents weren't exactly thrilled about her living with a man, but they understood both her and Ryan's need to take things slower. She and Ryan were happy with how things were going, and they were planning on hosting Ryan's parents for Thanksgiving, something Ryan still marveled at. "Ryan will be teaching at Pensacola University next semester."

"You didn't tell us that," Eden said with a smile.

"The job offer was made official today. He'll be going back into academia, but he's still running the charter boat service on the days he doesn't teach classes. He's excited about working with students, and he'll be collaborating with another professor on a research grant."

"Bet that made his parents happy," Rosemary said.

"They're pleased, but you know, I think they've finally accepted he's not interested in being a Nobel Prize winner. But he *is* rediscovering the nerd side of himself. Even dug out his *Dr. Who* and sci-fi movies from underneath *Rudy* and *Fast and Furious*."

"I love a sexy nerd," Eden said with teasing in her voice. "Does he know any single professors at the college waiting to sweep the manager of Penny Pinchers off her orthotics?"

They all laughed and kept walking toward the sinking sun, happy to be together for a few days.

"You'll have your turn," Rosemary said, looking over at Eden.

"I know," Eden said, sobering. "I haven't told you guys, but Sunny got some bad news about Alan. You know he's doing a tour in Afghanistan. The helicopter he was in went down."

"Oh no," Jess said, stopping and looking at Eden. "Is he okay?"

"They haven't found any survivors yet. They're still searching."

"That's horrible, Eden," Rosemary said, taking her hand. "How's Sunny?"

"She's hanging in there. She's three months along, and since she lost the last pregnancy around this time, I'm worried about the stress from all this. She's already on bed rest. I didn't tell you because I didn't want to bring a cloud along. Getting together will be harder now that both of you are settled down. And, honestly, I feel so selfish. Alan and Sunny were supposed to move back to Morning Glory once he finished his tour. I had hoped to finally go to college, and now I don't know what will happen."

"You're not being selfish," Jess said, wrapping an arm around her friend. Eden always seemed to get the short end of the stick.

They walked for a few minutes, none of them saying anything. Letting the unfairness of life peck at them. "Oh, hey," Jess said after a few minutes of walking. "I almost forgot."

Reaching into her cardigan pocket, she pulled out the paisley bag.

"The charm bracelet," Rosemary said with a smile.

"Since I'm now in love, with a new job, and living on the beach, I figure I did what Lacy wanted. I let go and got lost. I found Ryan and a part of myself I never knew existed. No, a part of myself I wouldn't allow to see sunlight."

"What do you mean?"

"I mean, I've always been snarky and sarcastic and practical, but beneath my scrubs I have a heart that's—"

"A little romantic?" Rosemary finished for her.

"Yeah, a little," Jess admitted, untying the strings that secured the ditty bag. She tipped the bracelet into her hand and extracted the small plastic bag that held a charm shaped like a flip-flop.

"Oh, that's cute," Eden said, taking the plastic bag and holding up the charm.

"Since I'm living on the beach, I figured it worked. Plus, I liked the little jewels in the thong part. A little sparkle in my life's not a bad thing."

Rosemary pretended shock with a gasp. "Next thing you know, you'll be wearing sequins and using glitter eye shadow."

"Ha-ha," Jess said with a smile, carefully taking the charm away from Eden and sliding it from the bag. Holding the bracelet, she clipped it on. "There."

She held the bracelet up and wiggled it. "Mission accomplished, Lacy."

Twenty yards or so out, a dolphin rolled over the gentle waves.

"Oh my gosh. Did y'all see that?" Rosemary said, chasing the sucking surf a few feet and peering out at the spot where the dolphin had emerged. "Do you think . . ."

She looked back at them.

Jess smiled and shrugged. "I'm living with the Brain. Anything is possible."

Eden laughed. "I don't think Lacy would come back as a dolphin. She hated getting her hair wet, remember?"

"That's true," Rosemary said, rejoining them. "But still, that was cool."

Jess slid the bracelet back into the bag and held it out to Eden. "Your turn."

Eden waved off the bag. "I'm not ready yet. Okay? Besides, if I take it now, my dream will turn out to be Gary on a motorcycle and me with five snotty rug rats living in a trailer beside my mama."

Jess wanted Eden to take the bag, but she understood. Eden was too scared to believe anything good would happen to her. But Jess knew it would because she now believed in the woo-woo Lacy had promised. Maybe there were guardian angels who wore blue wigs and drove orange pickup trucks. Jess tucked the bag back into her pocket and linked her arm through Eden's and then Rosemary's. "Come on, Eden. You've got a fairy tale in front of you."

"I don't want a fairy tale. I just want to quit working at Penny Pinchers. Prince Charming can wait."

"But sometimes he doesn't," Jess said, thinking about her own Prince Charming lying naked on the beach stargazing. Sometimes a gal trips over her Prince Charming . . . and finds he was exactly what she wanted, warts and all.

And as she and the girls returned to Del Luna, she caught sight of Ryan standing on the beach, looking out at the surf. It struck her that on her first night in Pensacola when she'd taken the moonlight walk on the beach, he'd been there. Waiting for her.

As he was now.

Ryan turned and smiled as they approached and held out his hand to Jess. He wore a plaid shirt and a lanyard from Pensacola University that said *Department of Biological Science.* "Who wants some tequila?"

Yeah, life was good with her frat boy nerd.

She lifted onto her toes and gave him a kiss. "I'll pass on the tequila, but wine would be excellent."

"Whatever you want," he said, wrapping an arm around her waist and following Rosemary and Eden up the steps to the walkway.

"Guess he'll always be your puppy," Rosemary joked.

"No, he's not my puppy. He's my prince." Jess looked at Ryan and then whispered, "I love you."

His answer was a kiss.

Yeah, just like a prince.

Acknowledgments

I'd like to thank Kim Law and Terri Osburn for their encouragement, advice, and friendship. Not only are both fantastic writers, but they excel in being cheerleaders, butt kickers, and overall decent human beings.

About the Author

Photo © 2016 Hartness Photography

RITA-nominated author Liz Talley writes sassy contemporary romances set in the South, where the tea is sweet, the summers are hot, and the men are hotter. Her first book, *Vegas Two-Step*, debuted in June 2010, and Liz has published nineteen romances since. She lives in northern Louisiana with her childhood sweetheart, two handsome children, three dogs, and a mean cat. Liz loves doing laundry, paying bills, and creating masterful dinners for her family. She also lies in her bio to make herself look like the perfect wife. What she *really* likes are pretty shoes, lemon-drop martinis, and fishing off the pier at her lake house. You can visit Liz at www.liztalleybooks.com to learn more about her and her upcoming books.